WITHDRAWN

THE GIRL WITH BORROWED WINGS

THE GIRL WITH BORROWED WINGS

by Rinsai Rossetti

DIAL BOOKS an imprint of Penguin Group (USA) Inc.

DIAL BOOKS

An imprint of Penguin Group (USA) Inc. · Published by The Penguin Group

Penguin Group (USA) Inc., 375 Hudson Street, New York, NY 10014, U.S.A. · Penguin Group (Canada), 90 Eglinton Avenue East, Suite 700, Toronto, Ontario, Canada M4P 2Y3 (a division of Pearson Penguin Canada Inc.) · Penguin Books Ltd, 80 Strand, London WC2R ORL, England · Penguin Ireland, 25 St. Stephen's Green, Dublin 2, Ireland (a division of Penguin Books Ltd) · Penguin Group (Australia), 250 Camberwell Road, Camberwell, Victoria 3124, Australia (a division of Pearson Australia Group Pty Ltd) · Penguin Books India Pvt Ltd, 11 Community Centre, Panchsheel Park, New Delhi - 110 017, India · Penguin Group (NZ), 67 Apollo Drive, Rosedale, Auckland 0632, New Zealand (a division of Pearson New Zealand Ltd) · Penguin Books (South Africa) (Pty) Ltd, 24 Sturdee Avenue, Rosebank, Johannesburg 2196, South Africa · Penguin Books Ltd, Registered Offices: 80 Strand, London WC2R ORL, England

1 3 5 7 9 10 8 6 4 2

Library of Congress Cataloging-in-Publication Data

Rossetti, Rinsai.
The girl with borrowed wings / by Rinsai Rossetti.
p. cm.
Summary: Seventeen-year-old Frenenqer lives a controlled and restricted life in the desert, like everyone else there, but when she meets Sangris, a Free, winged shape-shifter, everything changes.
ISBN 978-0-8037-3566-8 (hardcover)
[1. Flying—Fiction. 2. Shapeshifting—Fiction. 3. Deserts—Fiction. 4. Love—Fiction.] I. Title.
PZ7.R7212Gi 2012
[Fic]—dc23
2011027164

For the inspiration, Anju Suresh.

And for the Humane Society of Louisiana.
Nobody seemed to mind when I flew over to volunteer
and instead found myself inexplicably glued to my laptop
for two weeks, just typing and living in their backyard.
If they hadn't been so understanding about it, this
book might have been much harder to write.

Contents

THE BEGINNING
In Which I Am Made

I am unlike most other people because I began, not in the body of my mother, but in the brain of my father. He invented me, you see. He sat down one day and dreamed me up. I started out as no more than a figment of his imagination, and when he married my mother he set about making me real. I guess it's always true to say that a child is a creation of her parents, but I don't know anyone else who constructed their daughter as deliberately as my father did.

If you ask me, I'm more of an imagined person than a real one. I can feel him steering me through my spine. It's awfully hard, knowing that I'm just a construct of someone else's mind. The only part of me that wasn't placed there by my father—the only part of me that is *mine*—is the part that doesn't exist: the wings.

It's a fantasy I've told myself for years. I like to pretend that I should have been born with a pair of wings. But—and here's where reality seeps even into my private daydreams—something stopped their growth. Instead, ever since I was very young, no more than a tender little thing with a pumpkin for a head, I have had an *itch* right between my shoulder blades. It's because of that itch that I pace around my room at night; it's as though I have a finger in my back, pushing me forward. And I know who the finger belongs to. It's the finger of my father that digs into my spine directly between the two wings that never were.

CHAPTER ONE

In Which I Introduce a Greenless World

I'm called Frenenqer Paje. I know it's an odd name. It doesn't suit me. It doesn't suit anyone. It's like one of those frilly, too-exotic dresses that people buy for their unwilling daughters. My father's the one who dressed me up in it. He insisted on calling me Frenenqer because, in some language or other, it comes from a word meaning "restraint." My name will tell you all you need to know about my father.

I live in an oasis, deep inside a desert, deep inside the Middle East. If you've heard of it, my current home has a proper name, Al Ayren; you could find us on a map if you tried. To the people who live here, though, it's just "the oasis."

To reach me, you'd have to zoom over miles and miles of crusted sand, a flat blank plain where even the palm trees shrivel up and die. Pale sky, white land; like somewhere past the end of the world. In this nothingness, the only plants are the ghostly shrubs, as bare as clouds of gray scribbles. In one branch you might spot half a dead cat curled up, killed by boys with too much free time, or a slaughtered goat, gently dripping blood, hanging from another like a surprising fruit.

Beyond that is a softer, deeper kind of danger—the true desert. The sand becomes properly hellish, dreamily red, in long soothing curves. When the wind hits the peak of the dunes, they rumble, grinding under the pressure, and sand steams up along their tips like thin hissing smoke-clouds. The whole world seems on fire.

But then at last, the desert miraculously gives way to reveal, on the horizon, a patch of almost green.

Forget the lush greenness of northern countries. Here, everything has to be bone-hard and dry in order to survive. The colors are no exception. What passes for *green* is actually khaki, the color of bathroom tiles.

This is the oasis: a cluster of palm trees and stone buildings trying to escape the heat. The land is naturally dry and dead, but at least there's shade here, and some water. They call it a city, of sorts. My father the architect likes to think so. There's even a private school, owned by Sheikhs, run by expatriates, placed alongside one of the main roads. It's the only school for miles and miles around, so every child in the oasis is enrolled there. Including me.

I stood outside the dirty white school building, hair newly cropped to keep it from sticking to my neck and forehead, cheeks uncomfortably flushed in the heat, glasses slipping down my nose. I wore the unreasonable school uniform of Key Stage Four, black shirt and black pants and formal shoes. By this point, of course, they were stinging hot and gray with dust. No color lasts for long here, except for the sky.

I flopped down onto the sand by the side of the road and didn't move, watching with dull eyes as cars wavered past through shimmers of evaporation. It had been a bad day. Absently, I pulled an important-looking school newsletter out of my bag and tore it into strips.

Another girl straggled out of the school. She was also trussed up with a uniform and a name. Because she was younger than me, only in Key Stage Three, her shirt was blue. I envied her. Lighter colors were better in this heat. And her name—Reem, I think—seemed more comfortable than mine too. She didn't bow under the weight of it.

"Hey," she said, choosing to lean against the school wall rather than sprawl in the sand beside me.

I nodded with an effort.

"Frenenqer, right?" she said. "Where are you from?" She tugged at her sweaty collar, screwing up her face.

"Nowhere, really." But she still looked at me expectantly, so I counted the countries off on my fingers, choosing almost at random. "Thailand and Italy and Japan and New Zealand and some other places."

She nodded. "I'm Syrian and Mexican."

"Ah."

It was the equivalent of a handshake. In my school, what-country-are-you-from was our most common way of introducing ourselves. It was right up there with what's-your-name and the old favorite, how-long-have-you-been-here. Like prisoners, we kept track of the days. This was because

5

very few people ever *lived* in the oasis. Most of us were children of the expats who came, worked for a couple of years, saved money, and then, contracts complete, moved on to somewhere else. Perpetual foreigners, all of us. My family landed in the desert the same way. Except my father found steady work. And so unlike most, we stay.

Reem was one of the few who had been in the school for over seven years. I felt sorry for her. I myself had been here for six years, much longer than I would have liked, but my father's bosses loved him. Soon I would have people pitying me the same way I pitied Reem.

"I was here late for a club," Reem offered.

She said this with pride. It was unusual for students to be involved in extracurricular activities. I just nodded. Too hot.

"I was helping to plan for Heritage. I even wrote that article in the newsletter, if you saw it . . ." She trailed off, noticing the strips of paper around my feet. Furtively, I tried to cover them with sand.

"Yeah, I read it," I said encouragingly.

I hadn't been able to force myself past the title. I'd seen the word *Heritage,* and that had been enough.

Reem cleared her throat, tugging at her collar again. "Well, you know how it is," she said. "We're running out of rooms. And half the students are the only ones from their country. This year, we'll have to lump people together, and they won't like that."

I didn't look at her. Heritage again. People wouldn't stop

talking about stupid Heritage—and why not? They hadn't been trying a year to forget.

It was different for me. I heard the word around every corner. It ambushed me whenever my guard was down. And each time, without fail, a door in my mind thudded open, and I saw yellow eyes and burning mouths and spiders.

My father pulled up then.

His car, pure white with black windows gleaming, eased to a halt in the deserted parking lot. I got to my feet, brushed my clothes off, and reached up to adjust my wings before remembering that they weren't there. Hoisting my heavy bag onto one shoulder, I managed to flash Reem a smile. She grimaced back. And then I escaped from the pounding weight of the heat falling down on me from the sky—I could feel it building up over my shoulders—and slid into the air-conditioned relief of the car.

I won't describe my father. I don't feel like introducing him yet. So leave the contents of the car unseen through its dark-tinted windows. All you need to know is that he ferried me straight home, ushering me into a house made of old white stone, flat-roofed, with huge opaque windows to keep the sunlight out, and a door that had once been blue but was now bleached white and peeling.

And that was my life in the oasis. I only ever went three places: my house, the school, and the inside of the car. It made no difference that I was seventeen. Here, youth seemed unnatural. My universe was contained in a series of boxes. And all the while I lived my sheltered little life in the artificial air of those three boxes, I could feel my father's finger pointing into my spine, and the wings I should have had beating hard at my back.

The feeling had become worse in the past year. Caged by the heat that closed in over the buildings. Eyes lowered, avoiding the pain of looking up into the too-intense sky.

Other people seemed to bear the claustrophobia more easily than I did. My parents thought I was strange. Who could I explain myself to? I had a few friends, if you could call them that. For instance, I might have told Anju. But we always met in supervised settings. In the classroom, under the eyes of teachers; at appointed, carefully organized times in my house, with my parents nearby.

I did fight, at first. Six years ago, only a few months after arriving in the oasis, I tried going for walks when it was dusk and the heat had sunk enough to be merely stifling. I had a very narrow window of time before it became too dark. Maybe ten or fifteen minutes. I wasn't allowed to walk far, of course. Only to the end of the block. And anyway, there was nowhere else to go. So all I did was hurry along the street that ran in front of my house, pacing back and forth, up and down, until my ten minutes were up.

The first time I did it, I was elated. Even being stuck on that one street was better than nothing. There was a goat with its throat split open like a second red mouth, hanging in the acacia tree outside my next-door neighbor's house, and a pool of nearly black blood, with a stern, sick smell, was seeping slowly through the dirt and out onto the pavement where I might step in it. But at least the sky was wide open above my head. I spread my arms in glee, at the joy of being outside, alone, practically free.

Then I turned around and saw my mother standing over my shoulder.

She'd been there the whole time. My father had sent her to follow me. It gave me the shock of my life to see her. She'd kept impossibly close, walking when I walked, stopping when I stopped. Just watching. Mouth brittle. Hovering.

The next time, I fought—I still fought then—until my father said, "Fine, go alone. And whatever happens, blame yourself." So I left the house for my ten minutes of limited freedom. As I walked, I kept checking over my shoulder to make sure my mom wasn't sneaking after me. She wasn't.

Instead, there were cars.

Expensive-looking cars would follow at my heels, one by one. The windows would unroll, and men would lean out and shout at me in broken English. It was the other expats, men who had left their wives and children behind in their home countries, men who hadn't seen a girl up close in years. Sometimes I ran, and they laughed. Or cheap cars with no windows at all would stop, and the men inside would try to chat with me, asking where I had bought my clothes, what my number was, where I lived. Then I'd have to act deaf. Or boys on bicycles would stare an inch from my face. I'd act blind. Nothing worked.

I stopped going on walks.

"Frenenqer," my father said in secret triumph. "The sun is setting. Why don't you go walk outside the way you wanted to?" He looked at me steadily, and the breath was squeezed out of me. "Now you can't complain that I don't give you freedom. This is your choice."

I didn't tell him about the cars. I let him think I had merely lost interest, because otherwise I would have had to admit he was right. It wasn't safe for an almost-teenage girl to walk alone, even if it was right outside her house, even if it was up and down the same street, even if it was only for ten minutes each day.

For months after my "choice," I had a recurring nightmare. I would sit up in bed and see that my bedroom curtains were open, and that a man had climbed up outside in the darkness, a flashlight in one hand, the beam of light trained on me, and he was peering in through the glass, with a grin, watching me sleep.

Then I would panic.

I would feel the full weight of the heat above me, pressing in on my little bedroom, and I'd be too aware of the fact that, for miles and miles around, no matter where I turned, I was inside a circle of desert, and there was no place to escape. If I ran, I would find myself in an expanse of emptiness and sand and hell-heat.

So I got up each midnight and paced instead, around and around my room, rubbing nervously at my hands. It didn't help. It only made me more restless. I missed the color green. I missed fresh air. I missed grass that would grow naturally, without having to be planned and artificially sustained. I missed running. The itch flamed deeper into my back. Sometimes I climbed out the window, closing the curtains behind me, and just sat on the ledge, several stories above the ground, balancing dangerously and sucking in the air that almost isn't too oppressively hot in the middle of the night. I wanted to burst away.

The nightmare doesn't come anymore. But the claustrophobia is stronger than ever.

Because, a year ago, things changed. Just for a while, but they changed. I had a space of freedom.

I've pretended to have wings ever since I was a little girl, and when I sat on my windowsill in the oasis at night and took huge hungry gulps of air, I clutched hold of that daydream harder than ever. But last year, something happened that made it so real, I now have to constantly remind myself—whenever I'm alone, or leaning out the window—I can't fly off anymore, because he's gone.

He. Does there have to be a he? It seems weak and unoriginal, doesn't it, for stories told by girls to always have a he? Well, not in my life, nor in the lives of my friends. It's a very unusual thing for us. For my friends at least, their first relationship begins on their wedding night. It's a culture of arranged marriages—now, look, that's not necessarily a bad thing, and keep in mind that an arranged marriage is not the same as a forced marriage. Most of my friends are looking forward to the day when they will be shown a picture of their future husband.

But I won't have an arranged marriage, at least not officially. We all know that my father won't *arrange* anything for me, he'll simply . . . guide me, pulling the strings in the background, his finger pressed into my back, and everything will magically turn out the way he wants it to. So you see, for there to be a *he* in my story is a very unusual thing indeed, but then, the circumstances were unusual too, and the boy himself, if you can call him that, even more so.

When he came, things changed. There was no longer the shadow of my father in the background—or, at least, for a time, it was less noticeable. There was no longer the maddening proximity of walls on all four sides. Instead there were black skies, and sharp, stinging stars, and a window creaking open.

But first, I have to tell you how the thing came about.

CHAPTER TWO

In Which My Father Casts a Spell

The time: a year ago. Early morning, in an effort to avoid the full heat of the day. It was a Sunday, near the start of the week—weekends are on Thursdays and Fridays—but we had a short holiday off school, in respect of some Sheikh or other. This was common enough. Sometimes students get whole months off without warning.

The setting: the Animal Souk. It was my first and last time there. Needless to say, I was escorted by my parents. As I've told you, it was rare for me to go anywhere beyond my school or my house or the car. This was the first time in months, and then only because my father had decided that I should. Otherwise, left alone, he knew I would read, and he felt I did too much of that.

My father's colleague had an interest in camels, and by some twisted thread of logic, their rivalry had apparently metamorphosed into an undeclared I'm-more-knowledgeable-about-camels-than-you competition, somewhat in the spirit of men showing off their cars. This had resulted in my father's sudden decision to pay a visit to the

Animal Souk. He wanted to compare it to the Camel Market, that sprawling gathering of thousands and thousands of snorting, bored dromedaries that clotted the hard-baked highways each Friday. The Animal Souk had camels too, but also goats and miscellaneous, mysterious animals packed together in stacks of cages.

My father got out of the car and closed the door behind him with a polite click. My mom slammed hers, accidentally. He turned to stare at her, but I couldn't see his face. Still, I shut my door extra-softly. Chaos and loud noises hurt him, like lightning flashing into morbidly sensitive eyes.

In front of us was the main body of the souk, a low white building streaked with dust and wild pigeon droppings, and all along its base the lurid red sand was creeping up and eating away at its walls. An arched doorway was a solid block of shadow against the overwhelming light. Inside, I could just make out a mass of people moving through the relative blackness.

You might think I'd look forward to trips like these, since they get me out of the house. No.

It happened the minute I stepped into the souk. Hundreds of men were milling through the long white tunnels, weaving around the closely packed stalls if they were buyers, or standing by their walls of cages and shouting out if they were sellers. Eyes snapped up and fixed on me. As if in a spotlight, I walked between my parents and looked around uneasily. I tried to find another girl in sight, but I couldn't.

Back then, my black hair was long enough to reach my

waist, and I wore contact lenses instead of glasses. The hard thin body of my childhood was just beginning to miraculously soften like the cracked ground of a wadi when rain falls. I knew I didn't look the way a girl ought to look, at least in the oasis. My hair wasn't bushy, my face wasn't painted with makeup, and I didn't smell of strong musk and incense—I was too skinny, too delicate, and my straight hair was too flat. In some countries people like the way I look, but here, not so much. Not that it mattered. The men stared anyway; being female was enough. I tilted my face downward, hoping that their gazes would slide off it onto the floor.

"Stop slouching," ordered my mother.

I kept my shoulders the way they were. Slouching was the best way to avoid attracting attention. I was too tall for a girl. Almost five foot six. My friends teased me about it sometimes, calling me a giraffe. They wouldn't believe me when I told them that, in some parts of the world, my height was normal.

"Stay close," ordered my mother as my father led the way through the crowds. The footprints he left in the sand-strewn floor were perfectly even, as though he'd planned his steps ahead of time.

Hours passed. The day grew hotter. The sun, visible through an open area in the ceiling, throbbed like a migraine in the sky. There was no air-conditioning, only a few fans that lazily wafted the smell of fur and feathers from one stall to another. My father was absorbed in his new hobby. My mother played her part. She stood there and smiled and nodded and made silent faces. Superfluous, I trailed behind them like a dog on a leash. Dizziness began to spread through my head. I saw the world blurred through waves of sparkles and recognized the symptoms of dehydration, but I was used to them; I'd been through much worse before while waiting for my father after school. Sweating, I concentrated on the suppressed thump of my heartbeat. My wings—I pictured them as bronze-and-black falcon's wings, usually—lay sleek and imaginary over my shoulders, and fluttered once in a while when I had trouble breathing.

That is where I found the beginnings of freedom. In a hot, crowded souk, with the giddiness of dehydration beginning to bear down on me, where I waited, surrounded by walls and walls of cages, in a sea of trapped animals.

There were goats and camels on rope tethers, and stacks of cats—all skinny, flea-bitten, and probably half feral—in cages too small to stand up in. There was a bucket of baby crocodiles (there must have been about thirty in that bucket alone) balanced on the dirty floor next to the wall. There were parrots in cages and parrots on stands, hissing at anyone who came too close. Hamsters and rabbits and guinea pigs, no more than limp bundles of fur packed into boxes. But I felt most sorry for the dogs. There were only two that I could see, long-limbed, lithe desert-dogs in cages barely big enough for cats, and the men were gawking at them as if they were the most exotic animals there. In a way, they were. Here, dogs were regarded with a deep-seated fear, and the men tending them were treated as though they had the bravery of bear-wrestlers. There was no way those two dogs would end up with a good life. They would probably be bought by some macho man desperate to prove his courage.

Next to the dogs was another row of caged cats. The stacks of crates protruded out from the smooth white wall of the souk like a curved rib, and on the other side, behind the curve, was an area of filth and shadows. At the end of the row, I noticed one cage in a patch of darkness deeper than the rest; in it, a bundle of fur either dead or dying. The heat was killing the cat, squeezing it like a pulse in a tightened vein.

"Excuse me?" I said to the owner of the stall. He hurried over to me and nodded. It was clear he didn't speak English. First I glanced over my shoulder to make sure my parents weren't looking. They were still a short distance away, fussing over a rabid-looking baby camel. I swallowed. Then, quickly, I pointed at the cage.

He could see what I meant immediately.

He opened the door and reached inside. When his hand came back out it was gripped around the neck of the cat. It dangled in the air as he surveyed it gloomily. I wanted to point out that that probably wasn't the best way to hold it, but I kept my mouth shut.

The cat was enormous, about half as big again as the largest cat I'd ever seen before. The imprints of the cage wires were still in its fur, mixed in with dust and dead flies. The eyes were partly open without focusing on anything. They glowed yellow-gold, and the color stood out like a shock against the rich jaguar-black of its fur. The tip of a tongue lolled out of its mouth, bright red and flimsy, ready to be bitten off. The seller shook his head and tossed it onto the floor, where it would be hidden behind the row of cages. It hit the ground with a thud.

"Hey!" I said without thinking. But the seller had already turned away. He had no time for sick animals. I had seen that happen before, in a shop I'd visited with my father near Dawar Roundabout a few years ago. I had seen a dying chick in a cage full of baby chickens whose fluff had been stained green, red, and blue . . . the dye had seeped through its skin and poisoned its system, so it was lying on its side, one leg clawing at the air. I'd pointed it out to the owner of the pet shop, who had taken one look, pulled the still-living chick out, and dropped it into the garbage. I'd been too afraid to interfere. I had let the chick die. And, for weeks afterward, I had called myself a coward. Shouldn't a *life* be more important than my inhibitions?

I glanced over at my parents. Their backs were turned to me. I shot a look at the pet seller. He was talking to a customer.

It isn't stealing, I told myself. *He threw it away, so obviously he doesn't want it anymore.*

I slid behind the wall of cages. Some of the cats watched me curiously. The others were too far gone and didn't even blink their glazed eyes when I brushed past. The floor, normally tiled with white stone, was dusty here, stained yellow with some strange liquid in places. I didn't want to think about what that might be. Trying not to touch anything, I crouched beside the cat. Its eyes stared off at nothing.

"Hey, come on," I murmured to it, so softly that the words came out more like a hum. "You'll be all right, I promise. Poor thing . . ."

I could see its sides heaving as it panted. Its tongue hung out like a dog's, so far that it almost touched the filthy floor. "Yech, no, you don't want to lick that," I said, and, without considering whether I ought to or not, scooped it up. Ye gods (a phrase I'd picked up from some book), it was heavy. And completely limp, like a ragdoll. I shifted to get a better grip. As I did so, I noticed a tick on its back, close to my arm. And then another behind its ear. "Ye gods," I muttered aloud.

"Frenenqer!" my parents shouted in chorus, on the other side of the cages. I had been gone for all of ten seconds.

"Here," I called back before they could bring the entire souk down with their screams.

"Where?"

"Where?"

Possibilities flashed through my mind. I could ask my father for the car keys—say I had left my bottle of water underneath my seat, tell him about my dehydration—then sneak the cat into the trunk without telling them. But when we got home, my father would be watching. I'd have to leave it in the trunk until I could creep down and get it at night. I worried it would die before then, and, in the heat of the car, it might even explode, like that stray cat that someone had run over outside our house last June, and which had stayed on the street, swelling, in the sun, for days until—

What was I thinking? My father would never let me walk to the car alone. Either he or Mom, or both, would escort me. I was going to have to ask.

As if that would work. I may as well give up now.

But I didn't. I stood up, clutching the jaguar-like cat in my arms. It seemed to be unconscious, but its upper lip was drawn back so that I could see its teeth. What kind of cat had fangs like that? And ticks . . . I tried not to imagine them crawling off the cat and under my clothes.

I stepped out from behind the screen of cages. "I'm here."

My mother took one look at the thing I was carrying.

"Put it back."

"I haven't asked yet," I mumbled.

My father's mouth twisted a bit as he looked down at the mangy ragdoll in my arms. "No," he said. Just one word.

Well, that was it. You have to understand, my father's words have a way of shaping the world around him: Whatever he commands, somehow inevitably ends up happening. When I was younger I used to think he must be God. I was his creation, obviously. Just a part of his overarching plan. If he said I would grow up to be a businesswoman, I might as well buy the briefcase right now. If he decided I was ready to be married, then you'd better start planning the wedding. I was Frenenqer, the embodiment of his imagined, ideal daughter, and his imagined daughter did *not* pick up tick-infested, probably diseased animals, let alone bring them home.

"Put it down," he said.

My arms began to tremble despite myself.

"Don't tell me you expect us to pay for that," said my mother. "How dare you buy anything without asking for our permission first?"

"I didn't buy it," I ventured, seeing a chink of light. "It's free." Well, that was one way of putting it.

"No wonder," said Mom. "Is it dead?"

"No, it's just sick."

"Sick? It might be contagious! Put it down right now!"

"It might not be sick," I said, backtracking hurriedly. "I don't know. Maybe it's just dehydrated."

"Put. It. Down." My father's voice was flat. He was already looking away, back to the camels.

There. My father had spoken. The universe would obey.

"No," I said.

I listened to myself in amazement. I think the shock was so great that I had an out-of-body experience. Awestruck, I stared down at the skinny black-eyed girl as she stood on the crowded, dirty floor of the souk, holding a massive monster of a cat, and meeting the combined gazes of me and her parents. *The cat must have done something to her,* I thought.

I wanted to warn her how much trouble she would be in.

She heard my thoughts. *What? What can they do to me? If I'm grounded, how will that change anything? There's nothing to take away.*

She had clearly forgotten what my father had done the last time he was angry. I felt frightened for her.

No, she said, *I remember.* She looked back at her parents. Then the moment was over and I was her again, sweating in the oven-hot air, clutching the impossibly heavy body of the cat.

My mouth was dry. "Sorry," I whispered to my father, who had been slowly expanding with anger until he was twice as tall as usual, "but nothing is more important than a life, right?"

That was something my mother had told me, in one of her nostalgic, vaguely Buddhist moments. She recognized her own words and shifted guiltily from one foot to another. My father glanced at her. I saw the chink of light widen, and I began to talk faster. I felt as if I were balancing very high off the ground.

"If I leave the cat in this place," I said, "that'll be the same as killing it. I can't do that."

I tightened my grip on the animal. Unlike me and my mother, my father was a confirmed carnivore, so my plea didn't have much effect on him. But I saw him glance at my mom again. She avoided his gaze, studying the ground, and I almost felt bad for pitting him against her. Then he turned back to me. "I told you before," he said finally. "No pets."

"I won't keep it," I offered, still in shock at myself. "I'll find it a home as soon as it gets better."

He grunted and turned away.

Now pay attention. That part was important. I won, but

I didn't win. It's impossible to win against my father. He let me have my way for once, but his words—"No pets"—had been spoken, and their vibrations were already running down the spine of reality.

I carried the cat the whole time we were in the souk, even after my arms went numb; I kept it on my lap while we drove for three hours on a road through the desert to get back to our oasis; I pulled off all the ticks, waded through the books in my room, and laid it down on my bed; but those words of my father's would spread right to the ends of the world and come crashing back in a tsunami. I think that it was because of my father that things turned out the way they did. I think the universe couldn't help but obey him, even if I had refused to. In the end, his words came true, as always. The cat wasn't a pet at all . . . I'll explain, and then see for yourself whether my father is all-powerful or not.

It slept all day, curled up on the thin orange blankets of my bed. I settled it down so that its head was on the pillow, and it looked adorably luxurious stretched out like that, especially when I thought back to how I had first seen it in the Animal Souk—stuffed into its hot, tight cage. I began to enjoy my role as its savior. Inspired, I trickled water into its mouth. The water spilled all over my sheets and its fur, but it swallowed at least some. I saw its throat move.

That night we had dinner in silence. As usual, my mom cooked, but she didn't sit with us. She stayed in the kitchen, washing up, and ate her food there. When I was little, she did sit with us, but then, over the years, less and less. At some point she vanished.

I set the table for three anyway, the way I did every night. My father and I sat opposite each other, chewing slowly. At first, the only thing he told me was to adjust how my fingers held the fork, and to sit straighter in my chair. Then, when we were done eating, he said very quietly, "I'm worried that your interest in animals is becoming ridiculous. I wonder if I should ask your mother to buy anchovies again."

I shook my head without looking at him. When I was eleven and had first turned vegetarian, I'd answered back one time too many, and he hadn't let me leave the table until I'd eaten anchovies—whole, so that I could see their faces.

"Maybe you'll learn to be more moderate," he said.

He was just trying to stir up the memory. And it worked.

In a rush, I felt again the little eyes crunching between my teeth, and the dry, twisted faces, and the brittle bodies breaking as I bit—becoming slime on the back of my tongue. Salt, and scales, and hot acid. My first days in the oasis were soaked in that taste. I could remember the enormity of heat outside, how the cool, empty dining room had looked—we'd just moved in; not much furniture yet—and my father waiting, and the tears plopping off my chin. Now I held on to the table and concentrated on not throwing up.

"I'll have to see," my father said, watching the impact. Calm, resigned.

For weeks I hadn't been able to get the taste out of my

mouth. Eating anchovies . . . it was such a small, specific thing. If I complained about it to anyone, they'd just say "So what?"

So you see, in one deft stroke, he had isolated me.

It was a very private torture.

I stared at the floor.

Finally, my father changed the subject. I guess he was satisfied with my reaction. "I think your mother needs help. Go tell her you will wash the dishes."

And I thought, as I always did, *If you think she needs help, then you should help her, instead of sending me to do it.* But I cleared the table and washed the dishes without comment.

Straight afterward I withdrew to my room. This too was normal. I shut the door behind me, making as little noise as possible, and immediately went to check on the cat. It was still unconscious, but its breathing was less ragged than before. The air conditioner was blasting cold air right across it, and its fur was cool to the touch.

I could still taste anchovies. Ugh.

I made sure the curtains were properly closed—that there wasn't the smallest crack between them through which some man in the house opposite or down on the street could catch a glimpse of me as I changed. I threw on a baggy white shirt that was so oversized it almost reached my knees. That was all I wore at night. I didn't like to wear anything heavier because it might bring on a bout of claustrophobia.

Then I crawled over the sheets toward the cat, wanting to warm it, and smothered us both in blankets so that my parents wouldn't be able to see if they walked in without warning. I knew they wouldn't like it to be on my bed. But if it had a contagious disease, I'd probably caught it by now anyway, so why be cautious? That's what I told myself, cheerfully. I liked having the cat around. It was the most exciting thing that had happened to me in years.

I plucked a book off a towering stack beside me. At least six hundred books surrounded my bed, piled up like the walls of a fortress. I was only allowed so many because I got most of them for free. People often moved away and needed to get rid of their books, and my reputation as a reader meant it wasn't unusual for me to open the door in the morning on my way to school and find a big black garbage bag full of abandoned novels left lying across the doorstep. I just had to get to them before my father did.

I read one of my favorites for the tenth time, and then around midnight I turned the lights off to sleep. By that point I remember the cat was very warm.

I don't know what I dreamt that night. Something petty and annoying, probably. I don't have a lot of nightmares anymore, but I do have irritating dreams quite often. Of trying to walk while people keep tripping me. Of asking people not to do something, and then having to watch while they go right ahead and do it. Things like that.

At around four in the morning I woke up abruptly. Something had jerked me awake.

The song of the mosques? I had heard the mosques sing at their proper times for so many years that I should have been desensitized, but I was such a light sleeper that they still woke me sometimes. Although they weren't calling *me,* I liked to hear them anyway; they were the heartbeat of the day, providing a rhythm to the flow of time. I closed my eyes and listened. But no . . . I must have been mistaken . . . I couldn't hear the mosques. Something else must have awoken me. Oh, I knew what. It was the soft sound of my window being opened.

Ye gods.

That must be what it feels like to have a heart attack.

My eyes snapped open.

The predawn light was filtering in through the window. Right, it couldn't have been sunrise yet, because otherwise the mosques would have been calling. Only a faint, fresh whiteness came in through the curtains, making it light enough for me to see the details of my room.

Ever since that old nightmare of the man with the flashlight, I'd made a habit of keeping the curtains shut, for safety. But now they had been pulled apart, and the window was half open . . . that was all I could see at first, because I wasn't wearing contact lenses, and because my eyes were adjusting to the brightness of that glowing square.

Then I spotted the figure standing beside the window. He was half invisible behind the screen of white light that slanted between us. I could make out the curve of his body as he twisted around to look at me, and the very faint impression of a face. His irises were yellow gold.

I sat up slowly. My chest was solid with dread.

We were both frozen for a long, drawn-out sliver of time. Finally, I said, ". . . I think I should scream now."

"Don't," he said.

"Why not?"

"I'm just leaving."

"Don't," I said. Then I was surprised at myself. What an odd thing to say.

He clearly thought so too. "Why not?"

"Because . . . you have to explain what you're doing here. It's not fair to just leave." I sat straighter. The movement broke some sort of stalemate between us. We both unfroze.

"I'm not explaining anything," he said, shoving the rest of the window open.

"But you're in my room!"

He hissed. I don't mean that poetically. He actually bared his teeth and hissed at me, like a cat. "You brought me here!"

"What?"

One movement, and suddenly he was crouched in the window. The light framed him so that I couldn't see details, but his outline was very clear. He couldn't have been human. I thought he looked a bit like a gargoyle. But maybe I only thought that because of the wings: two arched wings at his back, with the skin drawn tight, almost transparent, over the thin framework of bones. They fit perfectly with the curve of his shoulders. He would make a really good statue, I thought, irrelevently.

He turned away from me; the wings shifted, like shadows sliding over his back; and with a quick, light movement, he tossed himself out the window. It really was a toss—the careless sort of gesture with which you would flick something not very important into the garbage.

I wasn't quite sure how I was supposed to react to that.

In the end, like a good girl, I got up and shut the window. My hands reached up and took hold of the heavy cloth of the curtains. Slowly I drew them closed, and the last of the light disappeared. My hands wouldn't relinquish their hold on the curtains, though, so I just stood there for a while, facing the thick folds of cloth and not looking at anything in particular. It was as if I were confounded by a weighty problem, only I couldn't have explained what it was. At last I let go of the curtains, turned around, and walked back to bed. I stood at the side of the bed for a while too, staring at it, my brow still furrowed. Then I got in and went back to sleep. There didn't seem to be anything else to do.

I woke up a couple of hours later. I stared at the ceiling for another half an hour. I thought to myself, *The cat is gone.*

This was true.

Then I thought—well, that's it for pets. My father doesn't want a cat in his house; the cat turns into a human thing and flees in the middle of the night. So much for my rebellion.

I thought for a while longer. Then I padded out of bed, changed, and went off to make myself breakfast.

CHAPTER THREE

In Which I Transform
Into an Eighty-Year-Old Saint

The day passed. I was unnaturally calm. I told my parents that the cat had somehow run away, and that was the end of it.

At noon, my friend Anju phoned and asked my parents for permission to visit me next week after school. I could imagine her flat, businesslike tone on the other end of the line. My father said he would have to think about it. From two to six in the afternoon I read another favorite book of mine for the fifth time. At six I set the table and we had dinner. Halfway through, my mother came into the dining room to check that I'd laid out the dishes properly, and knocked one of the placemats slightly askew. My father looked at it, frowned, and moved it back into the right place. Wordlessly, she retreated to the kitchen. This was their dance.

When I was done washing the dishes, I retired to my bedroom, closed the door, and sat for a while. Without looking, my fingers crept compulsively to one of my shelves and closed over the spine of a book. I drew it out, gave the cover a glance—I'd only read it twice before—and opened to the first page.

I was near the end and my parents had long since gone to sleep when the attack came. The itch on my back grew and grew, spreading fiery fingers right up to my neck. I dropped the book to the floor. My breaths came short and shallow. I felt that my bedroom was very small, hardly any bigger than a coffin, and it seemed to be shrinking even as I felt the walls to reassure myself that they couldn't be moving. I had to walk—had to run—but there was nowhere to go. I flew to the window and shoved the curtains apart.

The cat was sitting on the other side of the glass.

Two wide eyes stopped me dead in my tracks. I jerked back as if I'd been slapped. He was startled too, on his paws before I had recovered.

"Wait, wait," I said, regaining control of myself. I slid the window up. He withdrew, but at least he didn't flee.

What do you say to a cat? We studied each other in silence for a bit. At last I took a deep breath and said, "Do you mind if I sit here with you?" It made me sound a bit as if I thought we were in a public cafeteria, but at least it was polite.

"If you think you can fit," he said. Now *that* wasn't polite.

My mouth twisted, but I didn't say anything. I slipped myself up onto the window ledge effortlessly—I must have done it hundreds of times before. There was plenty of room for both of us. There would have been enough room for *three* of me. So there. I realized I was grumbling to myself—typical Frenenqer, getting distracted by irrelevan-

31

cies while sitting beside a talking cat. I tried to focus.

It was dark, but in the light streaming out from my bedroom, I could see that he looked a lot better. His black fur made him almost invisible, except that it gleamed at some angles. The eyes reminded me of magic lights in a swamp. Yellow, and savage, and seeming to come from very far away, even though they were right in front of me.

"Why did you come back?" I said to him.

"I didn't mean to," he said, looking away. "I was just thinking about it. You weren't supposed to see me."

"Is it necessary to sit outside my window in order to think?" Oh. That sounded more accusing than I had intended it to. "Sorry," I said quickly. "I mean—I'm glad you're back."

He didn't look convinced. I changed the subject. "Where've you been all day?"

"I went to kill someone," he said.

". . . Oh."

Silence.

He threw me a vaguely amused look. "I had a reason."

". . . Good . . ." I said.

Okay, so nonviolence had just backfired. That's the problem with doing good deeds. You work hard to save someone, and then they just go off and kill things.

"An old pest. Don't worry, it wasn't a human. He's the one who trapped me in a cage and sold me to the Animal Souk. He thought he was getting rid of me." He laughed to himself. It wasn't the wicked cackle I would have expected from a murderer. His laughter was only evil in a careless

32

way (as if that made it any better). He had an extraordinarily casual air about him. I'd noticed that before, when he had tossed himself out the window.

I said, "How come you were trapped?"

"Huh? Oh, he was trying to get revenge for some silly little thing he imagined that I'd done to him . . ."

"No, I mean—you're not a normal cat, so why couldn't you just escape from the souk?"

"I can't go *poof* and make the bars disappear. The only difference between you and me is that I was born free." He saw from my face that I didn't understand. "I'm a Free person. Probably the only one you'll ever meet. All the rules and boundaries and whatever"—he listed them as nonchalantly as if they were made of smoke; things that could be waved off in a bored fashion—"aren't applicable to me."

I stared at him for a moment, considering it. I had many thoughts. I thought of my stiff little life and I understood that there *must* be some people who were born differently, because otherwise reality wouldn't make sense. What would be the point of a world where everyone was caged? If I could be so trapped, then, in the interests of symmetry, there had to be at least a few people who were equally free. But the first thing that I thought, above all, was that I should shove this cat off the windowsill for taking his good fortune so much for granted.

"Lucky," I said, in a low tone. If I sounded bitter, he didn't notice.

He shrugged. "It's like that for all Free people. Some

animals are born without tails, some are born without aggressive instincts, and some are born without speech—and, well, *we're* born without rules. Simple as that. I'll still die, sure. But in the meantime, I can go anywhere and be anything I want. Extreme sizes are a bit tricky . . . That's why I couldn't slip between the bars of the cage in the souk. But anywhere between a whale and a mouse is fair game. I could go human," he added brightly, like a child saying "Look what I can do!"

So, without another word—that's exactly what he did.

And I almost fell off the window ledge. There was a sickly lurching moment—but before I could scrabble for a grip, before my heart had time to either stop or begin a row of frantic death-drumbeats, he'd caught me, and by the time I felt my first jolt of panic, he had already pulled me back to the window. With bare arms. Against his chest. And then I had more important things to worry about than falling to my death. "Let me go," I growled, before he had the chance to hoist me inside.

"What? Do you want to fall?" he said.

Better to fall than to be held by a naked— I closed my eyes. I didn't want to finish that thought. "I said to let me go!"

Blankly, he said, "Why?"

"Put some clothes on, will you?"

"Oh . . . right," he said as light dawned. He kept his hands on my elbows. "But I wasn't wearing any this morning, and you didn't mind."

"You weren't human this morning!" It was harder to

struggle with my eyes shut. I couldn't tell which side was my room, and which side had only the emptiness of air. I held rigid in the arms of the Free person.

He considered this, then sighed, as if hard-put-upon. "All right, all right. Keep your eyes shut, then." I was lifted briefly into the air, but before I could react, I was standing on the solid floor again and by the change in temperature I could tell I was back in my room. I heard my wardrobe door open and some things being shuffled around.

"There isn't much here that I can wear." He kept up a running commentary as he rifled through my clothes. "Oh, what's *this*? I'm not even sure how you're supposed to wear this . . ." I screwed my eyes tighter shut, wondering which drawer he was in. "I like this one. Nice color. You ought to put it on. It wouldn't suit me, though—far too girly. All right, let's see . . . Ah. I think I opened the wrong drawer. I definitely couldn't wear anything in *there*—"

"Okay," I snapped. "That's enough." To my horror, I thought I heard a noise in the next room. Ye gods, if my father found out I had a boy in my room . . . "I'll find you something to wear, but you have to either change shape or go stand in a corner while I do it," I whispered. I gave him a moment and then, without looking to see which he had chosen to do, opened my eyes and went over to the wardrobe. In the last minute he had managed to turn my mother's neatly stacked piles of clothing into a site of terrible devastation. Steeling myself, I picked a pair of pants out of the mess. They were loose and shapeless, neither particularly female nor male.

They'd do fine. And in the next drawer was one of my plain, oversized nightshirts.

That reminded me. I'd cuddled the cat last night, hadn't I, while I was wearing no more than a nightshirt? Had he been awake? I fiddled with the cloth, taking longer than necessary.

"Here," I said finally, throwing the clothes over my shoulder without turning around. "Put them on."

A second later he said, "Okay, you can turn around now. But I still think you're overreacting."

I turned.

I'm not going to gush. That would be demeaning. Even in the shock of the moment, I would rather stick to facts. I saw black hair and burning yellow eyes. The pupils were slightly slanted, and that, added to the sharp cast of his face and also the deceptively languid way he held himself, left a distinctly feline impression. I think a good way to describe it is—interestingly wicked. I would have been prepared to bet that his ears and incisors were just a tiny bit more pointed than usual.

"So the clothes fit," was all I said.

"Yeah, no problem," he replied. A breeze brushed the curtains apart, and moonlight flashed in his face as he grinned. "So, are we taking turns? Do I get to dress you now?"

"No!"

Great. I clammed up like some prim old woman. I folded my arms and looked off to one side of the room, as if to suggest that the peeling paint in the corner was a more interesting sight than he was. It was the only safe way to behave around his lounging, absentminded maleness.

I was really good at being humorless. Too good. I almost scared myself. And yet he didn't seem to notice my abrupt transformation into an eighty-year-old saint. "Just a joke," he said, casting his eyes around at all my books.

"Keep your voice down, will you?" I said.

"Why?"

"My parents are asleep next door." I used my best old-maidenly voice, still unable to look away from the stupid paint. I even tapped my foot. My mother would have been impressed.

"So?"

"My father wouldn't like you to be here."

"Sounds strict."

"Not compared to some of my friends' fathers," I said shortly. "But he does have a lot of control. He decides everything—he decided who I would be before I was born."

"Really?" he said. "Who did he decide you should be?"

"Not the kind of girl who lets Free people into her room! Especially male ones."

His eyebrows disappeared into the crush of black hair, which still looked rumpled from when he'd pulled his—my—shirt over it. "Free people? Unless you have some others hidden away, it's just me."

"Even worse," I muttered.

"I'll go if you want me to," he said, looking at me sideways. I couldn't tell whether he was testing me or not. He slipped

37

past me, closer to the window, and . . . grew wings. As casually as I would put on a hat.

The back of his shirt tore as the bat-like wings curled out. *So much for that nightshirt,* I thought. But my eyes immediately went to what was important. The wings. Two smooth dark arcs sweeping out of his shoulder blades. They seemed to fill the room with curves, graceful tapering points, an expanse of blackness, and I thought of the seas I had seen long ago, far away, during a time when I lived beyond the clinging dust of the desert. Those wings resembled the nights I could explore, if I only had a pair of my own. A faint flush came to my cheeks.

He noticed, of course. He paused at the window and a thoughtful look reached his yellow eyes. The corner of his mouth twisted. "You like the wings, huh?"

I jumped and jerked my gaze away.

"We could go somewhere, if you want," he said.

My mouth was dry. "Where?"

"Anywhere. I'm very fast."

Again I wondered what exactly he had done to deserve so much good luck. He was leaning against the wall, grinning at me slantwise, and steeped in his own freedom. The loose black hair was finally beginning to fall back into place. Messy. And he couldn't have been much older than me. No, he didn't look particularly superior; and yet there it was, the gift of wings curving behind him.

I wanted to answer yes. I wanted, badly, to just dive out the window. My skin tingled as I imagined it. The imaginary wings at my back beat as hard as a second heart, but there, exactly between them, digging tight into my back, was the itch of my father's finger, and from its tip came the command. It traveled through me, right up to my throat, where my father's voice spoke and said: "No."

"You sure?" he said, slipping up onto the windowsill. The line of his cheek was thin and eager from this angle, like the sharp edge of a knife. Then he turned to look back and ruined the silhouette. "I want to thank you for saving me, that's all. You should come. You don't have to be afraid of me."

I felt obliged to point out, "Well, you have killed someone."

"But I wouldn't kill *you*," he said magnanimously, as though he was going out of his way to do me a great favor. "I owe you. I don't take that lightly, you know. If you wanted to, you could hit me across the face right now, and I wouldn't do anything." He paused. "I'd prefer it if you didn't, of course."

I shook my head. *No, that's not how it goes,* I thought. My father's daughter could not just hop off over the horizon with a random boy. There were too many walls set up. The bricks had been laid down one at a time, day by day. Now they were built into me. And besides, "I don't know your name," I said. I used my stiff old-womanly voice again. I hated to hear myself.

He leaned more comfortably against the side of the window, wings shifting like a cape at his back. "Names are overrated," he said.

He seemed happy enough with that answer.

"So your name is . . . ?" I prompted.

"Don't have one."

"You must."

"Nope. This might surprise you, but not many people know me. I travel a lot, but I try to keep a low profile. I've been called, variously, Cat, That Thing, and 'devil' in maybe five different languages." From the look on my face I think he could tell that this news didn't exactly inspire confidence. "Look, if it's that important, you can choose a name for me. Whatever name you like," he said. I continued to stare at him with raised eyebrows.

"So . . . what's yours?" he said smoothly.

I hesitated before telling him. "Frenenqer."

"All right, Frenenqer," he said with satisfaction. He came forward, back into the glow of my bedroom, and his face shocked me all over again. I changed my mind about the statue. If he were a sculpture, then the artist would have to be locked up in an asylum—no sane person could create something like that. The boy wasn't beautiful, you know, any more than something bewildering, like fire, is beautiful; but, well, fire can be magical, and isn't that better than beautiful? He seemed to be lit with a different kind of light.

There were the eyes, for example. They were *wrong*. Eyes like that shouldn't be allowed in a human face. They broke rules just by being yellow.

"Are you sure you don't want to come with me?"

"Yes," I lied.

He grinned. "Go to sleep then. It's late." He reached out to touch my shoulder. I jumped back. "I'll see you later."

He hopped out of the window before I could reply, and the darkness of the night immediately swallowed him up. "Hey!" I whispered, a split second later. No response. He was gone.

And I was the one who had driven him off.

I said no, I thought in astonishment. *A Free person pranced into my room, offered me flight, and I said no. How stupid is that?*

But the truth was, there had never been a real choice.

CHAPTER FOUR

In Which I Cross a Land of Mirages

He didn't show up the next morning while I was serving myself cereal. At the usual time, I got into the car and my mother drove me to school. We were silent the entire way. I watched the white cars pass by, and the green-and-gold date palms slide away, and the dusty bleached houses, with their tinted windows reflecting dark blue or brown, vanish into the distance. Dirty stretches of pale sand by the side of the road. Rarely, a man bicycling past through the heat, if he was too poor to afford a car. Workers in their orange jackets toiling to keep the plants alive. The grass on the roundabouts, as artificial as paint, right next to the bare wadi, which was so dry that the ground curled upward in little flakes, cracked and scaly like the hide of a dragon. Nothing out of the ordinary that I could see. No enormous cats, no boys with wings.

He didn't show up while I was at school. I brushed through the schoolwork in the first few minutes of each lesson, then spent the rest of my time staring off into space. Anju sat beside me.

"What other classes do I have today?" I asked her.

I had a habit of treating her like a secretary, and, for some reason, she allowed me to.

"Double chemistry, then English," she said, consulting my timetable. "No, wait—afternoon classes are canceled today. You only have one period of chemistry, and then we have to organize our rooms for Heritage."

I doodled absently. Writing down names, then crossing them out again. "Great. What nationality did I decide to be this year?"

"Thai."

"Right," I said, sighing. "Are you sure you don't want to work on Thailand with me?"

"I can't. I'm Indian."

"They won't care. We'll just say you have a Thai great-grandfather or something."

She shook her head expressionlessly. "No one will believe me. Not everyone is from half a million different countries, you know."

"Whatever." I left it at that. "Tell me, do you like the name Sangris?"

"What?"

I showed her one of the names that I'd doodled down.

"It's weird," she said.

"Perfect. Do we have any tests this week?"

Again she consulted her notebook. "No. But you have an appointment with the librarian tomorrow. She wants you to make a list of recommended books for some of the Key Stage Two kids . . ."

I suppressed a smile. "If you ever want to be a secretary, Anju, I'll be more than happy to give you a reference. Just say the word."

She shrugged. That was another thing about Anju. She seldom spoke except in answer to a direct question.

Class ended. I wandered off to organize the Thai room for Heritage. On a sheet of paper, I scribbled about Thailand with the thickest pen I could find, to take up the maximum amount of space on the paper. Then I spent the rest of the hour reading a book beneath my desk.

He didn't show up.

And he still didn't show up when school ended and my father drove me home in silence.

I took no more than five seconds to run into the house. It was too hot to dawdle. In those five seconds, he failed to appear out of nowhere. A glance up showed only that an oncoming sandstorm had blanched the sky a coarse white, a few birds rolling past through the distant blankness. Over the wastelands, beyond the desert. I looked at them and a heavy, dry jealousy made my throat ache.

He didn't show up when I shut myself into my bedroom, picked a book at random, and read it. It was short. It only took me an hour or so to finish. I put it back and read two more in a row, like a chain-smoker.

He didn't show up while I had dinner in the cold white dining room with my father, and my mother ate by herself in the kitchen.

Then I made a mistake.

I was thinking of the sky, and of how I might have flown yesterday if I'd only been reckless enough, and as I left the dining room I closed the door behind me with a small *thud*.

Mom, still in the kitchen, sucked in her breath and turned away as if she didn't even want to see what would happen next.

"Frenenqer."

My father didn't shout. He never shouted. The call came as though he were performing a chore he didn't particularly like but needed to finish. Straightaway I *knew* what I'd done wrong—I wished I could just take the last few seconds back and do it over. Cursing myself, I returned to the room.

"You know how I feel about slamming doors," my father said, still at the table. "People will wonder how I raised you."

He spoke about it so sincerely. "I'll have to fix you," said my father. For the next half hour I stood closing and opening and closing the dining room door over and over again, making no sound each time. My face burned. I tried to think of something else until the routine was over. I dreamed of wings.

At last my father said, "You can practice some more later." But his lips were still thin with irritation at letting a disfigurement remain in me for even a day.

I went back into my bedroom and read another book until I felt less strained. My mother burst in twice to put freshly ironed stacks of clothes into my wardrobe, and to scold me for letting it get so messy. I jumped in alarm each time the door banged open and *thwacked* against the wall. For some reason my mother always entered my room—only mine—

as noisily as possible, but without knocking. It'd get us into trouble if he heard. Unfortunately, I couldn't lock my door. My father had taken away the keys.

I went to sleep early that night. I thought of leaving a window half open, then blushed at myself. It would be shameful to be so forward. I kept the windows and curtains as firmly closed as ever. If he wanted to come in, he could just knock on the glass, and I might open it . . .

But he didn't show up.

Typical boy, I thought to myself indignantly when I awoke the next morning after an undisturbed night of sleep. *They're all the same. Even the ones who can turn into cats.*

I didn't actually have any experience of such things, but I had read about them in books.

I had breakfast as normal, was driven to school as normal. The same views of dried wadis and date palms and artificial grass. I went into the school building as usual. "What classes do I have today?" I asked Anju, throwing my bag down and sitting in the seat next to her. She was reading a textbook, as studious and stolid as always.

She told me my list of classes. "But after break, we have more time off to plan for Heritage."

"Again?" I wriggled in my chair. I fiddled with a pen. The lesson began, but I was a good student, so I wouldn't get into trouble if I didn't pay attention. "One thousand, Anju. That's approximately how many days I've spent sitting in this same seat."

She shrugged.

"There was a Free person in my room the night before last," I said. "He offered to fly off with me, but I said no."

No reaction. Anju was used to me saying weird things.

"Pay attention," I ordered.

"I am," she said, not looking up from her textbook. "Why did you say no?"

"Because he's male and he scares me," I said.

"You should be used to that. There are boys in our class," she said.

As far as the Ministry of Education knew, our school was segregated. But there were only a few hundred students, so that really wasn't practical. As long as we quickly changed classrooms whenever Ministry inspectors came by, we could get away with mixing together.

"Ugh. They don't count," I said.

"True."

She lapsed back into silence. That was all I could hope to get out of her. Giving up, I pulled a book out of my bag and laid it in front of her. It was one I knew she'd like. Then I pulled out another and read it beneath the table. Another old favorite. I was reading it for the fifteenth time. To my everlasting regret, there were no public libraries in the oasis. Only the tiny high school library with about three rows of English books. I'd already read all of them, so I was stuck working my way through the shelves again and again. Still, it was comforting to open a book and see familiar words rolling past my eyes, in their proper order and at their proper rhythm.

There was one second I thought I saw something quick

and dark pass the window. But it was just a palm frond.

When the bell rang I went to stand in front of my shabby wooden box of a locker, rummaging, Anju having evaporated into whatever spirit world she inhabited whenever I didn't need her.

A few of my friends were talking nearby. Lots of whispers and raised eyebrows.

"Hmm?" I said, leaning over.

Some scandal had happened during a dinner. We don't have parties, you see, we have polite supervised dinners. A girl called Mitzi had wanted to show her friends a new dress. But the hem was above her knee, and so her friends had refused to look. "It wasn't even Mitzi's house," said one girl in an undertone. "She wanted to wear it in *my* house. My brother was there and everything."

I could understand her point. "What did you do?" I said.

"I told her the dress was inappropriate and asked her to change back . . ."

Suddenly I remembered myself in my nightshirt and my cheeks went uncomfortably hot. I withdrew to my locker before they could notice. My stomach began to squeeze. What would they say if they knew? And that, right now, I was actually *waiting* for him to come back? Dangling after him. Whatever they said, they'd be right, completely right. I walked away fast, face still burning.

"What's wrong?" said Anju, slipping back into place at my side, out of nowhere, in the manner of an experienced butler.

"It's not like I'm throwing myself at him," I exclaimed. "He has wings. Of course I'm waiting!"

"Um. Okay . . ." she said.

But already the stone in my stomach, the guilty feeling of shame, lessened a bit. Because it was true, I wasn't waiting for him, I was waiting for a chance to see those wings again.

"Sorry," I said to Anju, but already she wasn't listening. She didn't speak again until break, when she reminded me of my appointment with the librarians.

"Come with me," I said. She wasn't talkative, but at least she was company.

To get to the library, we had to exit the building and walk across an expanse of hot sand—the "garden"—before we reached the small stone hut. We walked quickly with our faces scrunched up in the blinding sunlight. Inside, the library was air-conditioned. I handed them my list of recommended books, restocked on reading material, and—done. Anju and I turned to go.

"Look at that," she said suddenly, pointing. In the dazzling, mirage-filled area of sand ahead of us, by the primary school building, was a gaggle of kids. They all wore the navy shirt and long gray pants of primary school children. Some of them were crouching. As we watched, one jumped up and burst into tears. His mouth became a small black O against the white-white sand and the bleached buildings.

Almost inaudibly, Anju chuckled.

"My dear Anju," I said, "sometimes you truly are evil."

"It's funny the way he was screaming," she muttered.

Nothing cheered her up like the tears of primary school children.

"Come on," I said, stepping out into the brightness.

The group of kids shifted worriedly when we walked up to them. It was unusual for so many people to be outside, out of the AC. Maybe they weren't allowed.

The screaming boy immediately stuffed his fist into his mouth. But I could see now why he had been wailing. There were three thin red lines cut into his cheek. "What happened?" I said, frowning. I was much older than they were, and I wore the intimidating light blue shirt of a student in Key Stage Three, so they didn't spit at me. Solemnly a little girl pointed into the middle of the crowd. They parted to let me through.

The cat looked up at me. Two yellow eyes burned in the haziness of the hot air.

He flicked his tail, and then I nearly fell over backward as the heavy black thing leaped neatly into my arms. I caught him just in time.

The kids' eyes widened. As much as they *could* widen in the overwhelming sunlight.

"How did you do that?" one demanded.

"It wouldn't let us near it!"

The crying one just pointed expressively at the claw marks on his cheek.

Among kindergarteners, I would be known forever afterwards as the cat tamer. "You have to be nice to animals," I told them, figuring that I may as well slip in a good lesson while I was at it. "Even the nasty, mean, smelly ones."

The cat purred comfortably.

They were still all staring at me. I turned and carried the cat away. Anju walked beside me without a word, but when we finally reached the air-conditioned relief of the building, she said, "So, do you have a secret way of taming feral cats that I don't know about?"

I shook my head and sat down cross-legged right in the middle of the corridor (I was a good student, I could get away with it) while Anju, never very interested in stray animals, drifted off to the side, flipping through my timetable.

"You," I said to the cat. "What did you scratch that kid for?"

He put his paws on my shoulder and leaned in so that his head was beside my ear. He was big enough that he could do this while standing on my lap. From where Anju stood, I must have been completely hidden behind warm black fur. "They were annoying me," he whispered.

"You didn't have to scratch him."

"He was trying to pull my tail. I could have done much worse, you know. I'm not a housecat . . ." he grumbled. I could feel his weight against me. I wondered if that was okay, if he was still a cat.

"Frenenqer," said Anju, "are you whispering to the cat?" She didn't sound very surprised. Anju had seen me act much more strangely before.

"Yeah," I said. I didn't mind if Anju thought I was a lunatic. "See, I've met this cat before. His name is Sangris."

"Not bad," he murmured.

"Okay. You can get off me now." I lowered him to the floor. "Sangris, this is Anju."

Unflappable Anju said, "Whatever. Look, the bell will ring in five minutes. I'm going to the room where the Indian stall will be. Okay? You should start heading to the Thai room too."

Ever the dependable secretary. "Sure. See you later," I said.

We both watched her walk off.

"Not very cheerful, is she?" Sangris said.

"No. She's very patient with me, though."

"Good—if that's what you look for in a friend," he said. "What did she mean, the Thai room?"

I was already getting to my feet. "Oh, that," I said. "I'll explain later. Anju's right, I have to go. They take attendance, you know."

He demanded, "What if those grubby little kids come after me again?"

"I'll only be ten minutes," I said. "I'm done organizing stuff for the Thai room anyway. I'll be right back." Without waiting for a reply, I took my bag and hurried up the stairs, leaving him to look after me in exasperation.

Good. Let him wait for a change.

CHAPTER FIVE

In Which Sangris Becomes a Poet

When I returned, I looked down the silent corridor. Empty. Everyone else was busy preparing for Heritage. Lockers pressed in on both sides, wooden, painted a garish green that had already begun to fade to khaki. At the end of the corridor was the exit. Two closed doors, with squares of glass glowing from the sunlight outside. The glass on the right was cracked from that time when Hassan had bashed his head against it because Jamila had refused to go out with him. (She was one of the girls who were allowed to date.) No cat. No cat anywhere.

I'm going to slap him, I thought. He did say I could.

At that exact moment, Sangris sauntered in from the direction of the stairwell. He was in human form, and he was impeccably dressed in the school uniform. "Hey, Nenner," he said.

A nickname. Really?

And just like that, I snapped back into an eighty-year-old saint.

"Did you know they have a uniform shop in the basement?" he continued enthusiastically.

Somehow, the uniform suited him. He could have been a student. A student from a bizarre faraway school with no regard for protocol, sure, where everyone was suspiciously attractive, but still . . .

"Wait a minute," I said, walking closer. I studied him with a frown. "Where were you keeping the money?"

"What?"

"You were a cat. Where were you keeping the money?"

"What money?"

"To buy the uniform."

"Buy?" He seemed genuinely surprised at the idea.

"You didn't!" I cried.

"They had plenty," he said. "They won't miss it."

"That's not the way it works!" I spoke too loudly. A door opened at the end of the corridor, and the incongruously British, tousled head of a teacher poked out.

"Frenenqer?" he said.

"Ah . . . yes."

His eyes turned, inevitably, to Sangris. "And . . . I don't believe I've met you before?" He came out into the corridor. That was a bad sign. "You're not a student here, are you?"

"This is my friend," I said quickly. "He's a guest. He wanted to see the school. He's thinking about coming here next year."

It turns out that I'm a pretty good liar.

"But . . ." The teacher looked Sangris up and down with a mildly bemused expression. I didn't blame him. "Yes, I'm aware that we allow guests to sit in on classes. But . . . why are you wearing the school uniform?"

"He's very excited about coming here," I said.

"But . . ."

"*Very* excited."

"Ah . . ."

"And he likes to dress up," I added.

Sangris went into a sudden coughing fit.

"Right, well . . ." The teacher backed away.

I watched until he had returned to the classroom.

Beside me, Sangris said plaintively, "Why did you make it sound as if I'm a cross-dresser?"

I ignored that. "What are you doing here anyway?"

"It's the only school in the area. Where else could you be? So I came to give you another chance," he said. Cheerfully. Fixing the collar of his shirt.

I took a step away from him. "What chance?"

"To take you flying somewhere."

I just stared at him.

"Don't you know that you're supposed to scream 'yippee' and throw your arms around my neck? You must have a heart made of sludge. Don't you have any sense of adventure at all?" He fixed his keen, slanted eyes on me. "When does school end for you?"

"Three forty-five," I said.

"I can have you back by then." He took a step closer, so that we were the same distance apart as before. He looked serious for once. "Do you want to go or not?"

He didn't know that there was a full-fledged battle being fought on my back, between the imaginary wings and the itch where I could feel my father's eternally pointing finger digging into my skin. Beating, searing, flapping, itching: I was the battlefield that bombs exploded across. I was sick of them by now, and I wanted them to stop, but I was only the ground over which the armies marched—I didn't have any part in the battle myself. I opened my mouth, but I couldn't say anything. I kept my eyes fixed on his. Couldn't he see that I was trying to say yes? Why couldn't he take my silence as assent?

But that was no good. I had to say it myself. Otherwise it would be no different from my parents driving me to school and back. Being driven, being flown, being taken here and there . . . *Answer,* I ordered myself.

"Yeah," I said, mouth dry.

His face split into a grin. I liked his grin. It was disturbing, but in a good way, a way that made my un-wings flutter at my back.

"Is there somewhere in particular you want to go?"

"Anywhere." I spoke quickly, before common sense could catch up and drag me down again. I was afraid I'd have second thoughts, so I ran ahead of them. "Anywhere, but let's go now."

He took my hand and led me over to the door. I didn't resist. I allowed him to touch me. On the fingers. I wondered if that meant I was already compromised.

When he opened the door for me, a blaze of sunlight

streamed in, illuminating the corridor like the flash from a camera. I stepped through into the heat. Grainy sand underfoot, the low wall that surrounded the school up ahead, the deathly blue sky above. We went around the back of the building, where no one could see us. "But I'd prefer it if you would turn into an animal," I added. I was still my father's daughter.

There was a pause. He looked at me for a long time with an expression of intense concentration, as if I were speaking a language he'd never heard before. He seemed to be puzzling out something very difficult.

Finally, he said, "Why do I have to turn into an animal? I thought we were leaving."

"We are, you idiot."

"I'm glad we're already close enough that you can call me an idiot with impunity," he said politely, "but I don't understand your logic."

"How do you plan on carrying me?"

"While we fly? Ah . . . in my arms, I guess."

"Now, see, that's far too intimate," I said. I got uncomfortable just thinking about it.

"*Oh.* I see. Well, that is a problem." The corners of his mouth twitched. "What do you propose to do about it?"

"First, you stop smirking."

"I'm not laughing at you," he said. "I'm just flattered."

That horrified me more than anything. "Don't be."

"Fine. I'm not. You just want me to turn into some hideous winged creature that you can ride on without feeling immodest."

That was a pretty fair summary of the situation. "Yes," I said.

"Huh," he said. "Hideous isn't usually my *goal*, but I'll see what I can do. Turn away."

"Why?"

"Well, I just thought I ought to take off these clothes—"

I whipped around, staring squarely at the blank white wall of the school. After a long moment, he said, "Okay, how's this?"

I turned back.

He had chosen a sleek, dragon-like form. Long yellow-gold eyes. Gray scales. He was on all fours, talons curled into the ground, and I had to look upward to meet his gaze. He would have reminded me of a lizard if his face hadn't been artistically framed by a few golden feathers. His tail and his wings were feathered too, with the same lush flame-gold plumage that blossomed smoothly out of the scales. I had no idea what he was supposed to be, but I didn't think he had made much of an effort to appear hideous.

"What are you?"

He blinked at me. "I don't know. I just made it up."

I couldn't help but smile at that.

Then, carefully, I put out my hands onto the most innocuous area I could find, on his side, just below the ridge of his spine. The scales felt small and rough beneath my fingertips. And the world didn't crack apart, my mother's voice didn't hiss into my ear, my father did not dig his finger harder into my back. I pulled myself up easily.

A wave of adrenaline—something I hadn't felt for a long

time, not once since my short-lived walks—surged through my stomach. The blood that had settled sluggishly some-where around my feet for the last five years began to beat through my body again. It was like a fizz in my veins. "Let's go," I said quickly, giddily.

"You might have to hold on to something," he said. "I told you, I'm fast."

I looked at my hands. They were resting lightly on the hollow between his shoulder blades, the fingers nicely folded, the way my father had trained me at the dinner table. That was no good. But no obvious places to grip came to mind. His shoulders were too sleek. There was a mane of feathers higher up, but it might hurt him if I grabbed those. And I wasn't willing to touch anything else. "Just go slowly then," I told him.

He sighed in disappointment. I couldn't hear it, but I could feel his sides move. For a split second I enjoyed the intimacy of being able to tell what he was doing without needing to hear or see; it was as if we were connected. Then I realized I could feel him breathe normally too—it was a rhythm between my legs. And that was *so* intimate that all at once there were nervous sparkles dissolving in my stomach. I almost jumped off.

But Sangris lifted his wings first.

Wings.

A lurch with the first, slow beat.

With the golden feathers rising on either side of me, I could pretend that they were mine.

They came down for a second time.

And a third.

Then the world fell away.

The school, the dirty sand, the stone wall, the dust, the spiky palm trees, the hard, glinting cars with sunlight on their windows, all sinking away. The long sun-bleached roads, gone. The scaly networks of wadis, gone. The white-domed roofs of the mosques, gone too. The weight of the heat, the claustrophobia, the little pockets of cold air that contained me as if I were a goldfish in a bowl—gone. And my parents—gone. I watched everything slide away. Only the itch on my back, no more than a pinprick, like the very tip of my father's nail, remained, an invisible fishing line linking me to him.

We were lifting, lifting. Pushing against the heat that fell from the sky. Then faster, finally, picking up speed, slicing through the blueness and the stiff folds of air. The sun stung on my back. Heat curled through my hair. Instinctively, I threw myself forward and wrapped my arms around his neck, bending into that hollow between his shoulder blades. "Faster!" I said.

"Really?" Sangris said. But the world blurred before I could reply. He took off, so fast that I couldn't open my eyes against the wind, but I didn't care. In the dark world behind my eyelids, I saw bursts of red excitement blossom in the blackness whenever his wings rose and fell, and the pit of my stomach rose and fell with them.

It seemed to take only a few minutes. Not nearly long enough. When I opened my eyes next, it was because leaves were brushing my face, and the air smelled new. Damp. "We're here," he said as I unpeeled myself from him.

When my legs recovered, I slid down, squinting. All around us was a network of curly, complicated shadows. Crowded trees, frizzy with twigs, leaned over my head. Branches blocked out the sky, like a roof; the place we'd come through had already closed over. It was so black up there that, where the layers of leaves happened to thin, a few unexpected edges of yellow, or a single warm patch suggesting green, shone out lovelier than any flowers. The only threads of light that managed to pierce straight through the foliage were needle-thin, hanging in the darkness like solitary, glowing white hairs.

Sangris bent his head down until it hovered over my shoulder. I didn't notice at first, because I was too busy gazing around the dimness, moving my hands through the needles of light, watching them splice between my fingers. Then I felt feathers brushing my cheek and jumped.

"Can I turn human now?" he asked.

"Have you got clothes?"

"No."

"Then no."

Sangris rolled his eyes and shrank into a cat somewhere around my feet. Then I relaxed.

"Where are we?" I said.

"Somewhere completely different," he said. "This isn't any country you could name. The people who live here call it Ae."

"Ae?"

61

"It means 'everything.' They're a bit limited—they don't know that anywhere else exists."

"And you speak their language?"

"I speak all languages," he said, flicking his tail. "Anything I choose. I'm a Free person, remember." He paused, then added, "I lived here when I was small. I liked it because it would be hard for anybody to find me in the forest. There are too many trees, branches, nooks, crannies . . . hiding places, basically. Ae is notorious for that. The people who *don't* live here call it Gans'ves, which means something like 'barely there,' or 'a place where things are lost.'"

"And you wanted to be lost?"

He didn't answer. "This place, here—I don't know what you'd call it—sort of a gap beneath the trees—was where I lived. You can't imagine what sorts of creatures are hiding in the branches, or wander in and then can't get out again. For instance, the forest seems empty right now, but I can assure you that at least ten things are eavesdropping on us. I say *things* because they might not be people—but don't worry," he added. "They probably aren't dangerous. Or if they are, they aren't looking for a fight—because they're hiding, see? And anyway, I—you might be surprised to hear this, but I actually am kind of deadly," he said modestly, "and I'm on your side, so there's nothing to worry about."

"I wasn't worried," I said. The situation was too unreal for me to worry about it. My head was still floating in the sky, and I, in my starched school shirt and proper shoes that remained warm from the heat of the oasis, touched a few scaly branches just to see if they were solid.

Right beside the place we'd landed, a couple of trees arched together in the crowded gloom, moss streaming down like gray mermaid-hair, to conceal the gap between their trunks. Sangris ducked beneath. I followed, pushing the moss apart and squeezing through, and was blinded momentarily by the sun at high noon.

I'd unfolded into another country. The forest had ended— abruptly, as if it had been slashed away with a knife.

A line ran through this world. On one side, the confused forest; on the other, this endless grassland. It must have just rained, because the sky was a living, breathing gray, and the ground shone intense green. Not khaki, but *real* green. Hills rolled over the distance. Light and shadows rippled down their sides, according to the clouds. Where sunshine billowed through, a few shallow puddles flashed like isolated spots of light.

This was a country of space and cool air and emptiness, different from the forest, though so close, and unimaginably different from the desert. The sky was open wide. Above me, a bird wheeled round and round with a high, piercing cry. Every time it came directly overhead, the light of the low sun hit the underside of its wings, and for a split second it seemed to be struck motionless, in full display, the bones glowing gold through its feathers. Then it would swing away again.

I felt some part of me lift right out of my body. A breeze blew in my face.

"Moorland. This is the other side of Ae," Sangris was saying, "but nobody lives here. They're all packed into the forest because they're afraid to be seen. Only the birds—"

"Let's run," I said breathlessly.

"What?"

I ran.

For someone who had not done more than walk (and walk slowly, at that) for five years, I was fast. In the back of my mind was a flicker of surprise. The ground swept past, thrumming lightly like the taut string of a guitar, beneath my feet. I suppose that, in the oasis, in my caverns of stone walls, I had forgotten how young I was. But my body hadn't forgotten. Somehow, in hibernation, it had managed to grow fluid and long and light. Ye gods, I thought, running faster and finding with joy that I could do so, I'm *young*. Who would have guessed? It was almost like discovering I could fly.

And I was *out of the oasis*. Past the desert—hah! I laughed without slowing down.

A jaguar loped beside me. I jumped before spotting the deep yellow eyes and realizing that it was Sangris. I expected him to look as surprised as I felt, but he seemed to think my mad dash was perfectly natural.

"I'm young!" I shouted at him in exhilaration.

"What?"

"I'm young!"

His gaze flickered over me. From my free-flying hair—I became very aware of it as soon as he looked at it; I felt it lifting off the base of my neck where the spine is tender, and streaming out behind me in tendrils—to the tightness of my stomach—I realized for the first time that I had a narrow waist and hips rather than the straight lines of my childhood; when had *that* happened?—and down to the legs. At that point he pulled his gaze back up to my face. "Yeah," he said. "Didn't you know?"

"No! And I—I'm strong! How's that possible? I'm light, I can run!"

This time his gaze wavered all the way down to my feet. "Yeah," he repeated, turning his face away. "Didn't you know?"

"How could I? I never left my bedroom! And I always wanted to look like my friends!"

A hint of amusement came to his voice. "What do *they* look like?" he said, keeping pace with me effortlessly.

I ran faster. The blood was pounding now, but I didn't want to stop, not yet. "They—ah."

"They're fat and lazy?" he guessed, beginning to grin.

"No! But they favor—more womanly forms, you know. They always say I'm too skinny," I said. I concentrated on my flying feet. I wasn't thinking about whether or not it was proper to tell him this. "A girl ought to be plump."

"I bet *they're* plump," he said.

"Yes."

"No wonder they say so, then."

My legs carried me up a hill. I was amazed they could still move, but move they did, and it wasn't even difficult. Then I hurtled down the other side, the heather billowing all around me, like the sea shocked by a storm. "They say I look like a boy," I panted.

"*That* you do not," he said, with another sideways glance.

"I know!" I said gleefully. "I look like a horse!"

He braked. "What?"

I went on for a while longer, shooting alone, a comet over the grassy world, and then finally, when my head was so light it was dizzying and I couldn't feel my legs anymore, I threw myself into a heap of hazy purple heather. I rolled over. The sky swam above me. My entire body had become a pair of lungs, heaving, but my breaths were luxurious, enjoying the fresh, impossible, unbaked air.

Sangris approached my head. I saw his face—a black cat's again—upside down. "Did you just say you look like a horse?"

"Uh-huh."

"Why?" he said, his tone baffled.

"Because I do. The way a horse looks when it runs."

"Oh. I think you mean 'graceful.'"

"No."

"Agile?"

"No."

"Glossy?" he said, obviously scraping the bottom of the barrel.

"I was thinking more a baby horse. Long legs, bony body, you know, but at least it's fast and it can run. My friends can't run. I didn't know I could." I grabbed at the plants all around me, holding on to them in fistfuls, to make sure they were real. I would never take grass for granted again. Breezes, like currents of water, slid lights over the heather as I lay there.

"Your body isn't bony," Sangris said blankly. "It's as soft and slenderly curved as the throat of a swan."

What?

I stared at him for a full minute.

"Um," he said.

I continued to stare.

"Never mind," he said.

"Did you prepare that phrase in advance?" I was genuinely curious. "Do you sit awake at night and write secret odes to the bodies of girls you've just met? Or was that stolen from somewhere? How many times have you used it?"

"I can't help it if I'm eloquent," he said. He studied one of his paws, grooming it.

"It sounded rehearsed," I said.

"Why would I rehearse? How could I have known that you were going to call yourself bony? Like you said, I've just met you." He fussed over the paw, licking it with a small red tongue tip. "You're the one who brought up the subject. It just so happens that I thought of the phrase a little while ago. I resent your accusation of plagiarism," he added virtuously.

"Were you in a particularly poetic mood when you thought of it?" I said, beginning to smirk. I felt as though I should have been embarrassed, and it was probably coarse of me to keep asking questions, but I couldn't pass up the opportunity to tease him. And besides, those concerns were far away, sitting with my parents in the distant oasis.

"I wouldn't call it poetic, no. Not particularly," Sangris said. He was still licking his paw. Having clean paws was evidently the most important thing in his private universe right now.

My smirk slipped away then.

Not because of what he'd said. Not because of anything logical. No, I stopped talking and scrunched up my nose because it had just occurred to me how easy it would be for him to turn human right now.

And the thought was more vivid than I would have liked. I had a mental image of Sangris grinning up at me through a screen of wavy black hair, eyes slanted and yellow the way they had been in my bedroom, and the way they were *now*. He was a cat. It didn't make any sense, except . . . well, except for the fact that, at a moment's notice, he could become something else, and—oh, gross. I thought the word loudly enough to drown out everything else. Gross. Maybe I made a noise, because he glanced up at me, and that made it worse. His eyes weren't catlike at all, at least not as far as their expression went. They were intelligent and far too male. That look was almost enough to make me go back to the oasis and shut myself in my cage, never fly again, and allow the cords of heat to bind me down to the ground— just because Sangris happened to have a knack of making me uncomfortable. I glared until he looked down again.

Then I had a cheering thought. He couldn't have been

talking about *me*; it must be someone else. I rolled over onto my elbows, preparing to be vindicated. I was up to my chin in the heather. "Who were you with at the time?" I said.

His eyes flashed up at me from his self-appointed task. "What?"

"I know it wasn't about me," I said. I tried not to sound hopeful. "What do you know about how soft, or how hard, or even how spiky I might be? I'm always swathed in clothes right down to my wrists and ankles. So who was that phrase really about?"

A pause.

"Um," he said at last. "A girl I knew. Before."

There. My shoulders relaxed. I'd been right.

"How long ago?"

"Months?" He said it as if it was a question.

I propped up my chin on my hands. He wasn't telling the story very well, I thought. "What was she like?"

"Beautiful, of course. She had fur like shining duckweed and big round eyes that almost popped out whenever anyone called her name." (*There's no accounting for taste,* I thought, but I was careful to keep my expression blank for fear of offending him. Duckweed, indeed.) "Her name was Loll," he continued.

"Loll?" I couldn't help but sound a bit disdainful now.

"Because of the way her tongue lolled out. She was a dog, you see. Sadly, she'd been spayed, but we decided that it was for the best . . ." He broke off, struggling.

Startled, I said, "I—I'm sorry."

"You idiot," he gasped out. He fell onto his side laughing. "It was you! I thought about orchid's stems and swan's necks and all sorts of other nonsense while you were cuddling me in your room, remember, because you thought I was a cat. You weren't swaddled in clothes *then*. You weren't even paying attention—you were reading *Of Human Bondage*. A tattered copy with a boring brown cover and so many pages that it was thicker than most religious texts. But you were absorbed in it for hours and hours, as though it was the most interesting thing in the world. I'd just woken up, and I had to wait there, held against your—ah—your nightshirt, until you finished the book and went to sleep, before I could try to sneak away."

I hid behind my hair. So he'd been conscious after all. I thanked my luck that he wasn't in human form right now. It was disconcerting enough to have a cat speak to me in this way. "But you didn't!" I said to the grass. "You didn't try to leave until hours later. I went to sleep at midnight, and you woke me up around four."

"I fell back to sleep when you did," he said, not laughing anymore. His gaze slid away from me. "You were—" He stopped.

"I was . . . ?"

Mumble.

"Was *what*?" I demanded.

"Warm."

That did it. I began to inch away. I hoped that maybe, if I did it slowly enough, he wouldn't notice.

"What?" Sangris protested. "It isn't *dirty*. I was comfortable, and I still hadn't recovered properly from the souk, so I thought, a few more minutes, and when I woke up it was almost dawn."

"Argh," I said. It was the only way I felt I could fairly sum up the situation.

"I should've stuck with the story about the dog, huh?"

"Mm." I hesitated. "That one was a lie, wasn't it?"

"Yeah."

Good. I didn't think I'd be able to handle any more revelations.

"We should probably head back," he muttered, pulling himself up to his paws, "if you want to be at school by three forty-five."

"I don't want to be, I have to be," I said. "My father's going to pick me up. If I'm not there . . ."

"Pity," he said. "You sure I can't just drop you off at your house? We could get around your father." Sangris had a way of saying things as though his suggestions alone were enough to solve all the problems in the world.

"My father," I repeated. The word sounded strange here, with the open sky and the purple-gray grasses, the green hills, and the black line of the forest just clinging to the horizon behind us. But it was as powerful a sound as ever, the strength of the rising *fa,* then the graveness of the *ther* bringing it back down to earth. Sangris didn't seem to understand that *want* was irrelevant beside the word *father*.

Without having to be prompted, Sangris changed back

into his feathered dragon form. I climbed up gingerly. What if he was thinking of more embarrassing phrases? *The taut instep of each tiny fairy-like foot . . .* or worse, *the orchid-petal smoothness of the skin on her palms was . . .*

"You're freaked out, aren't you?" He didn't say it as if he was looking for reassurance. He said it in acknowledgment of a fact.

I said, "No more secretly describing me in your head."

"It's called *thinking*," he said.

"Are your thoughts usually that flowery?"

"No, but I was trying to find a way to describe . . . You know how sometimes you just need to find a sentence that . . . Oh, all right. Fine."

He gave up.

But when we were safely in the air, another flush of warmth spread up through me, from the pit of my stomach this time. I thought, *The throat of a swan?* And I ran the phrase through my head once or twice to make sure I had it memorized.

CHAPTER SIX

In Which My Father
Tells Me About *Pfft*

Sangris lowered me back into the desert. Even though my eyes were closed, I could tell when the oasis began to crowd around me again, because of the heat. But it was more bearable now. I'd had my gulp of fresh air.

The daze of flying sank away and I set my feet down once more on the pale cracked stone behind my school. My watch read three forty-three. The sunlight was almost solid around us in walls of blinding white gold.

"Are you glad you went?" Sangris asked. Attentively. Like a chef taking the finished plate away from a diner whom he's not sure he has impressed.

There was no question about it. I said, "Yes."

With a talon, he picked up his stolen school uniform from where he had dropped it before. A film of fine sand had settled into the creases, and the fabric had already begun to bleach. "Ah," he said, "you might want to—" I swiveled around to stare in the opposite direction while he changed, and when I looked back, a very dusty and rumpled-looking boy was grinning at me. The white sand had stuck in his hair. "All right, what's next?" he said, rubbing his hands together.

"I'm going home. My father is picking me up."

"Okay, I'll wait with you."

"What? No."

He looked amazed. "Why not?"

"Because I don't want my father to see you."

"I'm a secret?"

"Of course."

He blinked, growing thoughtful. "What kind of secret? The embarrassing secret that you don't want anybody to know about, or the sort that's just too good to share?"

"The embarrassing kind that would get me into trouble."

"Oh," he said, looking a bit put out. "Well, all right then." The bell blared over our heads.

"Bye," I said, and, because that seemed to be it, I turned to leave.

I was a few steps away when he caught at my shirtsleeve. I turned. Abruptly, he said, "Could I come again tonight?"

"What?"

"Could I come again tonight?" he repeated.

I couldn't help smiling. "You have to ask?" I said.

"Oh," Sangris said, momentarily taken aback, before a pleased smile came to his face. He let go of my shirt. That's when I realized what I'd just said, and how it had sounded. Ye gods, I thought. I sounded cheap. Like those girls on TV my father always sneers at. I turned and hurried inside before I could say anything worse.

The halls were packed from wall to wall with the struggling, uniform-clad bodies of students. I slipped through the crowd, a fish through water, agile after years of practice, down the hall and up the stairs, my head seeming to float far above my body. At the familiar green door of my locker I paused to scoop up my bag. I was still thinking of heather and running and exhilaration. And tonight there would be more. Maybe this could be a regular thing. A new rhythm to my life, like the songs of the mosques.

"Frenenqer," someone said behind me. Anju slid into her accustomed place at my side. "Mr. Abass went around telling everyone that he forgot to give us homework," she said. "We have to do all the odd-numbered exercises on page ninety-one." She looked at me sideways with heavy-lidded, long-lashed black eyes, weary as a babysitter. "What did you do to the cat?"

Not *Where is the cat*, but *What did you do to it*. Anju always expected the worst.

"I didn't do anything. It turned into a feathered dragon and we flew off."

"Oh, okay," she said. We started back down the stairs. "How are your preparations for Heritage?"

"Done. I finished them yesterday. I'm not sure why everyone else takes weeks to prepare." I shifted the bag from one shoulder to another. It felt as if it were packed full of bricks. I peeped inside. Ah, that was right, I had ten novels stuffed in there. I'd forgotten that I had picked them up at the library. It was strange that the world hadn't changed while I was away.

"Everyone takes as long as possible because they want more time out of class," she observed.

"Sensible of them," I said, conceding the point. It was difficult to argue while my head was still full of the sound of rushing wings. I tried to focus. "I heard the South Africans are going to bring a grill and have a barbecue outside."

"So what? The Emiratis are bringing a camel."

"Camels are easy. Everyone has a friend of a friend who owns a camel . . ."

"But it looks impressive," she said.

"In our school, anything would look impressive."

"True."

As if OESS could buy our approval with *camels,* of all things. That's what my school is called: Oasis English Spoken School. OESS for short. The grammar may be worrying, but the "English Spoken" part is supposed to indicate that all students must have a fluent grasp of the English language. The sign in front of the gates, however, is misspelled, and proudly reads: "Oasis English Spaken School." Now you can guess the quality of the education I received.

But it was the only school on this side of the desert, so we had no choice, and we knew it. If anything, we were supposed to be grateful. "You can't expect to be pampered," my father had said when he'd enrolled me five years ago. "We're expats." I'd stared at the sign in front of the school and just nodded.

And Heritage always set my teeth on edge. Why should it be obligatory to proudly display our cultures? What about people like me, who came from everywhere and nowhere? And what had the administration ever done for us? But it was a chance to get out of lessons, and anyway the food was always good. I think it was the food, mainly, that made us go along with it.

"How many countries this year?" I said distractedly, hitching my bag higher. We stepped out of the building and, following the flow of students, went across the sand, out the main gates into the gaspingly hot parking lot. An airless, twisted haze of evaporation permanently swam over the rows of parked cars. Our faces were screwed up in the heat.

"Fifty-six," Anju said.

There were only two hundred students in secondary school.

"We won't have enough rooms."

"We never do. A lot of countries will be outside."

"I don't envy them," I said, squinting across the parking lot in search of my father's car. The rows of flashing car windows stabbed pain right through my eyes.

I spotted the hard rectangular white car in a sea of other hard rectangular white cars.

"There's my dad," I said. "See you tomorrow."

"Wait. Can I call you tonight?" Anju said. We always had to do it by appointment. "Remember, I want to come over to your house this week? To study for the math test. My parents need to talk to your parents."

I sighed. "Right. Did they give you their permission yet?"

"They're thinking about it. How about your parents?"

"They're thinking too." I shrugged to indicate my helplessness. "Call tonight."

We said good-bye and then I had to thread my way through the cars, heat steaming off them, to get to my father. Cautiously I pulled my bag off my back, steadied my face, and entered.

It was freezing.

When I shut the door behind me, the sounds of the parking lot stopped, and the calm drone of the air-conditioning was the only noise. The filtered air made the car smell of petrified sand and sour metal.

My father looked at me from behind a pair of sunglasses.

I pretended to be very absorbed in my task of putting my bag into the back. I didn't know why he was studying me like that. I'd made sure to move calmly, normally. *There's no way he could guess,* I promised myself, but my stomach felt jittery. Finally I said, "Anju wants to call again tonight. To discuss travel arrangements."

"What for?" He turned his eyes back to the traffic and we squeezed out onto the main road.

"She'd like to come over to our house this Saturday."

"I'll think about it," he said, just as I'd known he would. He always said that.

We continued the ride in silence. My fingers ached to slide a book out of my bag. But my father might get annoyed. And there were only ten minutes left before we'd reach the house. Surely I could wait ten minutes.

But I remembered hills and purple heather. And the heart-lifting flutter of speed as I flew, out of school, straight over the roads . . .

Just wait ten minutes.

I lasted five before I found myself twisting around to grab my bag. As soon as the reassuringly solid pages of a new book were between my fingers, a wonderful feeling of relief flooded me. I had already read this one twice, and I hadn't liked it much either time. But it would suffice. I rubbed the cover lovingly and kept my eyes away from my father.

Even so, behind the black painted squares of his sunglasses, I could sense that his gaze slid to my hands.

Turning my body a little to conceal what I was doing, I opened to the front page.

"That's a romance, isn't it," he said.

I stopped at the first sentence. No, it wasn't a romance, but the main character did have a boyfriend, and how was I supposed to read the book now, in front of my father, while he was imagining the worst? Silence and coldness seeped from his seat.

I tried to get through the first page anyway. But it was like force-feeding myself something that made me choke.

I shoved the book back into my bag.

"It wasn't a romance," I tried.

"And yet your face is flushed."

I'm sure it went even darker after that. The book *wasn't* dangerous, it wasn't even particularly interesting; it was about a girl who learned how to knit! But now I felt as though I was hiding porn in my schoolbag.

He took a long look at me and didn't like what he saw. "You *were* reading something bad."

"I wouldn't," I said, aiming for reconciliation. In my voice I heard the empty hopeful smile of a child, and stopped, sick at myself. It didn't matter anyway, because my father wasn't listening.

"My daughter! You're supposed to be better than that," he said, with real distress. I couldn't see his eyes behind the sunglasses, but I know it was real, because of his voice. It was as bothered as it got whenever there was a spoon out of place on the dining table, or Mom spoke too loudly on the phone, or he caught me opening my window. "Do you realize how people will point fingers? They'll *laugh*. You're at the ugly age when people make fools of themselves, and fall into all sorts of degrading mistakes—"

The memory of running wildly through the grass with Sangris shot through my mind, but it didn't seem liberating anymore. I tried not to look guilty.

"If you're all I raised you to be," my father said, focusing on the road, "you'll keep yourself above rebuke."

"Sorry," I mumbled, to end things.

We fell back into silence, but it wasn't a blank silence anymore. It was thick and prickly and I felt as though we were both wondering what the other was thinking.

I'd been so obedient for so long . . . but my *no* in the souk had flashed through the cracks, and now he was imagining a deep and concealed rebelliousness burning beneath my surface. I wondered if he'd always be suspicious of me now.

I had a quiet shriveling sensation inside. Heart curling up like the ferns in India, which close their leaves when touched.

When he spoke again, he sounded stiff.

"You should feel lucky you have a father who shows such concern for your welfare. Not all fathers do, and where do their daughters end up?" He made a dismissive noise with his mouth. "*Pfft.*"

That was where they ended up. In *Pfft*.

I only nodded.

Wordlessly, I pressed my nose to the window and watched the painful blue sky roll past. I didn't think of Sangris. I allowed my thoughts to approach him, in a roundabout way, and then at the last moment, just before I saw his alert yellow eyes, I jerked myself away.

If *Pfft* were a place, I thought, I probably deserved to be there.

CHAPTER SEVEN

In Which Sangris Makes a Proposal

The car stopped and I got out. I didn't own any house keys, so I had to wait until my father opened the front door and allowed me to escape from the oppressive heat, into a long, narrow hallway with cool white tiles on the floor. Mom was nowhere in sight. Both my father and I stooped to take off our shoes near the door. Then he disappeared to his computer and I hurried to my bedroom down the hall.

My room was painted yellow—no, not the same shade as Sangris's eyes—his were the bright yellow of those Danger signs you sometimes see on the side of the road—this yellow was more subdued, more feminine. Creamy yellow. But the paint in the corners of the room was beginning to peel in the dryness of the air.

There was my bed in a corner, surrounded by its fortress of books. I lay down and skimmed furtively until I finished the book I had started in the car. It was short, and just as dull as I had remembered.

"Frenenqer," my father said from down the hall.

He had a certain way of calling me, just saying my name

without raising his voice, as though he was sure I would hear.

It was like he'd *sensed* me finishing the book.

I scuttled over.

He was holding the phone in one hand, switching it off with an efficient click, and frowning at me. "I've decided to deny Anju's request," he said. Like a bank.

I nodded. Half turned to leave. And—

"Dad," I said on impulse.

"What?"

Something really odd happened then. A thought hijacked my mind: *I'll tell him everything.* Not that I'd flown with a boy (I was too scared to admit that) but that Free people existed, and that there was a place called Ae, and that I could give my father the sky. If he seemed interested. In the shock of something magical like that, he couldn't continue like this, he'd have to talk to me. I'd give up my secret for that.

"The cat—" I began.

"The cat!" he said, eyes narrowing. "You're still thinking of the cat? Is this more of your behavior from the souk?"

I shook my head.

His mouth was one tight line, restraining his fury at my imagined rebellion. "Frenenqer, I'm not going to waste my time listening to the complaints of a sulky teenager."

"I'm sorry," I said.

My breaths were shallow. I went back to my bedroom.

It was only five in the afternoon. I closed the door, lay on my bed, and stared at the ceiling. His words stayed in my head, and I felt compressed, kind of queasy. Like I was floating on top of a flood. I waited half an hour until the feeling was gone.

I could have read. I could have painted. If I were desperate, I could even have done my homework, although I usually had enough time to finish it in the few minutes before class began. I could have whistled. I could have sat on the floor and studied the wall. I could have paced. There were many things I could have done, but instead I fell asleep. For about an hour I dreamed of confused things. Halfway through, my mom burst into the room, but when I raised a bleary head off my pillow she said never mind, I could sleep. The next minute my head was full of blackness again and I thought I was racing through the sky. Until a tapping at the window, from behind the heavy folds of curtain, woke me up.

My contact lenses had slid around in my sleep. I rubbed at my eyes hard until I could see again. I was lying in bed, wearing the dusty school uniform I had worn all day, with the lights on and the curtains drawn closed and Sangris tapping behind them.

I got up and slid the curtains open. Sangris was sitting on the other side, cat-shaped. It wasn't even sunset yet; he was early.

I didn't let him in. "Can you wait a while?" I said in a low voice through the glass.

He gave me a look. "Why?"

"I've been asleep, and, see, I'm still wearing my school uniform. I need to change."

"You're fine," he said. "Let's go."

"No. Just fifteen min—"

My door banged open. I dragged the curtains closed and spun around.

My mother again. She regarded me closely a moment. "Dinner," she said.

"Okay."

She clicked the door shut, and I exhaled. There was silence.

Then from behind the curtains Sangris went on complaining, "Fifteen minutes? I bet if you said 'five minutes' you'd really mean twenty. I don't want to think how much time you're going to take if you say *fifteen*."

"Shh," I whispered, and left him outside on the window ledge. I heard him begin to paw against the glass as I left the room, but I was focused on slowing my heart rate.

I emerged to sit at the formal white dining table with my father, and didn't once ask what he would do if he checked my room tonight and I wasn't there. The little blue pulses in my wrists were still flickering quick. In the kitchen, Mom avoided us, only her silence seeping out.

"You must have had time to consider your attitude about the cat. You look ashamed," said my father, studying my face, and seeing his imaginary version of me. "Good."

I was ashamed. I was ashamed that I'd ever thought of handing my secret over to him.

We chewed for the next half hour without talking. Finished, I took care to look sleepy and say good night. I went out and shut the door gently behind me.

I grabbed some clothes from a spare closet in the hall and made my way to the bathroom. Lightly, for fear of drawing attention from my parents, I slipped inside. The bathroom had khaki-colored walls and a cracked, discolored sink, but I liked it; sometimes I even brought in a book to read on top of the washing machine. In here, at least I could lock the door.

By the time I returned, Sangris had managed to ease the window open. I walked into my room to find a wavy-haired boy lounging around, wearing the stolen school uniform with his shirt left untucked. I caught him leafing through the papers on my desk.

"Hey!" I whispered. "No!" I hurried over and snatched them from him. He looked at me in surprise. "You can't go through my stuff like that while I'm not here. I'm serious. This is just schoolwork, but it could have been something private—"

"Maybe it isn't so bad to wait," he said, softly enough that he might have been speaking to himself.

I opened my mouth to argue, then paused and realized I had no idea what he was talking about. I put the papers aside and looked up at him.

"You're wearing normal clothes," he said.

I glanced down at myself. "Yeah. I always wear normal clothes. Back to the issue of privacy—"

"No, you don't. You wear ugly loose cloth that could cover an elephant."

I couldn't take offense at that, because it was true. "These are clothes I wear around the house. I wouldn't walk on the streets in them, but, I mean, the only difference is that the sleeves are shorter."

He stared.

The clothes honestly weren't that different. The pants were exactly the same as normal. And the shirt was made of light, floaty material, not for fashion's sake, but because it was the best design for the heat. That was why my mother had bought it for me. But I usually only wore it indoors, since the sleeves were more like straps.

"I only cover up in front of strangers or people who come from that sort of culture," I said in confusion. "I thought you'd be used to seeing shoulders."

"Not *yours*."

My skin began to burn under his fixed gaze. I hate being stared at—I've hated it ever since that old nightmare of the man and his flashlight. My nervousness must have showed.

"Hey, it's okay," he said. "I only . . . Um. Honey?"

In shock I said, "Don't call me—"

"Not *you*," he said. "Sticky gold stuff. Honey. Am I right?"

"And are you being more incoherent than usual?" I was staring back now.

"No, really," he insisted. "Warm honey, or is it honeysuckle, and . . . musk?"

"Oh. Milk and honey. That's the scent of the soap I use. It's the soap I've *always* used," I added, in case he thought that this was something different too.

"Milk," he said. He was still hovering near, and still staring. "That's it. You smell like milk and honey. And warmth."

"How can someone smell like warmth?" I said sensibly.

"Maybe that part's you, not the soap."

"How should I know?" There isn't much to say about soap, but Sangris seemed to be suddenly obsessed with it. Slanted eyes taking in my wet hair, my throat, the shape of my shoulders. Only his pupils weren't so slanted anymore— they had widened, almost swallowing up the curve of color. Hold lit candles behind amber and you might get the same dark-bright yellow as his irises. I edged back. "Could you stop that, please?"

"Stop what?" he said, not listening.

"I don't like it."

That got through. He stepped back slowly. "I—sorry."

"You're kind of strange, aren't you?"

He gave a little laugh, pulling his eyes away awkwardly. "Well, I did spend the last six months as a cat."

I wasn't afraid anymore. It was sharp and sweet to see Sangris discomposed for once. He looked along the floor, at the desk, at the walls, everywhere but at me. It was rather like—having power. *That* was something I had never tasted before.

"You look very nice," he said finally, lamely.

"I thought you were supposed to be eloquent."

"Well," he answered, beginning to recover, "as a matter of fact, that hollow at the base of your throat does put me in mind of petals, and I'd probably use the words *tender* and *vulnerable* and *kissable* a couple of times too, but I thought I wasn't allowed to do that."

"You're not."

He had recuperated enough to grin at me. Sangris, I was learning, was nothing if not resilient. "Sorry if I freaked you out."

"Again."

"It's the last time, I promise," he said. He wandered back to the window, where he'd left the curtains hanging wide open. "Can we still go?"

My choice had already been made: The moment we'd lifted off, leaving school behind, it was decided. He could have jumped on me now and it wouldn't have stopped me from wanting to go. But I pretended to think about it. "Where do you have planned?"

"We could go back to Ae. Or any world you want. Or—I was thinking—maybe I could show you some of the other places I used to live." He looked at me tentatively. "You already saw Ae, and that's where I grew up. I could show you the place I ran away to after that. And the place after— and the place after—all the places that mean the most to me." He stopped. "Why are you smiling?"

"Places . . . not people?" I said.

He made a dismissive gesture. "Oh, well, *people* . . ."

I had to laugh. Whenever I thought of my childhood, I didn't miss people, not even friends—it was always places.

Sangris nodded, fiddling with the curtain. "It could be like a project, each night. Retracing my steps. I've been meaning to do that for a while, anyway. I planned it while I was stuck in that cage in the Animal Souk."

I paused. I understood what he was offering me. The enormity of it stunned me a bit. Then I said, "That's not really fair."

From the anxious look that crossed his face, I could tell that I'd guessed correctly. This project meant much more than he had admitted. It was his way of offering me—what? He was handing his childhood memories over to me like a gift. I knew I had him off guard. "Why not?"

"You have to give me a chance to retrace *my* steps too. It can't be all about you," I said, feeling the same lightheaded rush that had come earlier at school, when I'd let him take me to Ae. "Besides the oasis, I've lived in Italy, India, Japan, Canada, New Zealand, Thailand, Costa Rica, and Fiji. And for shorter times in some other places as well, of course. I'm from a long line of country-less people. My father grew up all over the place, like me, so we moved around a lot when I was younger, before he found steady work as an architect here. I'd like to see my old houses again . . ."

Sangris had been grinning wider and wider with each word, and, when I finished, he asked, "You'd do that for me?"

"It's not for you," I said defensively. "You egomaniac. I want to see them too, you know."

From his reaction, I may as well have been shouting "Yes!" He burst into laughter and reached out for me. "Nenner, may I please pick you up and twirl you around?"

"No." I couldn't trust him after that whole milk-and-honey episode.

"Could I at least kiss your hand?"

"No."

"Oh, all right, I'll shake it then," he said, doing so. "Nenner, you're absolutely right. Tonight you show me somewhere from your past. Where were you born?"

"Actually, I began before I was born . . ." I said. "My father first had the idea of a Frenenqer Paje in Spain."

"We should go there, then," Sangris said, refusing to relinquish my hand. "We don't want to miss any details."

"But I'm not sure where exactly he was. Somewhere along the Camino de Santiago."

"What's that?"

"A bunch of pilgrim routes that go right across Spain, from east to west."

"You were a dream your father had while he was hiking through Spain?" Sangris said. "That's romantic."

He obviously didn't know my father. "I'd call it more of a plan than a dream," I said. "My father doesn't dream. Anyway, he said it was toward the end of his pilgrimage. That means it must be near Santiago. I was flipping through an album once when he pointed at a photo and said, 'That's where I decided to have a daughter.' It was a place with sunflowers, and trees that looked as though they'd been painted by van Gogh."

"Can you get the photo?"

"Long lost. We moved around too much to keep that sort of thing. But I can remember what it was like."

"Then we'll find it," Sangris said. "I'll fly you there, and you'll find it."

We grinned at each other, and the dim dust-gray sky burned outside my window. "Oh, all right then," I said, too excited to not relent, "twirl me."

We spun around and around and I smothered my laughter so that my parents couldn't hear. Sangris had a faint smell, like rain and wood. That place in Ae, maybe; it had stayed in his skin. Finally he stopped, but my feet stayed off the ground. "Let's go like this," he said, hardly panting, holding me easily against his chest in the style of a newlywed. "I don't want to change form too much. It's a pain to have to keep taking off these clothes. If you want me to be hideous, I can become a gargoyle or something, but at least let me stay humanoid. Unless you want to carry my pants for me."

I wrinkled up my nose. "Gargoyle it is then," I said.

Without putting me down, he shifted into the lithe gray winged form he had used when he'd first tossed himself out of my window. The shirt ripped at the back, but other than that the uniform stayed reasonably whole. And once again, he wasn't hideous. Unusual-looking, yes, but I liked the sleekness of this form, the way his wings curved out of his back in one smooth line. There was beauty in his sharp demon-like face.

But maybe I only thought that because he still looked like Sangris.

At the last second, I glanced at the door, making sure it was closed. The house was hushed, sleeping. And then he threw us out of the window. My stomach plunged, then soared, and the restricting rubber-tight sky of the oasis tore around us, leaving a clean cold hole through which we escaped. I watched the desert pass by, the smooth shapes of dunes rolling beneath me like ships through a sea. Faster and faster. I closed my eyes in the wind.

CHAPTER EIGHT

In Which We Search for Sunflowers

Spain was a lot closer than Ae. From Sangris's point of view, it was right next door. He soon allowed us to slow down. "We're almost there," he said gently, like someone waking an infant. I opened my eyes.

Because of the time difference, the sky was lighter all around us. We were much lower than I had expected; the view wasn't at all like looking out of an airplane window. He was skimming, barely above the trees, the wheat fields a sunset-yellow blur rushing below, then lone houses, old villages, the occasional city streaming past, far off. It reminded me of Italy, except less languid. My impression of Italy, even when I lived there, was always of an old but very beautiful squid. Spain felt rougher, bolder. My skin began to tingle in the cool exhilaration of the air. Most of the landscape was agricultural, and the crops shone saturated gold everywhere. But here and there was a flash of green. Lush trees, wide fields bloodied with poppies.

"Are we near Santiago?" I asked, holding on to Sangris's shoulders with an abrupt change in my pulse, alive and almost unnatural, like an inward stagger.

"Yes. We're just east of it, so the road of the camino must be nearby. But I haven't found it yet."

"The camino isn't a road," I said. "It's a path. In the cities, it's not even a physical path. The way is marked with yellow arrows and seashells."

"You want me to search Spain for seashells?" he said, giving me a look that showed he had found the flaw in this plan.

"No. Keep an eye out for *albergues,* small white buildings, sometimes in the middle of nowhere, where the pilgrims sleep. And if there's a path connecting them together, we'll know we've found it."

"We passed something like that. Hold on—" He swooped to the left and in a few minutes, below us, beautiful, was an old stone house, strung like a bead on the thread of a long, wavering dirt path that ran from east to west right through the rich rippling acres of gold. "We're near Santiago, and this is the only building around for miles."

"That must be the camino," I said, kicking my feet in the air.

Sangris sped us low along the path. We flew between troubled lovely hills. They were raw, and ragged, on either side of us, frayed by the reckless wild plants. And there, underneath, untouched, were sudden secretive hollows where the countryside folded inward, absorbed into the privacy of its flowers. The land had an air of self-admiration about it then, and Sangris went as quietly as possible, as though not to disturb it.

"Okay," he said. "Keep a lookout for sunflowers and creepy trees."

95

"Van Gogh's trees aren't creepy," I said, swatting at him.

"Don't hit the driver."

"Don't antagonize the passenger."

"Are you always like this?" he said with a slight grin.

"It usually gets me into trouble, so I hide my evil talents," I said. "Actually, that's how you could come in useful. I need practice to keep my tongue sharp. You could be my scratching post."

He looked down at me and twitched his arms dangerously. "If I were smart," he said, "I would drop you right now, and fly away fast, while I still can."

"If you were smart? Good." I laughed. "I have nothing to worry about."

My stomach swooped then, and I gasped. Sangris had plunged several feet, leaving me falling through the air above him, like a child momentarily separated from her swing.

He caught me neatly.

"Hey! That's—"

But I lost track of my outrage, because, actually, I'd enjoyed the fizzy feeling of falling.

"Why do I have to be the scratching post, anyway?" he went on as if nothing had happened.

"Well, I do it to Anju sometimes . . . but she's so quiet, it's no fun."

I hadn't meant to bring up the oasis again, but there it was. It dampened my giddiness, just a little, and now I had time to worry about how awkward it could be to stay slung in Sangris's arms, in silence, as we flew over a field of rushing red poppies and delicate skinny trees. There was a risk that we might run out of things to say.

But Sangris seemed content to just keep going. He didn't say a word. I looked up, saw the black hair wild in the breeze, and, convulsively, I began to talk again.

"That's Anju," I said. "Even when I treat her like a secretary, she won't complain. I keep waiting for her to snap and tell me to organize my own timetable, but she never does. I wonder what her breaking point is. I keep pushing her; I can't help it. It's like holding a bendy twig. There's always something in you that wants to bend it all the way around and see how far you can go before it breaks, isn't there? But I don't know why she can't just tell me to shut up."

"I can do it. Shut up, Nenner," Sangris said.

"Right. See how easy it is? But she always just puts up with everything. She'd make a very good Frenenqer Paje. My father would have loved her."

"Uh. You don't think your father loves you?"

"Of course not. There's a list of things he wants me to be, and 'lovable' is not on it. But that doesn't matter. I'm *glad* my parents don't love me. It would make me feel uncomfortable if they did. We don't display affection in my house. It's not done."

"That explains a lot," he said, giving me a look. "But maybe they do love you and they just don't show it. Have you thought of that?"

"Yes," I said, a bit indignant. I hadn't expected him to question me. "I'm sure *they* think they love me, but their idea of love is forced and—and hypocritical. They've often told me that if I weren't their daughter, they wouldn't like me at all. What kind of love is that? Why should they only care about me because I happened to be born to them? If anyone else said, 'I'm obliged to love you because you're the daughter of so-and-so,' people would see through it immediately and say, 'Ah-hah! That's not love at all!' But when my parents say to me, 'We're obliged to love you because you're our daughter,' everybody thinks that's just fine. Well, I don't. My father invented his love just the way he invented me. And he doesn't actually like a thing about me apart from what he made up." I smiled. "You know what I suspect? I'm his failure."

I said all this easily. These were the facts of my life, and I was used to them.

"And you're okay with it?" Sangris said, winging onward.

"Oh, yes. I told you. Because, if they don't truly love me, then I don't have to love them."

"You don't?"

"No. I'm not stupid. I'm not going to force myself to love them the way that they force themselves to love me." I shook my head. "I did when I was little, but. . . ."

He gave up. "Okay, forget your dad. What about your mom? What's she like?"

That stumped me. I had to think for a while. "I don't know if Mom ever *had* a personality," I said at last. "If she did, then it's long gone."

"Oh, come on."

"No, really. I mean, she hardly exists. I've always suspected she was kind of hired for the occasion, but then after I was born, she became superfluous. And when someone's been erased, they can't be expected to be capable of love, right?" I said reasonably. "I guess it would be nice if Mom and I found comfort in each other, but it doesn't work like that. My father pecks at her, and she avoids me. But it's a good thing," I added, realizing that I was making it sound sad.

He looked down at me and frowned. "Have you ever loved *anyone* properly?"

I knew then that I shouldn't have suggested coming here. We could have gone anywhere at all. Why did even my escapes have to be planned around my father?

"Only when I was a kid. How about you?" I said, feeling like I'd answered enough questions.

I felt his fingers close around me as he swooped lower. "Nope," he said.

"What about your parents?"

"Never met them. Whoever they were, they wandered off straight afterwards. They could have been anything—I was too small then to remember. Free people like me just sort of . . . pop up in normal species sometimes, though of course it's rare. Or who knows, they may have both been Free people too . . . so it makes sense, they wouldn't have lingered. When you can turn into hundreds of different animals, family ties are whatever you want them to be. Child-rearing or independence at birth—monogamy or polygamy—all the options are open."

He sounded the same way I did when I talked about my

parents. Nonchalant, detached. I smiled up at him.

"See anything?" he asked.

We scanned the farms. Crops were twitching pink-gold everywhere. But no sunflowers. Nothing like the place in the photograph.

Our search lasted hours. We discovered treasures. A field of wedding-white blossoms, but with a few firework-colored flowers seething underneath, like rebels. An abandoned pair of boots on top of a hill. Odd spots where cobwebs had been spun between the trees, so that thatches of silver gleamed in midair like suspended pockets of rain.

I began to chatter about the silliest things I could think of. Sangris joined in at once.

"There is an art," I observed, "to artless chatter."

"People only call it artless because we make it look so easy."

"We? Sangris, you're an amateur. Your remarks aren't nearly irrelevant enough."

"How dare you!"

"You insist on imbuing them with meaning."

"I assure you that I don't know the meaning of the word."

"Of what word?"

"Meaning."

I grinned. "You don't know the meaning of *meaning*? My dear, you're talking nonsense."

"See? I told you I'm good at it . . ." He stopped. Distracted lemon-yellow eyes flew to my face and he dropped the act. "Did you just call me your dear?"

"Got you," I said in triumph. "You see, you can't sustain

meaningless chatter the way I can. Sooner or later you start paying attention, and then you're lost. That's the problem with you, Sangris"—I shook my head wisely—"you pay too much attention to what I say. The day you learn to ignore me, you'll be a better person."

He hissed and dropped me into the grass on the side of the path.

"Next time it'll be a pile of nettles."

I bounced up onto my feet. "I'm sick of being carried like a newlywed anyway. Let's run."

"You've got running on the brain."

"Try to catch me," I said.

"No."

He was evidently still sore. I smirked at him. "Sure you don't want to?"

"Yes."

"Even though I smell like milk and honey?"

"I could just buy a bar of soap and carry *that* around," he said.

"A bar of soap wouldn't call you 'my dear' either."

It was like poking a bear on the nose. He hissed again and turned on me.

I fled down the path, shrieking like a delighted little kid who has finally managed to trick someone into playing with her. I only got a few steps before he swept me up.

"Cheater," I said. "You flew."

"Call me your dear," he demanded.

"Nope."

"Just once."

"Nope, nope, nope," I sang.

"You're acting like a five-year-old."

"You're acting like the grumpy boy on the playground who pulls girls' pigtails."

He flew me a little way off the path, staying low to the ground.

"What're you doing?"

"Trying to find a pile of nettles."

There weren't any, so he got impatient and just dropped me on the spot.

This time I lay there and refused to move.

He commanded, "Get up."

"I can't. I think you broke my arm."

"Liar."

"I have weak bones." I peered up at the sky through a screen of the huge, dark undersides of flowers. "It hurts."

"Liar," he said again, but I heard him land cautiously beside me, pushing leaves apart. I prowled through the stalks as he changed to human. Then I attacked, grabbing at his elbow, and tried to knock him over. But I was too light, or he was too heavy, so instead of dragging him down, it turned out that I pulled myself up. We ended up face-to-face in the chest-high field of flowers. He tried not to smile, twisting his head away so that I couldn't see. "You're such a pipsqueak."

"I'm normal-sized," I panted. "It's just that you're too fat to budge."

"You don't get to call me fat unless you call me your dear as well."

I thought about that. "My fat dear?" I said at last, laughing.

"If that's the best you can do, I accept," he said. "At least until the day I find a bar of soap that can be programmed to talk."

I looked at him, but he wouldn't meet my eyes. There was the heady, sticky smell of upturned dirt, and a cold wind, and mixed underneath all that, the faint sleepy smell from the forests of Ae, which seemed steeped into Sangris's skin. It took a while for us to realize that we were standing in a vast field of sunflowers, thousands of them, stretching up and over a hill ahead of us. The path of the camino was now hidden somewhere far to the left.

"But no trees," Sangris said. "This can't be the place."

"Maybe my father went off the path. Let's check. The sunflowers seem to just keep going and going."

We pushed through the huge, crackling dry stems, which towered around us like a garden designed for giants.

I heard the trees before I saw them. At first I thought it was the sea. Millions of leaves all moving as one. We reached the top of the hill and saw, on the other side, a row of trees that had been planted on the edge of the sunflower field. They were each shaped like the flame on a candle, pointing up at the sky. The leaves rippled together in long curling waves like brushstrokes of paint. At their base was a little well of dirty green water, and a stone bench where my father had sat and posed for a picture years and years ago, thinking of the person his daughter must become.

"Is this the place in the photograph?" Sangris said.

"Yes." I walked ahead and showed him the place where I had begun. We sat on the stone bench, looking back at the sweep of sunflowers that hid the camino.

"It's a good place to be invented," he said.

"Maybe. Except that my father imagined a daughter who—" I hesitated. I'd never told anyone this. My father had only said it to *me* once. I was nine years old, and we had just moved to Sardegna, an island in the Mediterranean. I was in trouble for getting into a fight at school, even though the other kid, a boy, had started it. He had kicked my shins and grabbed my bag, so I calmly kicked him back and a teacher saw. At home that night, my father looked at me and stated, in that voice of his that could change the universe: "My daughter is a girl who would never raise a hand in anger, not even to save herself from death. My daughter is meek, above all things. She would jump off a cliff if I told her to. That is who you should be. That is the *point* of you. It is the daughter I decided to have. A truly gentle, noble creature. If you cannot be her—if you ever fight against anybody again—then you are not Frenenqer Paje. You are nothing, you are nobody. Understood?"

Sangris frowned around at the oil-painted trees and the dry sunflowers and the well of cold water. "I don't see how jumping off a cliff is noble."

"Because it requires willpower," I said, "and discipline. My father gets uncomfortable with affection, and putting yourself forward, and all of that. So his ideal daughter has to be quiet, submissive, restrained. Kind of the perfect woman."

"Who, *you?*" Sangris said. He gave me a sideways smile.

"Don't," I said worriedly. "Don't make fun of it."

"Why not? You don't love your father anyway. You should make fun of it with me."

"But I think I agree with him. Sort of. See, he's—powerful," I said. "He scares me."

"But obviously he taught you to think that. It's the only way he could hope to make you the sort of person who would jump off a cliff on command," Sangris said. "Why else would you do it?"

I'd thought of this before, and I had the answer. "Because there would be no other choice," I said. "My father has all the power, and I have none. Simple as that." I looked at my fingers and saw with vague surprise that they were shaking.

Sangris saw them too. He put his own hands, long and brown, over them. I'd never noticed a boy's hands before, and it was strange how different they were from mine. "You wouldn't actually jump, would you?"

I shrugged. "I believe that my father's words have a kind of inevitability about them. Everybody obeys him. I think that if he told the sky to rain, it would. And as for me—I live in the oasis with him, don't I, even though I hate it there, even though I get attacks of claustrophobia, even though I have to stay inside all the time? And I still put up with it, because I have no choice. It's my father's way or nothing."

I stared at our hands. "Living somewhere suffocating . . . how different is that, really, from stepping off a cliff? It's slower, that's all. I have enough time to live my life before I hit the ground."

"And then it's over, and you've spent your life hating every minute," Sangris said, frowning at the sunflowers.

"Maybe not *every* minute," I said. "My books help. And you. You're helping." His hands tightened over mine. Before he could get a big head, I added hastily, "A bit."

Silence. I peeked up at him. He didn't look back; he was watching our hands. "I'm being overly dramatic, aren't I?"

"Shut up. You meant every word."

"That doesn't mean it wasn't melodramatic."

"Shut up," he said again. "I was just thinking . . . It's funny, but this isn't at all the sort of place where I'd expect your father to invent his idea of you."

"No?"

"No. The sunflowers, for instance." He nodded over at them. "They're strong, bold. The least delicate flowers you could imagine. And there are thousands of them. Your father would probably call it an immodest display."

True. I had to bite back a smile.

"Could he sit here, listen to the leaves roaring, smile for a photo, and then say, 'Huh, I think I need to ruin my daughter's life'?"

"He wasn't trying to ruin my life, he was trying to *bring* me to life," I said, "and he wasn't smiling in the photo, though he looked sort of optimistic—"

"We're in the Spanish countryside," Sangris said, "by a centuries-old pilgrim route. Fresh air. Those enormous flowers, so many of them that they cover the entire hill. Trees that look as if they've been painted. They make a sound like a flooding river, don't they? A stone well, in the shade. Dark green, gold, black." He paused. His hands were still over mine. "I can imagine someone sitting here, thinking of you, but a different you. Different from what your father wants, I mean, and more like you are now. Your father's Frenenqer seems like she'd be thought up in a dull drawing room somewhere. But here . . . everything is ancient and lovely and bold and dusty and romantic. It's the sort of place where a poet would be born. Either a poet or a revolutionary."

I tried to brush it off. "Are you calling me ancient and dusty?"

"And lovely and bold and romantic. You conveniently left those out, didn't you?"

"I'm not any of those things."

"Well, actually I was trying to describe the place, not you. As it happens, you're only bold on occasion, when you feel comfortable enough; you're the opposite of ancient and you're definitely not romantic; as a matter of fact, you're so determinedly unromantic that I think you do it on purpose; and I haven't noticed any dust on you. But you are lovely. One out of five—at least it's something."

"I'm not lovely," I said seriously. "Anything with the *L* word in it doesn't suit me."

"Liar. Why do you think I haven't been able to look you in the eyes since you called me your dear?" He ducked his head and added, "Even if that was only a joke."

Ye gods, he was serious too.

"You didn't notice, did you," he said.

I looked over at the straight line of Sangris's nose, and the black hair that hid most of his face right now.

Well—

Of course I had noticed. No one with eyes could have missed it. But it was better to fake blindness. "No," I said slowly. "I didn't."

I'm not sure whose benefit I was acting for. Not my own. (I knew that I was lying through my teeth.) Maybe not even Sangris's. I think I was talking to the presence of my father, which hovered behind my shoulders. *See that?* I told it. *I didn't notice a thing. So I don't have to shove Sangris away, and I don't have to run back to my room, and I don't have to go to* Pfft, *because . . . because I didn't notice a thing.*

I shrugged, I looked away from Sangris with a show of disinterest, and I did everything I was supposed to do; almost everything that my father would have wanted me to do. But I couldn't quite make myself slide my hands out from under Sangris's. That was too much to ask of me. Instead I turned away and gave the sunflowers a last look.

He was right. The place didn't make sense. It was so pretty, so peaceful, it seemed to deny all the cold little facts of my life. The beauty here was the exact opposite of what must have been boiling in my father's head when he'd visited. But

I'd told Sangris the truth. Everything I knew. My father *had* sat here, and, somehow, he'd come up with me.

When the time came, I didn't stop Sangris from picking me up and flying me home, over the lightening landscape on the other side of the night. And if I ought to have said no when he asked if he could hold me while in human form—well, that was also too much to ask of me.

CHAPTER NINE

In Which a Bird Is Wadded Up

The desert looked pale and perfect at dawn. The dunes lying in vast interlocked patterns. Almost pink—but that didn't fool me. Nothing was alive down there, nothing soft. Even the trees were armored. The acacias buckled under the weight of their spikes, and they grabbed their leaves close and stingy around themselves, refusing to spread out green, keeping gray instead, as if the color were a hoard of treasure they were afraid to share.

And beyond that, on the horizon, a flat yellow sun sliding up into a dull white sky, a cardboard sunrise.

Sangris lowered us into the oasis. I spotted my house from far off, a cube of crumbly stone, flat-roofed. My window had been left open. It seemed miserably small.

Sangris brought us level, and I slid out of his arms, through the window, into my room before I had time to regret it. When my feet were safely on the hard marble floor, I turned and looked back.

"Could I visit you at the school today?"

"It's the weekend," I said.

"Oh." He hovered in the window frame. "At night, then?"

"Not on the weekend."

"Why not?"

"Too dangerous. My father doesn't keep a regular sleep schedule unless he has work the next day. And he's home the entire time."

He thought I was exaggerating. "I'm sure your dad won't figure it out—"

"As a matter of fact, you'd better go now."

Sangris frowned a bit. He leaned on the windowsill, black hair waving all around his face in the breeze from his wings, and burning eyes fixed on me. "What are you worried about?"

"He might hear something."

"What, do you think he'd guess if he did? Is your father the type of person who'd say, 'Oh, it must be a shape-shifting non-cat'?"

"Just go."

"I'll try to visit anyway," he warned, and then before I could change his mind, he slipped away and the faint color-less light closed in where he'd been.

For a moment I just stood there. The stupid Free person didn't understand what it was like to have a father . . .

I shut the window, then the curtains. I got into my night-shirt and crawled into bed. I thought I might as well try to sleep. After a few minutes the tension dropped away. Sangris wouldn't do anything rash. He knew I'd kill him if he did. I could handle this. I shut my eyes, and for a few hours the world went black and secret.

Later in the morning I went through my routines. I consciously tried to be a machine. When I came out of my room, I thought my father would be able to look at me and see something different at once, as though the Spanish sunlight and the smell of the sky had left their marks on my skin. But he didn't look up.

My mother poked her head into the dining room once, but when she saw the two of us sitting together she slowly withdrew it.

As I ate cereal, my father concentrated at the other end of the table, working on his laptop. Long spidery fingers pecked back and forth. He had never learned to type properly. The pallid sunlight came in through the window and lit the marble floor, the white walls, his crinkled black hair.

I said, "Good morning."

He glanced at the clock on the wall to check that I was accurate. Luckily it was still eleven.

"You should make your voice go up on the last syllable," he said, "not down. It's more polite."

I wondered again about Spain. He must have thought he was doing the world a duty, creating me. I remembered the sunflowers. The invention of one girl, someone who'd always be right, and always be blameless. It was a grand thing. My father had spent years of his life struggling in this tiny effort to improve the human race. Except that I'd turned out so shoddy, still a work in progress.

"All right," I said, my voice going up on the second syllable.

"Better."

Peck, peck, peck. His index fingers moved in nervous little jolts over the keyboard, meticulous and precision-perfect.

When I began to leave he stopped me. "Show me how you close the door."

Like a toddler trained to go potty, I demonstrated.

The thing about being an expat is that you can pick up fragments of the cultures you pass through, like a crab covering its shell with pieces of its surroundings, choosing whatever appeals to your personality. My father has adopted guidelines for me from all around the world. Whatever strikes him as refined. Apologize to anyone you brush against, that's from Canada. Act shy, that's from Thailand. Don't smile at men, that's from the oasis. I do admire these graces, it's not that I'd rather be coarse and cultureless . . .

Ten times I shut the door quietly, cheeks flushed, until he said, "Bend a little too. In doorways, keep your head low in case someone's passing through." (You see, that's why it's such a pity I'm tall: My head's not meant to be higher than my superiors'.) "You don't want to lay yourself open to reproach," my father said to me.

But I'm not as much of a machine as I should be. Hidden in my room later, it didn't take very long for me to regret sending Sangris away.

By noon I was sick of my books and their fantasy worlds. I wanted something new. Again I thought of Sangris. Then I heard my father pace past my door, and I jumped, as though he might have sensed my thoughts.

But that didn't stop me from tossing my book aside and going to the window.

I winced when I peeled back the curtains. The glass was too hot to touch, and outside, everything shone hard and white. I could see the air rippling over the cars on the distant road, and I could almost feel the ground curling up and stiffening in the dryness. I scanned for any signs of life, any movement—particularly in the shape of a black cat. But there was nothing.

I tried to summon the memory of Ae, and the openness of the sky there, but it was like a dream that becomes more faded and disjointed the harder you try to remember it. I thought maybe Sangris was a lie that I had told myself to keep from going crazy. Free people?—an impossible idea; impossible exactly because I wanted it to be true.

Come on, Sangris . . .

I caught a scrap of movement. My eyes focused. Down there, somewhere. I scalded my fingertips when I tried to lean closer to the windowpane.

Yes, there. On the sun-sucked gray pavement along the road, in the direct and dangerous sunlight, there was a tiny thing struggling. I squinted. Just looking outside gave me a headache. The atmosphere was toxic. But I saw it, near a shriveled-up tree, out of the shade. A bare patch of skin burning on the pavement.

I should have looked away. It was only a baby bird. You

find them all the time, normally as no more than papery skeletons littering the balconies and the roads. The desert is a place well-suited to turning small creatures into dust.

But this bird hadn't died yet.

I swallowed and it hurt my throat. My eyes were fixed on the rare living thing down there, on the other side of the glass. It was so small I couldn't see any details. But I could tell that it had no feathers, because it was pink gray, the color of bones showing through bare skin. I knew that the stone of the pavement would be flaming. God help anything that fell out of the nest; it would be cooking on the ground.

Nothing on earth matters more than a life. Right?

I think everything would be easier if I didn't have a conscience.

I pulled away from the window, headed to the door, stopped at the last second and looked down at myself to check that I was wearing enough. The pants were long, but the sleeves were a bit short. I got nervous at the sight of my arms. But there was no time for that. I hurried out, walking on the balls of my feet, I slipped on the first pair of shoes I could find, and *let myself out the door.*

I would pay for it later. I spent a precious moment trying to close the door as quietly as possible. Then I ran.

The heat squeezed at me. Nobody else was outside, not at noon. No one was stupid enough for that. A few cars slowed on the street so that the people inside could watch me run past, and they honked in appreciation. I ducked my head, trying to hide behind my hair. But I didn't slow down.

For a second I was afraid I might forget where I had seen the bird. But my feet carried me there. With relief I spotted the pink-gray dot wriggling around on the stone up ahead. For that dot, I had left the house. Maybe I could get back before my father noticed what I had done.

I knelt down on the pavement, and even through the fabric of my pants, the stone blistered me. I couldn't stay kneeling for more than a moment before it became painful. I can't imagine what it must have felt like for the bird.

It was a nestling. Its wings were crooked bare bumps like those on a baked chicken, and part of its skin was raw, mottled red in a way that made it look more like a monster than a baby. I felt queasy at the idea of touching it. I did anyway. Its head was too heavy for its neck, and flopped back as I slid my fingers underneath. The brittle bones were bulging beneath the skin.

"Shh," I said. The bird was gross and I would have died for it willingly. It couldn't have been more than a few days old. It stank of something musty. The beautiful thing. It waggled its head back and I whispered to it again. I got up, turned, and almost walked right into my father.

He'd followed me out of the house.

I staggered back, opened my mouth, then shut it again. On the palm of my hand the broken bird wriggled.

"It was going to die," I explained.

My father watched me. His face was screwed up in the heat and the bright light. Sand was already beginning to stick to the streaks of sweat gathering in the creases on his forehead. I saw him like a stranger, leveling his gaze at me, straight and unemotional as a bullet.

It would be easier if he seemed angry sometimes. But there's never any uncontrolled feeling behind the flat glaze of eyes. Or if there is, it's something alien—something so far removed from me that it's unrecognizable. His feelings are made of metal, and I'm only meat.

"I came out to help it," I said, starting to babble when he still didn't speak. "I saw it through the window—"

"Get inside."

"Going now."

He stopped me. "Put that thing down first," he said.

I hesitated. "This?" I said, holding up the lopsided bird.

His face screwed up even more when he saw it.

"That's disgusting," he said. "Don't you see how *wrong* your conduct is? I wouldn't have believed it. Do you think it's smart to run outside without supervision and pick up dirty animals off the street?"

I glanced up at him and then down again, quickly, before he could think I was staring. Staring is rude.

I was taken off guard when he reached out and pulled the nestling away from me. He stepped back with the baby bird somewhere inside the fist of his right hand. He wasn't holding it very carefully. There was one bony leg sticking out from between his fingers and waggling in the air, blindly.

"What are you doing?" I said. It was difficult to breathe in this heat.

"You'd disobey me for this?" he said, opening his fist and looking at the crumpled nestling on his palm. "This . . . *thing?* It's hideous. Allowing you to save that cat must have encouraged you. From now on, no helping animals. You're not a child anymore, Frenenqer. You can't just run outside whenever you see some filthy half-dead creature. People are staring from the road . . ." And he grew paler, as if he'd been insulted.

I wished I were a Free person. Instead I was a skinny girl on the hard blaze of street with bearded men in cars going past. My father looked down at the bird as it thrashed, featherless and burnt, on the palm of his hand. There was only repulsion in his face, tight lines by the side of his mouth.

"I never want to see you outside during the day again," he said. "We agreed that you could go on walks at sunset. Not earlier. You have broken your promise."

The bird began to cheep, high-pitched and sudden.

"All right," I said, "I'll go inside, just let me put it back first—I'll put it in a tree—"

"Stop answering back."

"The bird—"

"Frenenqer!"

But I had to speak. I didn't want him near the nestling. I didn't like the way he was looking at it, as though it was a lump of dirt. If he didn't give it back soon I would go frantic. "The bird, can you—?"

He crumpled it up in his hand like a used tissue.

Then dropped it. Dust puffed up around the crooked mess

as it landed on the pavement. My father's face was calm, as though he'd done nothing worse than litter.

I stood there for a moment looking at it.

"It's only a bird," he said. "Now go back inside—"

I brought my foot down hard on the pavement. I hoped it would make a loud noise. I wanted to stomp and destroy the world and make a terrible, enormous racket that would be impossible to ignore. But I was too light. Nothing happened.

I pulled away from my father. I ran for the twitching thing, to pick it up. But he grabbed me. He held my arms to my sides and said, "Frenenqer, stop!" and I struggled without being able to move—his hands felt as if they were made of iron, and he said, *What is wrong with you?* and, still holding me pinned, he picked me up and carried me away from the twitching thing as if I were a lawn chair he wanted to move to a more convenient location.

He put me down outside the house. When he was satisfied that I wasn't showing any resistance, he quietly pushed open our front door. Then he waited, watching, until I stepped inside.

CHAPTER TEN

In Which I Jump Out the Window

It was cold inside. He made me take my shoes off first. Then my room—I ended up there somehow, my feet on the chill floor, looking straight ahead as I heard the door close behind me. My bedroom looked exactly the same as I'd left it. I stood delicately balanced on a high wire above hysteria.

There was a big empty space inside of me struggling. I wanted the sun to explode and swallow up the world. I wanted the universe to be dark, all the tiny stars to be snuffed out, as easily as my father had rolled the bird up, like a bit of scrap paper in his hands. He'd constructed me—he'd crushed the bird—it was all the same to him.

It's true that I've always been his creation, as if I'm a project he put together for school when he was young. I'm the child, the miracle of life, the baby who has to be fed, kept clean, and told what to do. But he has never thought of me as a thinking, feeling person. Around him, I'm not real.

I considered throwing myself onto the bed and crying. But that was too dramatic.

And then I was disgusted at myself for calmly trying to

calculate the best way to express my grief. It made everything seem so artificial. That was the worst thing. Even alone in my bedroom, I was too inhibited to cry.

After a moment my bedroom door opened. I turned to see my mom stick her head in.

"What did you do now?"

"Tried to save a bird," I said tonelessly.

Her eyes widened, just for a second, but then she threw me a look of exasperation. Probably my father was in a bad mood now, taking it out on her, and she blamed me. She didn't say anything, only sighed and left.

Suddenly a bubble of cramped anger swelled in my chest.

I wish we could be like animals, abandon our young after a certain age. I'd like to just wander off one day, over the vast plains, and never come back.

I wouldn't mind if my parents outright hated me. It's the fact they pretend to love me that I can't stand. Could *that* be love? It's a crippled, painful, sour, unnatural thing. But I know that's only how I feel because I'm unnatural myself— because my heart is as clean and empty and unfeeling as the open sky.

I saw now that it had been dumb to go outside.

The door opened again. This time it was my father. He had his sternest face on.

"I hope you've learned your lesson," he said. "Have you?"

I nodded, not trusting myself to speak.

"I don't know what's got into you lately, Frenenqer. It started with the souk," he said, in the tight voice of a sculptor watching a masterpiece developing flaws, growing cracks. "I've decided that you must be reading too much. These books are teaching you disrespect."

"But—"

"No answering back."

I fell silent again.

He said, "I am sick of this teenage rebellion phase."

I didn't answer back.

He took that as insolence too. "You think you're smart, don't you?" he said.

The problem is, there's always something inside me that's watching, and thinking, and judging. God knows I try to hide it, but I can't turn my mind off; and my father *hates* to be judged. Leaving the door open behind him, he came in and heaved a stack of my books off the floor.

"What—what're you doing?" I said.

No answer. He left the room with the stack and I stayed standing there, awkwardly, like an idiot. After a moment he returned for another armful. And another. And another. It took a long time. He didn't glance at me as he worked. There was a dark closed-up look on his face that reminded me of a soldier. Steadily, he dismantled the walls of books that protected my bed. I watched it all fall apart. Some of the novels he didn't bother to carry. There were too many of them, so he kicked them along the floor instead. As he was lifting up the final stack of books, one—*The Innocence of Father Brown*—slipped off the top and fell with a quiet thump to the floor, pages splayed. I bent over and picked it up. I slid the book on top of his stack and stood aside as he carried it away. Then the door closed and he was gone.

My room looked very bare without the books, smaller than I had remembered. There was dust all over the white floor. And cockroaches. A black wave of them rippled away into the walls.

I stared at the new emptiness around my bed.

In Spain last night I'd told Sangris that, when I was a little girl, I used to love my parents, but that I had stopped. And it's true. Now I remembered the exact day, the exact moment, when I stopped.

It was the day my father took away a book I was halfway through. I forget why he was angry, but that was his punishment. He didn't even bother to hide the book properly. He knew that I wouldn't dare to retrieve it. And I crawled into the bathroom and I cried—I still cried freely in those days. My mind was like a whirlpool when I was younger, constantly sucking me down. Nowadays I have myself under better control.

I remember the bathroom and the cracked khaki sink. I knelt on the floor, held on to the sides of the sink to keep myself steady, and shook hard with hatred for half an hour. I muffled the noises coming from my mouth so that no one would hear.

I don't know why it affected me like that. Such a small thing, and I dreamed of running away. I was eleven years old. New to the oasis. I remember that incident because it was the first time the feeling didn't go away afterward.

It stayed, and it's still there, a round hard lump where my heart muscle has cramped.

After that, I felt very alone and cold and miserable, but in a good way. Everything became better once I stopped caring for my parents. Things hurt less. Though for months afterward, whenever I went outside, I expected the sky to spit on me, because no matter how much improved my life seemed to be after the emotion stopped, I knew perfectly well that children *should* love their parents, and that I was a monstrosity. But I'm okay: With time, I settled, I grew used to it—after all, people can get used to anything—and it became mere background noise to my life.

But now I stood in the middle of my room, stunned by the flat blankness of the floor. And slowly, slowly, my mind caught up with what had just happened.

I'd handed my father the book that had fallen. I'd practically held the door open for him.

The anger and bitterness stirred up inside of me then. I can ignore the feelings if they're left alone, but a gust of wind sends them all whirling. I felt the sparks catch fire. My back—the emptiness where there should have been wings—ached. Itching so that I could barely breathe. I shut my eyes. I was trapped. I stood in the center of the room, walled in. Then I remembered. There was one thing that my father hadn't forbidden me to do, because he hadn't known about it. I went to the window, shoved it open. I felt my ribs screaming under some enormous pressure. I didn't allow it to reach my mouth. I couldn't. He would have heard. I shoved my head and shoulders out into the heat. Above me was the chemical blue sky; up ahead, the road with rows of white cars sleeking across it; below, the mingled dust and sand by the side of the pavement. Now that the bird wasn't moving, I couldn't spot it, and I was glad about that. I'd hate to see.

I wanted Sangris to come. There were many things I wanted. I couldn't believe anymore that out there, somewhere, were the wide lands of Free people, and the coolness and the open spaces of eternity. Right now the world felt about the size of the trunk of a car. I shut my eyes hard and the blaze of red almost knocked me over. I held on to the ledge tightly until the wave passed.

How was I supposed to grow and live stuck in a place like this? Even weeds couldn't grow here, so what chance did I have? The bird was lucky that it had turned to bone—it suited the desert better now. Bone and dust is natural. Flesh isn't. I could tell that the desert sensed me as something impudent and short-lived, and it was slowly creeping around, sucking the air out of me, turning me into a part of the place I hated. A dry hard land and a dry hard girl to match. I wanted shadows and movement and mossy things, and a living sun instead of a dead one, but it was all out of reach and my body was useless, wingless. I don't know how long I stood fixed there. The pressure building up. I couldn't think.

Then the familiar voice, clear as a sudden stream of cool water: "Nenner?"

I opened my eyes and there he was. His eyes were like lemon ice, and that was all I could see of him against the white blaze of light. But I reacted as if I had expected him to be there. At once the frustration snapped and I pulled myself up onto the windowsill. "Sangris," I said, "quick!"

"What?"

His eyes widened in surprise. He was human, but I didn't pay close attention. It was enough to see that wide, dragonfly-transparent wings were glimmering at his back, moving so fast they were a blur.

He was studying my face with a frown. "Nenner, are you okay?"

"No, I'll explain later, but I need to get out of here," I said, all in one breath.

He looked bewildered. "It's daytime. What if your father needs you and can't find you? You said he'd—"

I had to crouch. The window frame was too small. I was inside that square, tight and trapped, the glass above me wouldn't move when I touched it, and claustrophobia was squeezing me, and the heat pushed at me, trying to force me back into the room, and Sangris was being irritating, so I jumped.

Beneath me were the dry pebbleless stretches of sand, and pale roadside, flaking like a diseased skin, and the hard knots of acacia trees, prickling and curling as if in pain. My room was in the highest floor of the house. The dead white light roared below—if I fell, it would be like falling onto the surface of the sun. But the next moment I thudded into him and he caught me.

The wings blurred and sent a breeze into my face until I

could nearly breathe. He'd caught me awkwardly, one arm under mine and the other around my waist, and the sunlight was so bright, it was making it hard for me to see anything. "Let's go, let's go," I said, clinging on, afraid to slip.

Sangris shifted, getting a better grip. And catapulted us away. I left the window open behind me, and the curtains parted, and my house abandoned in broad midday with my father awake inside. Anybody in the cars going past could have seen us too. It was the most reckless thing I'd ever done and none of it mattered. I had to breathe.

CHAPTER ELEVEN

In Which I Climb a Ladder Out of the Desert

Everything inside of me was coiled tight. I struggled to draw the air in. But very soon the sky became cold and smooth, streaming pearl gray around us, like swells of water. I breathed deeply, hungrily, my pulse fluttering. We'd entered a space of low cloud. All around us was blurry paleness, as though the sky had cataracts.

This might have seemed a dreary place, the two of us lost inside the clouds, but sometimes, through a gap in the mist, the sunlight suddenly slanted through, splattering us with rainbows, gone in an instant. Sangris flew so fast, my hair billowed out in our trail, cape-like. The air was clean, the sunshine rolling like a white ghost below our feet—*that* couldn't belong to the same sun that had beat me down just a few moments ago.

"Now are you going to tell me what happened?" he said.

"Nothing happened," I muttered.

"Right. It's normal for you to hurl yourself out of windows."

"A claustrophobic moment."

"What set it off?"

"The usual."

"And what's the usual?"

I wrinkled my forehead at him. But this impressive argument didn't convince either of us. Sangris flew on, quiet. Waiting.

Still I wouldn't meet his eyes. "I want to forget about it, that's all," I said at last. Even as I spoke the words, I knew I wouldn't forget. Instead of withdrawing my arms, I tightened them around his neck. I felt him studying me.

"You look tired," he said after a moment.

"Yes, last night I had a nightmare that I was stuck in Spain with someone who wouldn't stop throwing questions at me."

The words were meant to sound light. They didn't. I regretted them instantly.

Sangris didn't say anything. I watched him focus on the sky ahead, his face unreadable. He glanced down at me. "The wind's got your hair," he said.

"Yours too." There was a long pause. "I'm glad you came," I said finally. "I don't know what I would have done otherwise. I'm glad you can fly."

"Well, I like making myself useful," said Sangris.

"Really? You don't seem the type."

"You think I'm lazy?"

"No—" That caught me off guard. "I think you're free." I pursued the change of subject. "What's it like to have a life without rules or responsibilities?"

"Fine, I guess."

"Just fine?"

"It gets old."

"You'd rather be cramped?" I bit my lip. My voice had sounded too bitter. His eyes were still roving over my hair, then my face, and it was a long time before he focused on the sky again. I stayed silent for a second, listening to the lonely flappings of my shirt in the wind, and the steady thump of Sangris's wings. Then I told him.

I would tell Anju too, later on. Anju would blink and *mm-hmm,* and for all the comments she'd make, I may as well have told my story to a particularly unresponsive block of wood. She tended to accept all suffering as ordinary.

But Sangris listened. I wasn't used to people paying attention to me. Each word dropped into the yellowness of his eyes and changed their expression somehow, as though he were a lake I was sending ripples across. When I came to my father's hand, the crumpling, his forehead creased up and he said, "Nenner—" And because he was showing emotion, it was easier for me to be matter-of-fact. I heard my flat voice going on and on into the vacant gape of the fog.

It was better than crying. It didn't make me feel weak or ashamed.

When I was done, he said, "Do you need to head back now?"

I thought of going back to the oasis and my heart gave a dull thud, like machinery grinding down to an end. "My parents will leave my room alone for a while. They'll want me to stew," I said. "Keep flying. Please."

"Oh, good," he said, not as if he was doing me a favor at all, but as if I was doing him one. And he zoomed faster, until the fog burst, opening up around us, and we shot out into clearness.

The clouds gave way so abruptly that by the time I'd gained my bearings, Sangris had already landed with a soft patter of wings against leaves. He put me down and I felt smooth wood beneath my bare feet. Pulling away, I wasn't quite stable. Sore, aching, my mind had the thinness of new skin growing over a cut.

But then I looked around.

We were in a rainforest. A river curved soundlessly through the clustered trees, with a low wooden dock for boats tethered to one bank. Sangris had landed on this. It rocked gently beneath our weight.

The river waters were bright honey, as intensely colored as paint. A faint mist drifted over its surface. The forest massing on either side was so dense it looked black, except where, strangely delicate, a slash of flowers glowed white, or tear-shaped mangoes dripped pale green. Strange smells seeped out of the foliage, savory and disturbing. There was the sense of unknown things hiding beneath that painted-honey water, behind the screen of trees, even below the slowly creaking planks of the dock we stood on. Animal noises rumbled together in an ever-present background thunder, but no life was actually visible, apart from a single butterfly tumbling over the water, its wings flickering red as a racing heart.

It was the most beautiful place I'd ever been in, and I'd been in a lot.

"Nenner," said Sangris, who'd been staring at me while I was staring at the jungle. "Listen—I'll help you. I'll stick around the oasis. As a cat, or something small, like a lizard. And if you ever have a moment like that again, if your father, you know . . . I can take you away. Anytime you want, whenever you need it. I'll never be far. I'm your ladder out of the desert, my dear."

"Don't call me your dear," I said faintly.

"I'm your ladder out of the desert, Nenner," he said, offering me a smile. When I didn't respond, he rushed on. "Listen, I've thought about this. I lead a pointless sort of life. It's about time I put myself to good use. And—well, that's not really why I'm offering." He hesitated. Then he took a deep breath and lowered his voice until I could barely hear it. "You saved me from the souk."

But his speech was still too much, too sudden. I found myself answering the way my father had trained me. "There's no need for that," I said, with vapid politeness.

There was another reason too: I didn't believe him. Sangris thought promising "I'll never be far" was enough to solve everything. But it's impossible for a person to always be there. I've moved away from too many countries, and from too many friends, not to know that. And Sangris was a Free person, bound to be unreliable.

He rubbed his head, caught off guard by my reaction. I didn't blame him. I'd caught myself off guard too.

We were both quiet for a while. I pretended to be very interested in the throbbing red of the butterfly over the river. My heartbeats felt muffled, still adjusting to the change from the claustrophobia of my bedroom. A few seconds ago I'd been so walled in, and now I was in a rainforest—

"I used to live here," Sangris said.

He was pointing downward.

I looked at him blankly. "What, on the dock?"

"Under the dock. Inside the river. That's why I brought you here, to show you. I got sick of Ae, the same way I got sick of everywhere I'd ever lived. I'd never spent more than a couple of weeks in one country. So I flew here to the jungle at random, and I forced myself to stay for an entire year."

"Why?"

"I was hoping that if I lived in one place long enough, it would become a home. Stupid idea, didn't work."

He spoke as though this information was somehow logically related to his offer to become my ladder out of the desert. A thought struck me. "You can't possibly want the oasis to become your home?" I said in disbelief.

"Not the *oasis*," he said. I blinked when I realized what he meant. "I mean—getting to know someone . . . That's almost the same thing as belonging, right?"

I didn't know what to say to this. Sangris frowned slightly at the curls of humidity sliding over the water.

133

"The thing is," he said to the river, "places blur together after a while. Everywhere's the same. Imagine how bored you can get if all the worlds are scattered like marbles at your feet . . . Free, and alone, that's the life of a Free person. It's like flying inside a bubble."

I hesitated. "It used to feel that way before we settled down in the oasis. When my family moved around a lot."

"Then you know what it's like."

"But I was with my family."

"Still alone."

"You're sharp today," I said, raising my eyebrows.

"Oh, I know exactly what I'm talking about," he said, shrugging. "Limitations give things meaning, but Free people don't *have* limits. It's like living without the outlines that would define your shape. There's no rhyme or reason for us."

I'd never imagined he would complain about it. "Don't you like being a Free person?"

"Oh, sure. It has its perks," he said, still casual as ever. He probably wouldn't mind if he had been born as a cockroach. "But you give up a lot of things. No ties, no background. You're always lost—because if everywhere's the same to you, it doesn't matter where you are. Free and light as air, and just as empty—" He stopped for a moment. Then he made a small motion with his hand, as if brushing it all aside.

I frowned. Evidently, Sangris wasn't a cat who could shape-shift. It was more difficult than that. He was a nothing who occasionally pretended to be a cat. "I wish I could know what it's like for myself, that's all," I said. I felt rather the way a jail inmate would if a bird flew up and shouted through her window bars: *This freedom thing? Yeah, not so great.* "Is it just you? Or do most Free people think this way?"

"No clue. It's not like Free people organize social gatherings. Lone wanderers, remember? Part of having no species. Though there are exceptions. I have noticed from a distance—among the older ones, sometimes when the coldness gets too much, they try to find some normal species and settle down with them. Once in a while it actually works. With migrating bird-people, normally."

"Not humans?"

He scrunched up his nose. "Humans . . . ugh. No offense, but your species isn't very popular." Then he brightened. "But you, you're kind of like a migrating bird, aren't you, Nenner?"

I didn't say anything, but secretly I liked the idea.

He went on quickly. "Anyway, me, I never did get along well with big flocks. A Free person couldn't truly fit in. It's just exchanging one kind of loneliness for another."

"Ah, so that's why you don't have any other friends. I thought it was just because nobody else can stand you."

For some reason that made him crack into a huge grin. Turning away from the river at last, he looked straight at me.

"It's just my luck that my only friend can't show affection in any other way than by insulting me."

"Affection? Me?" I began indignantly, but he plowed right on.

"And that's what I've been leading up to. You know what I realized that other day in your room, when we made our deal? You're practically a Free person yourself, Nenner."

I started laughing. "Are you kidding? I'm the most un-Free person I know."

"Yes, but how many countries have you lived in? Okay, you can't fly, and you're not much of a wild spirit—"

"Thanks a bunch—"

"You're welcome—but still, I've never met a non-Free person so unrooted."

Smiling, I shook my head. "You mean I have all of the bad bits without any of the advantages."

But then the thought snuck up on me: *It's true.* No human could be more like Sangris than I am. After all, I don't know where I'm from or what I am; to be honest, I'm not anything at all. I have four passports and none of them mean much to me. When people ask "Where are you from?" the question doesn't even make sense.

I looked at Sangris with an odd feeling, almost like a shock of recognition. He had no species, but I had no ethnicity. He had no world, but I had no country. Why had I felt amazed that he was a constant alien? I *knew* what that was like.

His head was bent, and he was looking at me more seriously than was usual for him. The hint of wickedness in his face, the sharp cheekbones and the black straggles of hair, now just gave him an earnest look.

"It's a weird feeling," he said, "having a connection to someone."

And he actually flushed as I stared at him.

"So," he said, rubbing at the back of his neck, "so, as one foreigner to another, Nenner, now tell me—am I allowed to stay with you?"

I wanted to shuffle my feet and refuse to look up from the creaking wood of the dock. But I thought he deserved a proper answer, especially when he was making so much effort to keep his own eyes steady. So I met his gaze as I nodded. "Let's go back," I said. "If you come, I think I can handle the oasis until tonight."

Before I could even finish the sentence, gravity dropped away. He had scooped me up and we shot into the cool, sticky white sea of the sky again.

Too soon, I felt myself being lowered back into the tightness and heat.

"Remember, it's just until tonight," said Sangris into my ear. "Then we can get out and go somewhere new."

This time I didn't say "No, it's the weekend." I nodded and we submerged ourselves into the airless oasis.

Sliding back through my window, I was struck by the cold. My room looked so hollow without books. But the next second Sangris distracted me. He shrank into a cat, leaving his uniform in a careless heap on the floor, and I shoved his clothes out of sight behind the bed. I sat cross-legged on the ground with my back against the door. At least, this way, we'd have prior warning if my parents tried to burst in.

"If the door knocks me over," I said, whispering, "you jump out the window. Got it?"

"Yep."

My shoulders grew a little less rigid. But then Sangris added: "I promise. Although, you know—"

"No ideas!"

"Just thinking," said Sangris innocently. The huge black cat flicked his tail and tried to ease himself into my lap. "If your dad annoys you, I could always turn into a tiger and rip his face off. If you want. It's a possibility to keep in mind, that's all."

I tried to picture my father fighting a tiger. Instinctively I felt that the tiger would lose, but I couldn't quite picture how.

"No."

"Oh, all right. If you say so," he said cheerfully, and flipped himself over onto his back. With his paws sticking up in the air that way, he looked like any silly cat waiting to be petted.

Having Sangris in the same house as my father, separated only by an unlocked door, was enough to make my nerves ripple, but it was better than the alternative. While Sangris was here, the claustrophobia couldn't get hold of me. And even if my father burst in, he would only see a cat, right? I kept my back against the door. Slowly my fear turned to dark-sparkling adrenaline.

"You," I told Sangris, "are living proof against the existence of a well-ordered universe."

"Really?" he said, flattered.

"A Free thing in the oasis? Doesn't make any sense. You're going to be struck by lightning any minute now."

"Oh, come on. This isn't a bad place to be in. As far as prisons go."

I looked around the room, at the exposed walls where my books had been. "Easy to think that, if you haven't been stuck in here for years."

"Pssh. Shut in a room with you? If this is a prison, it's fine with me." He nudged my hand with his head, and immediately a low, warm rumble came from his throat.

"Are you *purring?*"

"No," he mumbled, and purred louder. After a moment his eyes slid shut.

I sighed. "Lucky Sangris," I said, still listening at the door for my father's footfalls. "Must be nice to be so easygoing. Nothing ever matters to you, does it?"

"Oh, I wouldn't say that," he said, eyes still shut.

CHAPTER TWELVE

In Which I Walk
Through My Childhood

Everything changed after that.

In the dimly lit back of the classroom, Anju said to me, "What's going on with you?"

"What do you mean?" I doodled intently in my notebook. "Here, look at this." I shoved the sketch over the table to her. "Is it any good?"

I had covered the page entirely with straight lines, but in such a way that, through the bars of ink, you could make out the impression of our teacher's face. Bald head, curved nose, a toothbrush mustache. It was, I thought, a pretty good resemblance. I had captured his half-wild expression as he ranted about moving vectors.

She glanced at it. "Very artistic," she said, in her rounded, monotonous voice. No matter what she was talking about, that voice of hers made it sound as if she were reciting quadratic equations. "But what's going on with you?"

I rocked back in my flimsy orange plastic chair. On two legs, and then only one, tilting as far as I could without falling. "What do you mean? Am I acting weird?"

"Yes."

"You know me. That's normal."

"A different weird," she insisted. "You're acting almost . . . happy." She said the word with distrust.

"Sorry."

But I couldn't help it. In those days, I don't know which I valued more: Sangris, or his wings. Walking through my school in the tiny oasis, I'd come across a thousand different memories of places I'd been with him—a piece of juice-sodden fruit tasting like the jungle, sunlight splashing my classroom walls brilliant cloud white, the air suddenly smelling of Spain. And I'd want, instantly, nothing more than to fly again.

Even my father was struck by my new mood. One day at dinner he laid down his fork and gave me a long look over the table. "You haven't been pestering me to return your books," he observed.

And he was right, I realized, surprised. I had almost forgotten about them.

"I didn't want to annoy you," I said simply.

A pause. "Well . . ." he said. He didn't look pleased, but there was something on his face: hope. Like somebody working on something massively important, who doesn't dare to believe it when the pieces seem to be coming together. "Maybe you're improving."

My lungs expanded. He had no clue. He hadn't seen the inside of my head. He didn't know me well enough; his thoughts were full of a mythical Frenenqer Paje.

That night I held my breath until my father had gone to

sleep. Then I dressed with a quick-beating heart, and stood on the cold marble floor of my bedroom, pushing the window up.

Furtively, I climbed out onto the sill. Under my hands the stone felt coarse and crumbly, as though it might give way beneath me at any moment.

I sat inside the square of that window as if I were a painted girl in a picture frame, trapped and unreal and static, and I looked at the black forever waiting just outside. In the silence I could hear the faraway sands giving off a high-pitched seething noise like a steaming kettle. I kept thinking of what my father would say if he saw me now. Then a movement in the darkness, and a gleam of eyes, and Sangris said, "Ah, waiting for me, are you?"

"No, I'm waiting for some other maniac with wings."

Then I got to my feet, and, taking my arms, he drew me out of my picture frame, into the darkness and the heat, to a place where the ground was frighteningly, thrillingly far away, and the sunless sky was burning and trembling all around us. The stars were faint tinsel, and the air, smooth—not the dry sawdust stuff I had to breathe in the oasis, but sweet and full. Far, far beneath us were the manic lines of streetlights. They jagged over the oasis like stray fantasies. My prison was beautiful from the outside. And then, with one easy glance, Sangris gave me the earth.

"Name a country," he said. Like a conjuror. *Pick a card, any card.*

"Thailand," I suggested, naming my birthplace this time.

My family had lived there a few times too, but I'd already forgotten so much about the sounds of rattling tuk-tuks, the smells of moist earth. It was a bright humid night in Chiang Mai. Sangris and I trotted toward the night bazaar, stepping over the basketfuls of fried red chili that the sellers had spread out on the streets like open bowls of flowers.

Finding a canal on the fringes of the market, we fed enormous gold carp. They curled through the water like submerged flames beneath the heavy tropical-black sky. Acting innocent, I bought him orange juice and watched his face change when he realized that the sellers had filled it with salt. A trick to prevent dehydration, I explained, and ran off cackling before he could get revenge. I wanted to go into the orchid farms and the butterfly gardens, but they were closed, and I refused his offer to break in (of course Sangris had a way of assuming that rules didn't apply to him, but, I said, they applied to *me*), so we walked along a half-lit street instead, warm greenness and humming insects all around us, and spent hours trying to catch the guppies that swarmed in innumerable pots by the roadsides. I was better at it: I could lift my hands out of the green-tinted, plant-filled water slowly, without startling the fish, and show him the flashes of yellow and orange and violet and red guppies that flickered through the water cupped in my palms like a strange and magical treasure.

We were in the same neighborhood as one of my old houses. Sitting on the curb and resting my cheek on the cool rim of the guppy bowl, I looked around at the buildings.

Some were Western style, but many, like the one I'd lived in, were small curly-roofed boxes on stilts. It was too dark to see much except their black outlines, and the lights glimmering through slots in the wooden panels that served as windows.

"The last time I lived here was for six months," I said. "That was pretty long for me, when I was little."

"How old were you?" said Sangris, still peering sorrowfully down at the elusive guppies in the water. He'd failed to catch even one.

"Eight. A couple of years before moving to the oasis." As I spoke, the neighborhood seemed to become more solid. I grew uneasy listening to the murmur of human voices in the houses. It had just occurred to me that I might know some of these people, that I was really here. It seemed to me that if I peered through the chinks in the wooden shutters I would see myself curled up inside, barefooted, loud-voiced, smelling of bug spray.

"My dad had a work contract in Saudi. That wasn't a good place for Mom and me, so the two of us stayed here in Chiang Mai, to be near her family. It was wonderful . . ."

Mom, busy running the house and squabbling happily with relatives, had left me to my own devices. I was eight years old. My father wasn't around. So I talked myself into only remembering the best things about him, boasting about his travels to my friends, claiming that he owned a camel (a lie, but I liked believing it). I even called him Daddy. Then, at the end of six months, he came back.

I remembered—I'd been incredibly excited for days, unable to sleep. The night he returned, I was awed by him in the airport. His face had become unfamiliar to me; he looked so different from the version I'd developed of him, so remote and stern. I didn't make a peep, just huddled big-eyed in the back of the car while he took over the driver's seat and Mom moved to the side. But I wasn't fazed. I still believed. I was only waiting for him to unbend when he got home, to give me presents like Mom's relatives always did.

When we'd arrived back in this neighborhood, and sat inside our little building, Mom just served dinner and my father stayed silent. Impatient, I wriggled on my seat. Since I didn't dare talk directly to him, I started chattering to Mom, raising my voice on purpose to be sure he heard me.

He said, "She's very loud."

I was delighted. He'd noticed me. Immediately I began babbling to him, describing everything that had happened to me in the past six months, absolutely out of my mind with excitement, not noticing as his replies grew more monosyllabic and his face hardened. When he went to the bathroom, I followed, still talking nonstop, and when he shut the door in my face, I stood there calling through the wood: "And then I told my friend Pee-Mei that I never step on ants, and she said I was silly, and I said she was silly, and—"

Then my father came out and said, *"Shut up."*

I stopped dead.

"She's grown completely wild," he said quietly to my mom. Then he took her aside, and the two of them had a very

145

serious grown-up conversation in an undertone, in which Mom seemed to bridle at first, but after an hour of steady murmurs from my father, finally gave up.

Well, after that he never left me alone with my mother again. Wherever he went, we followed. He started training me properly around that time too. And I think he still blames those six months of his absence for my long-lasting imperfections.

"You actually did love your father that much, then?" said Sangris, staring at me.

I flushed in the darkness. But I couldn't lie, not here. It had taken years before I was able to purge my heart of that pathetic yearning. "I guess I did." I shook my head. "Come on, let's go."

"Now?"

"Yeah." I got up and scrunched my face, looking into the night where my old house was hidden. "Ye gods, I'm glad I'm not that kid anymore."

He'd been fiddling with the pot while I told my story, but now he scrambled to his feet as well. "Cheer up," he said, pulling lightly at my shirtsleeve.

"I don't need cheering up," I said, forcing a smile. "*I'm* not the one who was too ham-fisted to catch a single fish."

Solemnly, Sangris pulled out one hand from behind his back. The world's ugliest little guppy was flopping around in a small puddle on his palm.

"It's for you."

Its fins looked deformed, and I was sure that's why he'd

been able to catch it; but he was watching me hopefully. I accepted the gift like a bouquet, then released it reverently back into the water.

The next night it was Sangris's turn, so we visited *his* country of birth—a flat, flat place where the horizon seemed so far away it made my heart ache. It was nighttime here, but he found a hole in the ground and crouched down. "Listen," he said. I lay on my stomach and heard a song, a bubbling, high-pitched song, reverberating somewhere deep inside the hole. He explained that it was the sound of stone-creatures below the surface. In this world, nobody lived above the ground. He got on his stomach beside me in the darkness, panting slightly from our long flight. "I was born way down there, in a groundwater lake. At least, I think I was. My first memory is crawling out, so . . ."

"Alone?"

"'Course. All the normal creatures stayed. It's like Ae. They're too afraid to come out."

"Except the birds," I said, remembering what he'd told me before.

"No, there aren't any birds in this country," he said, but I pointed upward. High above, I could just make out a massive animal, its wings navy blue dotted with white, for camouflage against the stars.

"That's not a bird," said Sangris, coming convulsively closer to me. "It's a Free person."

"Another one?" I jumped up in excitement. "Isn't that rare?"

"For somebody who can't fly, maybe," he scoffed, staying on the ground. "But we move so much, trails are bound to cross once in a while . . . Depending where you go. There're some favorite spots that can even get sort of crowded." He frowned up at the creature.

"Hm," I said. We'd never come across someone else before. Keeping my eyes on the shape overhead, I asked, "What do you consider crowded?"

Sangris looked aggrieved. "Sometimes three of us on a world at a time. Can you imagine?" He shook his head as if unable to express the horror.

"Oh, the audacity of some Free people," I said gravely. He looked at me with suspicion, but I kept a straight face. Never mind all that, I wasn't about to miss this opportunity. I tried to tug him up. But, fanning out its midnight-colored wings, the creature had already glided away.

"Showoff," muttered Sangris.

"Let's follow it."

"No."

"Don't you want to say hi?"

"Why should I?"

"It's your own kind."

"Free people are not my own kind—I don't have an *own kind*. I told you—'Free person' is a description, not a species, all right? They're no closer to me than any animal."

"No need to be defensive."

Sangris subsided a bit, enough to look sheepish. "It's a territorial thing," he mumbled. "Like I said, we take up an awful lot of space . . ." He shrugged as if shaking away the other Free person.

When it was time to leave, Sangris remained human, his favorite form nowadays. He simply grew an assortment of wings: sometimes dark sculptural bat wings that curled above his back and made him, with his wavy black hair and yellow eyes, look like a veritable demon; sometimes big soft feathery wings that made him look like a little boy playing dress-up. In the hot afternoons when I took naps alone in my room, I could still feel the rocking of those wings, up and down, before I went to sleep, and I'd drift off on a sea of imaginary waves. The beat of flying had become the rhythm of my dreams.

The next night we found that we'd both once lived in Glasgow, so we went there. Dying leaves shivered down from the trees along the street, falling around us like showers of sequins. We were running, in a rush, toward the city's cold milky river, when I stopped suddenly. I'd spotted a bush so transparent in the wan sunshine that people on the other side were visible as floating shadows, like ghosts. "Here! I used to walk here," I exclaimed. "When my father was at work, every day, after school."

"Really? I was a pigeon just over there . . ."

On the other side of the city, for a couple of weeks. But he'd been so nearby.

"And just think," Sangris said, "I felt completely pointless at the time! If I'd known—"

"Don't worry, I'm sure your feeling was accurate," I said

kindly. But I had a superstitious thrill too, and I couldn't help adding, "I always fed the pigeons here. If only you'd come to this side of the city instead, we might've met sooner."

Some dog took a dislike to Sangris and barked madly, chasing him along the river as I giggled and refused to help. Finally we took refuge in a shop that for some reason sold only Nepalese skirts. He insisted I buy one—"In Scotland, nobody will care if they can see your knees, Nenner." I remembered the days, before I went to the oasis, before my father got extra-protective, when I used to wear normal clothes, even shorts sometimes, and, in a moment of weakness, I did buy a skirt. But then I was too embarrassed to wear it in front of him.

"Don't be dumb," he said. "I'll drag you into the changing room and put it on you myself if I have to."

On being threatened, I finally went away and changed. When I returned, in my floaty short-sleeved shirt and new Gypsy-like skirt with its ragged hem that swirled around below my knees, I watched as Sangris's eyes slowly flushed dark amber. He looked away and didn't speak to me again until we reached the river, although I caught him sneaking glances. When he lifted me up to fly me home, I could feel the heat of his skin against mine. Without a word, he turned into a gargoyle-thing for the first time in weeks. "Why did you do that?" I said.

"Being human is a bit too complicated right now," he muttered, then added, "But I think I could be a *slug* and it still wouldn't help."

"You'd look better as a slug, though."

It was an unthinkable thing to tell someone with a face as clear and keen as his. But he was being gushy, and he was the one who had forced me to wear the skirt in the first place, so I thought he deserved it.

He groaned. "Could I please have permission to kiss your ankles? Just your ankles."

"No," I said, my insides leaping with something like fear.

"A knee?"

"No."

"A foot?"

"No."

"Oh, come on. You won't allow me to kiss your *feet*?"

"No."

"You're cold, Nenner."

"Yeah. You should learn from me," I said.

I have the suspicion that some girls would've been thrilled by Sangris's attention. But I'm not like that—I never have been—and I'd feel disgusted with myself if I were. I don't belong in *Pfft*. I don't gush and allow boys to . . . That's as much a part of me as my bones are. Really, I ought to have kept my distance from him after that—withdrawn as soon as he mentioned kissing. And yet I didn't. I had to grab what freedom I could while it was there, or that would be the end of cool, clean, wet skies waiting untouched and untouchable over another world.

. . .

The nights were magical, the days remained tight. But who cared what happened in real life? Day was only a murky moment of sunlight, soon over; then I could escape through my window again.

Back in the classroom, going through the motions of Heritage preparations with the taste of the chilly sky air still in my mouth, exhausted and giddy, my distraction must have showed. Anju continued to regard me with suspicion, as if she thought I might have caught some rare tropical disease. "You're smiling!" she kept saying, jumping out of nowhere and surprising me at random moments, when I was doodling in the classroom, or eating my lunch, or talking to the stray cat that was Sangris. "You're *smiling!*"

I said, "Well, sorry, but you don't have to look so disgusted."

She stared at me in shock.

My other friends, the beautifully plump ones, told me, "You shouldn't go around smiling like that. It's as if you're trying to get attention."

"You should learn how to hold it in," one of them said. "A boy back there thought you were smiling at *him*. You weren't, were you? You don't want to be a . . ." Delicately, she didn't finish the sentence.

"I'm not," I said, my eyes widening.

They looked at each other. "Hmm," was all they said, and then they left, in a cloud of heavy perfume.

It should have been a reality check. But it was easy to disregard them, because Sangris was very much on my side.

"'Plump and curly-haired'?" he spat at me afterward, quoting something I'd once told him. "Fat and frizzy, more like! Who are they to lecture at you?"

I was sitting cross-legged on top of a table at the back of the school, its surface all dust and peeling paint. I'd gone there to hide from my friends. Sangris sat beside me with his tail curled around himself, the light almost blue where it hit his fur. "What do they know?" He paused, his venom momentarily distracted. "Ah . . . you weren't *actually* smiling at that boy, were you?"

"No idea," I said truthfully.

There was a pause at that. After a moment I looked up from my lunchbox to find Sangris studying me. He didn't seem angry anymore. A new expression was there, incongruous on his cat-face.

No, actually, I realized, it had nothing to do with the fact that he was a cat. It was incongruous on his face because he was *Sangris*. Sangris the Free person, who could fly, who shrugged as he talked about being constantly lost—this same Sangris was studying my face with eyes as canary yellow as ever, but different in one way: For the first time since I'd known him, he looked tense.

CHAPTER THIRTEEN

In Which I Am Not the Right Way

I snuck out the window with Sangris one night, straight after dinner.

Just quickly, I thought. Fifteen minutes of floating between the stars, then I'd come back around bedtime, show my parents my face to prove I was still in the house, and whisk away again.

But the sky was so wonderfully cold, and the air so open, and Sangris so exuberant, we took longer than I'd planned. Finally he swooped us back down outside my window. It looked square and black at this hour, not at all like a return to normality. More like a tunnel to some underground world.

I'd left the window open, but closed the curtains so that my parents couldn't see, just in case. I reached out to pull them apart.

Sangris jolted us back. I wasn't expecting it and I went crashing against his chest. When I looked up to complain he hissed between his teeth.

Then I heard it. Inside the room, just on the other side of the curtains, was the sound of breathing.

It was distinct and slow. There was almost enough time to die of suffocation between each breath. I couldn't move. I thought that at any moment my father might pull back the curtains and see us, but I still couldn't move. Then I snapped out of it, and I had just put my mouth to Sangris's hair, to tell him to fly us away, when there was movement behind the curtain and I heard the familiar footsteps going away. The door inside shut gently.

Immediately Sangris deposited me on the windowsill. He was very dark in the starlight, except for the eyes, which always burned, and the gleam of the whirring wings behind him. "Quick," he said. "He'll be looking for you. He probably thinks you've left the house."

"I'll handle it," I said, steeling myself. "You'd better not come back tonight."

Sangris nodded and hesitated as if he wanted to say something more. But he only watched as I slipped through the curtains back into my bedroom. I closed them behind me, shutting off the sight of Sangris and his wings. The room was empty. I changed in a rush, throwing on my nightshirt, ran to the door, and then went sedately out. My father was in the corridor, and when he saw me he turned around and gave me a hard look.

"Where have you been?" he said quietly.

"I was in my room," I said.

"You weren't."

"I was sitting on the windowsill," I said. "I like the fresh air."

He was very still for a moment.

"You realize how dangerous that is?" he said.

I hesitated.

"You realize what could have happened?"

"Yes," I said, discovering that he was worried, "you're right, I could have fallen—"

"And if you'd fallen, then what?" I could only see his outline in the dark corridor. With a *click,* he folded and unfolded the delicate metal legs of glasses he held in one hand. "Do you know how much effort I've put into raising you? And would you like to waste all that?"

A needle-pain slid into my heart. Okay, so he wasn't worried.

"Frenenqer," he said sharply. "You've been sheltered in the oasis, you're lucky not to know much. I've traveled, I've seen. If you manage to grow up *right*, you can add a true beauty to a world that desperately needs it . . . Or you can plunge out the window and end with stupidity. Which do you think is better?"

Without waiting for an answer, he strode away. A dim figure down the corridor poked its head out to watch me where I stood. Mom must have overheard the whole thing, but when my father went past her, she only nodded at him and followed.

And I slunk back into my room.

My throat swelled and I swallowed down a lump tasting of sour iron. Staring up at the blank ceiling, I lay flat. Too tired to move. I had a hanging, unfulfilled feeling. Like the sky had a hole in it. Like, all at once, everything was wrong.

I don't know why I'm not used to my father saying these things, why I'd expect anything else.

I couldn't sleep for a long time. I'd grown too used to taking naps during the day. For a while I distracted myself by reciting a story in my head—one of the books I'd memorized by reading it too many times. But after a few minutes I lost track. I wished I hadn't sent Sangris away.

I closed my eyes and passed the time by thinking of him as he was in Spain, his mouth puckered in a self-satisfied smile, like a child's, eyes gleeful, flying over a gold-tempted field of wheat hiding the breathless blue flowers underneath. And the clouds deepening the sky over Ae, a pink gray like a sheen of icy purple, a color without a name . . . and the carp curling like underwater flames in Thailand. All those things we shared together in our private impossible world. He was my air, and that was, I told myself, enough.

But when I finally fell asleep I dreamed of my old house in Thailand.

In the morning:

"You look tired," said my father.

I jerked my head up from about an inch above my cereal bowl. "I'm not really."

His mouth became one tight line.

"Just didn't sleep well," I said.

The line grew tighter.

"Honest," I said.

I was shy of him this morning. The dark air from all my travels was still around me, I was carrying the memory on my skin. He'd only have to look at me here in the light and he'd see it.

And he was looking. Over the newspaper, observing me mechanically, he saw just about everything except my face. As I raised my spoon from the cereal to my mouth, careful not to let the soy milk drip, his eyes checked that my fingers were placed properly on the handle, that I was sitting with my back straight, that I chewed with my mouth closed. I tried to concentrate, but he was watching me too closely.

"Don't let the milk drip from the spoon," he said abruptly.

It didn't make sense. I'd been sure that the milk wasn't dripping.

"Don't let the milk drip," he said.

Losing my head, I put the spoon down, back into the bowl. At least it definitely wouldn't drip that way.

But he wasn't satisfied. "Show me again."

This time even I noticed the drop of milk that plopped from the wet underside of the spoon.

I couldn't do it right this morning.

My father began working on his computer with his forehead ominously creased, convinced that I was being this way on purpose. I left the rest of my cereal untouched and threw it away in the kitchen.

A loud, disapproving *tut* from the corner made me jump. I hadn't realized Mom was there. She looked at me, and then at the empty bowl, shaking her head once.

"Frenenqer," came my father's voice, peevishly. I was supposed to be waiting at the door five minutes early. I returned to him.

We got in the car to go to school.

"You're not wearing socks," he said.

I hated wearing socks. They were part of the dress code, which the school administration had copied straight from England without considering that socks were worse than useless in the oasis—they only made you hotter.

"Nobody wears socks," I said.

He switched the car off and in the abrupt silence, there was something huge and dangerous. I stayed seated for an instant. My father tugged out the keys and threw them onto my lap, where they fell with a chill clink. The message was clear. I wasn't going to school unless I repented.

I hurried upstairs and put on some socks.

During the drive to school, my chest suddenly heaved, and all I wanted was to break the stiffness between us. This cold weight wasn't worth a quibble over socks.

"Sorry," I said, looking over.

"Words are cheap. There's something not right about you lately." Without taking his eyes off the road, he pulled a neatly folded piece of paper out of one pocket and tossed it to me. Not the way Sangris tossed things, but accurately, like a missile.

"This morning I printed out a list of rules for your benefit. You'll study it, memorize it."

So that was what he'd been doing on the computer. I

looked down at the paper in my hands. "Frenenqer's rules." The list began with "1. You will smile and act pleasant when spoken to," and ended with "10. You will not make a fool of yourself in public anymore"—a reference to the bird incident. There were other commands too, basic things like "You will not be selfish" and "You will not act out for attention." As I read, my cheeks burned as though they were being stabbed by a million tiny pins. I said, "Oh."

"Was that a complaint?"

I shook my head.

"You're going to be better," he said to the windshield, not like a promise, but like a resolve without alternative.

My pulse thudded. The thing about being treated as a child by my father is that I always believe him, and it makes me a worse person instead of a better one. When he calls me selfish, I always think, *All right then, I'm selfish,* and I have no choice but to proceed with my selfishness. That's what I hate most. He turns me into whatever he thinks I am.

I studied the list with my face still flushed. I memorized it. I absorbed each hated line. I needed to. When my father quizzed me later, I couldn't fail.

The bad feeling would have gone away after a few chapters of a book, but I was stranded in the real world. Staring out the window when I was done, I caught sight of my own reflection. I turned so my father wouldn't see my face. If he spotted my expression, he'd probably despair of me ever becoming his ideal daughter.

Neither of us said good-bye. I don't think he wanted me to speak to him anyway.

I went through the straggling crowds into school, holding my bag tightly in one hand, and the list of rules in the other. Anju was the only person already in my homeroom, reading the book I'd left on her desk so many weeks ago.

"I wish I were over eighteen," I said to her.

"That's nice," she replied.

When attendance was done, I got sent to the empty classroom I was meant to be transforming into the Thai room for Heritage. But Heritage was the farthest thing from my mind. I kept looking at my father's ten rules. I wished for a pool of deep water, an enormous bath, which I could jump into and come out completely clean, my heart washed as wonderfully blank as the desert after rains.

Sangris had made a habit of sneaking in to meet me at school sometimes, especially when I was supposed to be working on Heritage, since it was basically a free period. So I wasn't taken off guard when the door whammed open—*he* had never been taught not to slam it—and a weirdly light-eyed and messily good-looking student came bouncing in.

"Notice what I'm wearing?" he said, popping his collar. "I'm going to start making a collection of these school uniforms, just to see how many I can get away with. They suit me, eh?" He slowed down in front of me. "Why aren't you yelling yet? Go on, lecture me about the immorality of theft."

I handed him the sheet of paper. He read it.

"What *is* this?" he said after a moment. "'You will bear

yourself with composure'? 'No more ugly faces; smile when you are looked at'? What's that supposed to mean? No, let me guess. Your father wrote this?"

I nodded.

"Well, that's stupid," he said, and held it out to me.

I shook my head.

"Oh. You're actually upset about this thing?" After a second of studying me, he read it more carefully, raising his eyebrows when he got to the end. "Well, in that case—" He began to tear it.

I lunged forward. "What're you *doing*?" I snatched it back. "Are you crazy? Do you realize how much trouble you'd get me into?"

"It's just a sheet of paper, Nenner." He leaned back against one of the abandoned desks, watching as I folded the list and shoved it safely into my bag. "I don't see why you care anyway. We're at school, no one else is around, you can turn that paper into confetti. It'll be good for you, I promise."

I burst into tears so violently that Sangris stood up, alarmed.

"Nenner!"

The next second I'd swallowed the pressure down again. The tears were gone. But the storm behind them was still shaking. Sangris was *right*, I ought to be able to laugh at the list my father had made.

Sangris moved closer and lifted a finger as if he was going to touch my face, hesitated an inch away from the skin, and then, awkwardly, lowered his hand again. I'd slapped him the last time he'd tried; he'd learned his lesson. And it was a pity. "What did I say?" he was asking, not in his usual voice, but a worried one. "I didn't mean to, I was only joking—"

I wished he'd stop being nice. It was making it harder not to cry. I sealed myself up. There were three images in my head, and my thoughts kept flashing between them. The glimmer of light coming through the window slots of my old house in Chiang Mai, that was one. And a cracked khaki sink, the cool, clean floor shining, me on my knees in the bathroom. The third was the look on my own face when I read my father's list in the car.

But it wasn't true. I couldn't possibly be so stupid—I had more control over myself than that. I might still have managed to get my mind tidy and composed again, if Sangris hadn't chosen that moment to murmur:

"I don't understand, Nenner, you told me in Spain that you're fine with the way things are."

"Well, I lied, didn't I?" I snapped, then stopped dead. Why had I said that? "No, I didn't lie," I said.

Gingerly, Sangris petted my shoulder. I pulled away, still feeling the hot itch of tears in my throat, and I was horrified. Crying, here in school—in front of Sangris. I scraped at my face. It would be fine as long as I didn't talk.

But keeping quiet meant that Sangris was allowed to fill up the silence.

"If someone gave me a list like that, can you imagine I'd ever take it seriously?" he said, giving my shoulder a little shake. "Just think of that night in Thailand. You were all right then, weren't you? We'll go back, and you'll remember what you told me, and you'll see—"

"I don't know," I croaked, and what I felt when I heard my own words, above all, was terror.

"What?"

"I'll never be the right way, will I?" I whispered.

No guppies to hand over and cheer me up this time. Sangris's hands hung helplessly. "What?"

"I'm not the girl he imagined. The one on that list. But he won't give up. He's trying to—" Then I got it, the best way to make a Free person understand. "He wants to pin me down into one shape, Sangris."

Sangris promptly abandoned the no-touching rule, wrapping his arms around me and holding me in. He felt warm and solid and I wished I could enjoy it, but I didn't know how. I think it was the first time I'd been hugged.

It was too hard to look at him; I fixed my eyes on the wall. I didn't have the first clue how to respond. So I just kept mumbling. "If I improve in one direction he'll only pick on something else—trying hard doesn't work, not when there are a million tiny ways to be wrong. It's impossible; I'll never be the right way, he'll never be satisfied."

"Nenner, please," said Sangris, leaning his head against mine. He sounded almost as miserable as I was. "I only wanted to know why—"

"So are you happy, Sangris?" I said in a hoarse voice. "Are you glad you know now?"

His eyes widened and that's what made me get a proper

grip on myself at last. "No, it's not your fault," I said. "I didn't mean—"

Sangris let go of me and went to shove open the big classroom window. Heat and dust streamed in. For an awful second I thought he was just *leaving*. But no sooner had his wings spread out, huge gray wings fanning out the tips of their black-barred feathers against the dazzling sky, than he twisted around and reached for me.

Taking his hand, I stepped onto the sill next to him. The next second we fell out of the window, plummeting upward, and the air was roaring around me; leaving behind the stone vault of the air-conditioned classroom, and my schoolbag with my father's ten commandments inside.

CHAPTER FOURTEEN

In Which Frogs Are Captured

My heart thundered. There was no way I'd be able to sit opposite my father at the table every day, *wanting* to please him, and stumbling. It would be like going into battle without a shield.

All he'd have to do was flick a finger and I'd fall.

I'd have to work harder at not caring.

I felt steadier once I'd made my decision. It was something solid to grip.

"I've thought of an ideal place," said Sangris, unaware of the resolve I'd taken. Curled up in his arms, I nodded. Already it was working, I really did feel stronger. But this wasn't enough. I needed a way to reach out and turn off the last light inside me, like flicking a switch: something absolute and reliable.

"Where are we going?" I asked.

"It's in Oman."

The sky around us was now so feverishly bright that I had to shut my eyes. When the painful light subsided a bit, I was able to look down and see enormous dusty white plains and mountains, with a few thin mountain goats and some shriveled gray trees.

Sangris swerved toward a peak, then set me carefully, in my ridiculously formal school shoes, down onto the flat, dust-coated stone.

"I suppose," he ventured, "that if I ever asked for your hand in marriage, your father would say no?"

I shook my head at the idea of Sangris ever meeting my father. "He'd kick you out the door."

Sangris brightened. "We'd just have to elope, then."

"Actually, I'm planning to be a spinster, if I can."

"What," he said, "even if I took you somewhere as amazing as this?" He took my face in his hands and lightly turned it so that I could see what he meant.

We stood on the cliff at the edge of a wadi. Not a dried-up, cracked river like the one behind my house. This wadi was set deep into the valley walls, a smooth, hollowed-out area hidden from the heat of the sun. The water lay folded into those crevasses, gray and deep, as though the mountain had secretly bled it out. It didn't have the blue brilliance of a lake, but it was protected by the valley walls like something pure and precious, a cold pocket of liquid. It was as miraculous as a living world in deep space.

All around the edge of the water, green plants grew. Three date palms, dark in the shade, long grasses, and even a little shrub that bravely spat white flowers out into the world. There was something like glitter in the air, which might have been the wings of a dragonfly. And the faint sound of water lapping over stone.

The instant my eyes focused on the wadi, I lit up. I imagined jumping into that bottomless pool of water and coming out clean, washed colorless, a ghost.

"Ah," I breathed. "Then I might have to reconsider." His hands were still holding my head in place. I turned, and he withdrew his fingers, more slowly than he should have. We stood face-to-face.

"I was hoping for somewhere new," I said. "How did you know?"

"I guessed."

"Really?"

"Well, I guessed that you needed a place without memories," he said, watching me. His eyes were almost translucent in the strong light, like amber. Because of the heat, there were drops of sweat on his temples, staining the skin a richer brown. "No human's ever even been in this wadi before. It's completely untouched."

The idea, uplifting and airy, like a wave of cool water, lapped through me again. I stepped up to the edge of the rock. Sangris automatically grabbed my arm to keep me back. "Don't worry," I said without looking around. "I just want to see the water."

"Why?"

"I want to jump in." I twisted around to look at him. "Do you think I could swim?"

His hair ruffled in the same breeze that had spread the idea through me. "Your uniform," he reminded me. "It'll get wet, and we have to be back by three forty-five."

"Well, yes," I said. "You're going to have to promise not to look."

Sangris gaped.

I smiled at the expression on his face. I had never before seen anybody who could accurately be described by using the word *flabbergasted*. "I'm not going to swim naked," I said. "Don't worry."

Sangris didn't look worried. He looked disappointed.

"But I need to borrow your shirt," I said.

"Why?"

"I *do* have to take my own clothes off," I said. "I can't swim in them. Even if the uniform dries in time, my mother will be able to tell when she does the laundry—"

Sangris wasn't listening to my treatise on laundry. He had already pulled off his shirt. "Here you go," he said quickly, thrusting it at me.

I was very steady. I'm sure of it. I didn't even look at him. As a matter of fact, I impressed myself. Rock and ice couldn't have been more indifferent. I gestured at him to go away. "Turn around and close your eyes."

He did, but not without complaining, "Why do I have to close my eyes if I've already turned around?"

"Just to be safe. Do it." I waited. And then, with a furtive look around at the bare white mountains, I changed, savoring the warm air that moved over my skin. I tucked my own clothes out of sight beneath a bush, where I could retrieve them later.

His shirt fell down past my thighs, just like one of my

169

nightshirts. It was, on the whole, I thought, much more modest than a swimsuit. The cloth had the light, woody smell of Sangris. I was never sure whether that was his natural scent, or whether he just had a habit of prancing around in forests a lot and the smell happened to rub off on him. Either way, I wasn't about to ask. Glancing over, I saw the subtle shadows under his shoulder blades. Beneath the skin, between the muscles, there was a suggestion of his spine.

"Okay," I said, looking away quickly.

Sangris turned and an ill expression crossed his face as he stared at me. I call it ill because it looked unnatural and flushed, as though he had a fever. I stepped forward instinctively. "Are you all right?"

"Fine. Ah. Actually. Give me a second."

I waited for ten. Then, when he continued to study the ground without saying anything, I said, "Are you dehydrated?"

"Maybe. That must be it," he said, a tinge of sarcasm in his voice. He must have been starting to recover.

I took that as a no. "Well, what is it, then?"

"Nenner—you're wearing nothing but *my shirt*," he said huskily.

"But it covers everything—"

"Nothing but *my shirt*," he repeated, in exactly the same tone as before.

"I'm wearing stuff underneath," I said indignantly.

"Stuff?" He looked as if he was going to faint.

Oh. This could be a problem. I watched him for a moment.

There is a hardness inside of me. I know that better than anybody else. When all's said and done, the bit of me called *Frenenqer* is an impenetrable lump, and it's almost a comfort to feel it there, because if it's cold, then it's also strong. I chewed at my bottom lip. I tried to see if the telltale shadows beneath his eyes had darkened. They had.

"Sangris," I said, "maybe you should go away. Pick me up later?"

No. He shook his head without looking at me. He wasn't going to leave me alone in the mountains.

So that was the choice. Sangris's peace of mind, or—I glanced back into the wadi. More than anything, at this moment, I wanted to wash away my father. Inside the water was everything I needed. If I could just be free for this moment, and leap—that was the way to ease that old, old itch on my back, to shake off Thailand. It would be my good-bye to caring. Just at the thought, I lightened; the heavy parts of me rolled away.

Sangris was still unable to face me. Briefly, I wondered if I was sacrificing him. And the thought felt knife-sharp, but . . . at least it wasn't heavy. I made my choice. And everything that followed afterward was my fault, I admit that. But at least I got to clean myself in the dark water of the wadi first. And, at the time, it didn't seem so bad. It was easy to decide. This was silly, wasn't it? I'd just had a breakdown, didn't that entitle me to attempt a recovery? Anyway, Sangris had already seen my legs. And, most of all—he was being a bit of a pain, wasn't he?

"You do what you like," I said. "I'm going to swim."

"Just a minute," he managed.

I gave him another ten seconds. Then, "Better?" I said.

"Yeah," Sangris said, giving me a glance and looking quickly away again. "Uh . . . Should I pick you up to take you into the wadi?"

"I don't think you could handle it."

He leaned over and put his hands on his knees, like a marathon racer recovering from a long run. "I don't think I could either."

"I guess I'll climb down then."

"Fine," he said, without really listening.

"You're useless."

"Nenner ? . . what *stuff?*"

I didn't understand at first. When I did, I glared at him until he said quickly, "Sorry. That just slipped out."

I wondered if all boys were like this.

I turned away and lowered myself over the wall of stone. The surface was heavily pitted, with ledges and pale puckered caves, and I had no trouble picking my way down. The only difficulty was that the larger stones had grown too hot to hold or step on. I had to rely on the covering of pebbles that had enough air and dust between them to make touch bearable. When I was a few feet above the water I inched out into a precarious position, checked that the water was deep enough, and let myself fall.

I had an airborne second with my shirt rushing around me.

Then there was the momentary chaos of a splash, and I sank into a deep, clean, silent world. The water was cold against my skin, like fluid frost. When I broke the surface a breeze went to my face and made me shiver. I reached up to a nearby boulder and pulled myself partway out of the wadi, my wet hands sticking to the dryness of the stone.

I was floating in the water, and the bitterness and the yearning dissolved away. I ducked under again, just to make sure. And when I came back up the air was still fresh and calm-smelling, and the flowers by the waterside were still white, and the palm trees rustled in faint applause. I would cut out my heart again and again, as many times as it took.

Sangris was sitting amid the grasses by the waterside, watching me.

"You can come in if you want," I called.

He shook his head firmly. "Nuh-uh."

I let myself slide back into the water. My hair was plastered flat and sleek against my head, but the minute it was submerged it fanned out like black seaweed, twinkling near blue in the direct light. I watched it wave around through the sun-threaded water. A fish darted away. "Are you sure?"

"It's not a good idea," he said.

I ducked under. Oh, this was liberating. The water was so clear I could hardly see it. I felt as though I was gliding through air. I resurfaced at the edge of the pool, where it was too shallow to swim. I had to get up and walk out. And the itch on my back hadn't exploded. I could barely feel it at all. Letting the warm breeze cool me and the cool water warm me, with a sensation of complete relief, I sat beside Sangris. "You're my best friend, you know," I said to him. I watched as a little smile came to his face, but, noticing my gaze, he wiped it away at once.

"I'm still not coming into the water with you," he said, his hands resolutely clutched around his knees.

"Why not?"

"Because I might do something stupid," he said. "And don't ask what."

"Why can't I ask?"

He shot me a sideways glare, then went back to staring straight ahead.

I grinned at him. "You can't beat me at this, you know. I'm a champion at asking questions. I can bring a teacher to his knees within a minute."

"I bet you can," he muttered. Again came the little smile, and again it was wiped away.

"Seriously, you should try the water. I feel so much better, it's incredible . . ." I had a brilliant idea. "We could catch frogs! I'm sure there are some around here."

"Nenner, we're not little kids." He swallowed. "And your shirt's clinging to you."

Why did he have to insist on embarrassing me? But the cool water and the purifying peace of the wadi kept me calm. The school uniform was made of heavy material, anyway, so

174

I knew it didn't show anything. "*Your* shirt, actually," I said, matter-of-fact.

He started to ask something, but stopped.

"What?"

"Am I going to wear it afterward?" he said without looking at me.

"Not if you're going to be weird about it," I said. "Come on. We have an hour. Let's hunt for frogs. If Anju were here, I bet she'd hunt for frogs with me."

"Yeah, well, Anju's your little slave, isn't she," he muttered. "She'd do anything you asked."

I frowned. He owed me—or at least I thought he ought to. I'd defied my father for him, albeit briefly, but he was still acting as if catching frogs was too much to ask. "You mean you wouldn't?"

His eyes shot to my face at that.

"I'm pretty sure you would," I said.

I meant because I'd saved his life at the Animal Souk. But the words sounded different, spoken out loud. I was met with silence. Sangris looked at me for a long time, his expression unreadable. The slow warm wind rested upon the gray surface of the water and the wadi walls rose upward around us into the sunlight, and in the shady heart of the valley, as water lapped and shadows waved and grasses moved, Sangris finally got up and said, "All right, I'll catch you a frog."

To hide my relief at the sudden breaking of the tension, I tried out my wickedest laugh. "Mwa-ha-ha!" I grinned up at him. "What do you think? Does it need work?"

"A bit. But please don't practice it on me."

But Sangris allowed the little smile to steal over his face again. He held out a hand and pulled me to my feet.

He behaved more normally after that. I spotted the first frog, a grayish speckled lump with its feet pumping like pistons, shooting through the water with a stiff expression on its face like a determined old man. Sangris managed to catch one before I did. Overall, though, I captured the most, and at some points I even had two at the same time, one in either hand. He couldn't beat that. We found tadpoles too, tiny black scraps of slime wriggling over the submerged surfaces of the rocks. Sangris joked and splashed and satisfied me by acting the way that a friend should.

Still, occasionally, when I came too close, or smiled at him unwisely, and sometimes for no reason at all, there was a sudden silence, a break in the atmosphere, and I would look up from my task to find Sangris watching me with that strange, intent look in his eyes, not breathing, as though it was his vital organs that I held in my hands instead of a protesting frog.

CHAPTER FIFTEEN

In Which I Have My Feet Kissed

The unwinding of the thread can probably be traced back to those first moments when we tussled over the frogs and Sangris watched me. And maybe it went farther back too. Ever since Ae and ever since the sunflowers—oh, all right, ever since Sangris had entered my room that first time, and the useless curtains had parted to let him in, and he'd messed up all my neat stacks of clothes, which had taken me hours to set back straight, and had grinned at me as if my attempts to ignore him were funny beyond words. From the moment I'd first seen him as a human, in fact, there had been a sharp and uncomfortable little spark between us. I'd hoped that it would disappear on its own, but if anything, it seemed to be growing. I didn't like that at all. He stepped closer, and I stepped away. And the thread continued to unwind.

But things didn't come to a head until, appropriately enough, the night that we completed our project. When I opened the bedroom window one Friday Sangris slipped inside and said, "This is the last place I can take you."

I'd been waiting for him, probing the place where I was trying to turn my heart into a clean gap like a lost tooth. My father had given me hope tonight at dinner, because, when he'd been disappointed in me for not keeping my back straight, it hadn't hurt much at all; I hadn't even felt humiliated.

"Why?" I said to Sangris. It was one of his nights. I had already finished showing him my memories throughout the world. We had finished in Sri Lanka, in a city where the sky flooded with hundreds of giant bats each evening, and where, in a parking lot five years ago, my father had informed me that we were moving to the oasis. But I'd thought Sangris had plenty of places left to show me.

He was human tonight, as usual, but with sleek white wings at his back. They were edged in black, similar to an albatross's. He also, for some reason, looked nervous. I caught the emotion darting through his yellow eyes like a fish through water. "A few years ago, I started . . . going to risky places. And I went too far. Why do you think I ended up in a cage in the Animal Souk?" He glanced down at me. "But I won't take you to the really bad worlds. This is the last safe place, so it's the last place I can take you."

"Why would you go to 'really bad' worlds anyway?" I demanded.

He shrugged one shoulder. "It was kind of inevitable. We Free people wander, and we're drawn to the edge of things." He offered me a winning smile. "We like being all dark and mysterious."

"Dark and mysterious," I muttered. "Dim and inexplicable, more like."

Sangris laughed. "I used to work for some creatures called Trappers. They make a living by capturing and selling rare animals."

"The wild animal trade?"

He raised his eyebrows. "Excuse me? For all you know, those frogs you viciously manhandled in Oman might have been rare six-toed speckled mountain frogs or something."

"At least I let them go afterward."

He decided to press on with his story, taking no notice of me. "You can imagine how a Free person would have come in handy for the Trappers. But in the end I got bored, as always, and moved on. I only did it for a couple of weeks, and it was more trouble than it was worth. We stole a crystal-toothed boar from the wrong person, and I accidentally made an enemy. He knew a guy who knew a guy, and, long story short, years later, when I wasn't expecting it, I ended up in a cage myself, dropped off in this lame world. And then I was rescued by a heartless little slave driver called Nenner. A fate more terrible than death. So, don't worry, I've learned my lesson." He waved it away, the lesson dismissed with a flap of his hand. "The point is, I had some messy years. Before I met you. And I'm over it."

I frowned. "And?" I said. That couldn't be why I had spotted nervousness flashing a fin in his eyes. Sangris was shameless. He didn't care about his mistakes. This, I thought, with suspicion, was something else.

"And so this is the last place I can show you." He scooped me up without warning.

"We can go exploring," I said. "We'll find other places."

"Yes," he said, hesitating. "We will. But, since this is like our anniversary—"

Sternly I said, "Sangris, we don't have an anniversary."

He wilted. "I just want to tell you something," he finished in a mumble.

That didn't sound good. I tried to turn it into a joke. "You have a third eye. You have an evil twin brother," I guessed. "You don't know how to play chess. You can't knit. Don't worry, neither can I. I don't follow the rules because I always want to invent my own way to knit, and I end up with a massive—"

"No, nothing like that," Sangris said, interrupting my ramble. He stepped out of the window into the darkness of a desert night, and just kept on walking, across the air. His wings made hushed sweeping sounds. "I'll tell you once we're there."

I squinted at him. "This is one of your Free people attempts to be all dark and mysterious, isn't it? It's not working."

"Nenner," he said, "just shut up."

"Touchy, touchy," I said. Something was definitely wrong.

In silence Sangris took me up into a deep blue sky, so deep and so blue that sometimes I forgot we were in the sky and began to think that we were down below the sea instead. It was a long flight. We went farther away from the oasis than we had ever gone before. Even zooming so fast that the wind shut my eyes for me and rioted in my hair, it took nearly an hour, and as we plunged farther and farther into the clear blueness I almost fell asleep. At last, through half-closed eyes, I saw the place where Sangris meant to take me.

It was an island in the sky. Simple as that. A jagged piece of land, shaped almost like a crescent moon, in the sea of sky. It was small and bare, with nothing on it except for a tree. The tree grew out of its corner at a crooked angle. With relief, I noted the lack of moonlight and roses.

Sangris set me down in the twisted boughs of the tree. It only had about three branches, but they were surprisingly strong. For such a little tree, the leaves were huge too, like pale-green flags drooping around me, and the flowers were as big as my head: silvery blossoms that smelled faintly of almonds.

"I used to come here to think," he told me, landing beside the tree. It was so short that my head was only a few inches above his.

"Sangris," I said in shock, "you think? When did this start?"

"Shut up," he said again. "Stop joking around, okay? This is serious—"

"All right." I held on to one of the branches for support. I hadn't meant to annoy him. But he was too close. There was a familiar twinge between my shoulder blades. The itch was back. I shifted slightly, until I was farther behind the branch.

He noticed. One hand went to fiddle at the collar of his shirt, then dropped again. "Sorry."

I said generously, "It's okay."

"I'm kind of tense," he explained.

"I've noticed."

Reaching out, he played with a strand of my hair. He watched it as he did so, without meeting my eyes. I considered tugging it away from him, but the fact that he was on edge made me uneasy too, so I just held still. The tiny tree waved its branches in a wind that didn't exist.

"The thing is," he said, "the thing is, you probably already know this. Unless you're willfully blind. But you are. You're so determinedly oblivious sometimes—"

Maybe he'd brought me here just to insult me.

I began to inch backward again. Insults, I could handle; but Sangris's eyes had those shadows beneath them, and the yellow was glowing in contrast, and he was either too distracted to take a hint, or he refused to. "I'm not the only one who's willfully blind," I muttered. He disregarded that. Maybe I'd overplayed my hand over the last couple of months—insulted him too freely. It didn't affect him anymore. He let go of my hair and leaned forward, into the almond-scented shelter of the flowers. "Nenner," he said softly, "pay attention."

I *was* paying attention. I was paying attention to all of the danger signs. Sangris, watching me; eyes glitter bright, keen marks between them, as if he'd been bruised there. I'd never seen the shadows that sharp before. I held tighter to the branch. It was thin and coarse in my hand, and firm enough to make me feel more secure. My heart, on the other hand, had turned into a messy wet lump flying hard in its cage of meat. Some vicious little animal had fallen into my chest. I set my teeth, trying to think. "I'm hungry," I said, in a flash of inspiration.

Sangris stared at me for a moment and then, evidently deciding that I must have the attention span of a particularly dim duckling, ignored me. He leaned farther into my nest of silver flowers. "Nenner," he persisted, "you must know by now that I—"

"No, no, really," I said, "I'm hungry. I need food. Are there any restaurants around here?"

"We're in the middle of the sky," he said. "Now *pay attention*. I'm trying to—" I felt his hand at my chin, gently tilting my face toward his. I hadn't realized how near he'd edged again. If I leaned any farther back, I would fall out of the tree. I looked straight into anxious amber-yellow eyes. "Nenner—"

"You need to go get me food, then," I said. "If there aren't any restaurants around here. I'd like—" I needed something rare and specific. I couldn't think of anything. Fried olive oil ice cream? Naan with yak butter? Emu eggs? "Falafel." *Stupid.* "Not just any falafel," I added. "It has to be from a shop in Puerto Viejo." Better. There weren't any falafel shops in Puerto Viejo.

But Sangris wasn't buying it. "Why," he demanded, "do you keep changing the subject?" He drew a deep, shuddering breath. He was close enough now that I could feel it rather than hear it. "Just give me ten seconds and then you can babble all you want. Ten seconds. That's all I ask," he said.

"Um." I drew back, unwinding his fingers from my hair as I did so. His hands had been moving stealthily to the back of my head. I said, "But I can't pay attention to you while I'm hungry." He was going to think that I must be deficient in some way. Oh well. I decided to run with it. "I can't think of anything except falafel. It's a craving. If it's not satisfied, then . . . then my ears won't work. They shut down. All systems fail, and hearing is one of the first things to go. That's how starvation happens." Did anything in that argument make sense? I gave him an earnest look.

"Falafel," said Sangris.

"Yep," I said, in my newest role of a food-crazed starvation victim.

"You ate earlier at school," he pointed out. Trust him to be observant at the wrong time.

"That doesn't mean anything. Sloths can starve to death on a full stomach," I informed him. "They have slow metabolisms."

He paused to process this news about sloths.

"But what does that have to do with—"

"Just go!"

I was holding on to the branch so tightly that the bark had cut into the skin on the palm of my hand. Sangris eased himself away from me at last. With relief, I pulled myself back upright. I'd been hanging almost horizontal out of the tree. "Falafel," I said with a nod. "Puerto Viejo. Don't forget. I'll be here waiting."

And then, when you get back, I'll send you out again for

strawberry juice from a specific restaurant in Vietnam.

"Fine," said Sangris, standing back. He was still holding on to the branches on either side of me, though, and I had the impression of being caged in by his arms. One lock of twisty black hair fell into his right eye. "But when I get back—"

"After I finish eating—"

"After you finish eating, I want to talk with you about something."

"Fine." I hoped I looked innocent.

"I'll hurry." He turned, and the wings spread out. Blue light caught in the sleek white feathers along their upper ridges for an instant. Then he was gone.

Well, my genius plan had worked. I should be able to drag this out until dawn, when he'd have to return me to the oasis. Tomorrow . . . I'd figure that out when it came. For now, Sangris had been successfully distracted: Off hunting for falafel in Costa Rica. No more leaning close and touching my hair and wanting to *talk* about things. I was safe! Ha-ha!

Safe, and stranded on a tiny island in the middle of nowhere.

I looked around, sobering. The ground on the island was crumbly and silver. It seemed to be made of silky powder, not dirt, and nothing grew on it except for this dwarf tree. Now that Sangris had flown away, I felt ridiculous on my flowery perch. I eased a foot down and found that the ground was firm, so I jumped. And only got a few steps before I reached the edge of the land. I looked all around. Stranded in the sky. I'd almost forgotten that I couldn't fly off on my own. If for some reason Sangris didn't come back, I was done for.

I paced in circles. Couldn't Sangris have at least tormented me somewhere with a library nearby? I waited and waited. On this island, time didn't appear to go anywhere. It just seeped around my feet, like the light. I was thinking of my father, reminding myself how clean and remote and triumphant I'd felt when I'd cut my heart away in the wadi, when I spotted the fish.

It was swimming above me, through the sky. The scales were green but the fins had a tongue of orange running through, and its lips were orange too. I stood there and watched it glide past like a bird. It floated weightless in the air and I became disoriented because now I wasn't sure if I might not be underneath the sea after all.

It was as long as my arm. I thought I could see the sky churning in the wake of its fins, ever so slightly, the blueness blurring behind it in a way that reminded me of disturbed ink. And yet it didn't look like anything more than a large, strangely colored goldfish. It was like a helium balloon with fins stuck on.

I was so absorbed in figuring this creature out, I didn't notice, at first, that it had changed course and was swimming right toward me. Then, before I had time to feel more than a faint flutter of worry, it slid to a halt in the air, a short distance away from my widening eyes. It bobbed a little, up and down.

Its irises were green.

"Hello," I said, disconcerted.

The word fell alone in this quiet empty island. The fish drew closer. It circled, spiraling around me, not in a menacing way but beautiful. I turned to keep it in sight.

Its fins, up close, were feathery.

So what was it? A bird or a fish? Sky or sea? Air or water? I could breathe, but that didn't seem to mean anything. In dreams, people could breathe underwater, and I thought I might have fallen asleep in the tree. Good. When Sangris came back he'd be forced to carry me home without any fuss.

The bird-fish settled to a halt in exactly the same position as before, at eye level.

There was something not quite right about its eyes. It sounds silly to wonder about something so small when faced with a flying/swimming bird/fish. Still, the feathered fins, the way it glided through the greasy sky, okay, I could accept all that. But green eyes? Could fish have green eyes? Could birds? I knew that some of the specially bred fish in Thailand could have blue irises, but their eyes weren't this wide, or this intense . . . the fish was *staring*.

"Sangris?" I called, as if saying his name would bring him back. My voice wavered.

"No, I like to be called Juren," said the fish.

I don't like girls who yelp, but I admit it—when he spoke, I shrieked like the best of them. I even clapped my hands over my face.

"Relax," said the fish, and it exploded. At least, that's how it looked to me. It burst open. Billowed out into a person.

The next second, there was someone standing there and looking pleased with himself.

I stumbled back. The ground was lumpy underfoot and I fell. It wasn't a dramatic fall: I caught myself with my hands and I ended up un-bruised, sitting sprawled in the powdery grayness with my legs stretched out in front of me. "Stupid Free people!" I shouted. "Going around pretending to be animals! Exploding in innocent girls' faces! Do you have any idea how traumatizing that is? I'll never be able to own a goldfish again!"

He laughed.

"It's not funny," I said. "First a cat, then a fish. I won't be able to trust any animals ever again. The next time I see a puppy I'll have the urge to run away screaming. I won't be able to ride horses in case they turn out to be men. I won't—"

He interrupted my laments. "You have a bit of a random thought process, don't you?"

I lost track. "Sometimes. In moments of stress."

At least now I knew why the fish's eyes had been green. Another Free person! I wondered if all Free people kept their original eye colors no matter what animals they happened to be. His were still glittering bright and emerald. They were slanted like Sangris's. As a matter of fact, he resembled Sangris overall, though his face was too innocent to be feline. Maybe all Free people had certain bone structures in common.

I began observing him in earnest. Wouldn't it be funny

if he turned out to be a distant relative of Sangris's? His hair was in loose curls, light brown, which fell across the curve of his cheek, the straight line of his nose, the long sweep of his exposed throat. Although he was mainly human, luckily a covering of soft white feathers concealed his body, running from his collarbone right down to his feet. The wings too were white, a plumy white that reminded me of doves. They curled, unlike the hard sleek wings that Sangris favored.

And he was still laughing. Clearly, I was a riot.

"It's not funny," I repeated. *Stupid Free people.*

"Oh, come on," he said. He had a wide smile and a dimple in each corner.

"Huh," was all I said.

"You mad?" Another minute of that grin and I'd do something immature, like stick my tongue out.

"You did it on purpose," I said.

"I was in the neighborhood. You looked bored. I wanted to help."

This island must be a favorite haunt of Free people, one of the "crowded places" Sangris had mentioned to me before. "Next time, don't." I realized that I was still sprawled on the ground. No wonder he couldn't stop laughing. I pulled myself into a proper sitting position, and I was about to stand, but instead Juren dropped to his knees in front of me.

I frowned at him. "Can I help you?"

"Are you really angry?" he asked.

No, I didn't care enough to be actually angry. But it

seemed that I finally had the upper hand, so I lied. "Yes."

His smile drooped, and for a moment, he looked like a chastened kid. "Really?" Then he brightened and the grin popped back up. "What if I say sorry?"

Shrugging, I sensed that we were playing now. Except I didn't know the rules, or what the prize would be. I certainly didn't know what was going on in Juren's happy little head. Because before I could say anything else, he bent in a great show of penitence, and kissed my feet. I opened my mouth to say "Hey!" or something equally intelligent, but no words came out. I gaped at him. Immediately I felt queasy. All I could think was, *Ye gods, if my father knew what—*

But my father wasn't the one I had to worry about. When I looked up, I saw Sangris standing on the opposite side of the island.

He had clearly just landed. His hair was still tousled from the wind of flying. His eyes were pale yellow and in one hand he held a paper bag. Seriously? He'd managed to find falafel in Puerto Viejo? I stared at him over Juren's shoulder.

Not a good time to send him away again for strawberry juice. I closed my mouth and bit the lips together.

"Nenner," he said.

Juren raised his head at the sound of this new voice. He pulled away from me and I jumped up.

"He was a fish," I said quickly, pointing at Juren. I'm not sure why I felt the need to give Sangris this irrelevant piece of information. Maybe I wanted to make him stop staring at me. And it worked. He turned his eyes, slowly, to Juren instead.

Juren turned. "Oh," he said. "Is this *Sangris?*" He rose to stand beside me.

I didn't like being shoulder to shoulder with him, facing Sangris. The body language was all wrong. I inched away until I was in the shadowy drooping shelter of the dwarf tree. The smell of almonds was all around me. The two Free people didn't notice. They continued to watch each other. I felt the thread of growing hostility twanging tight. Juren's eyes were now very green. I thought of the Siamese fighting fish in Thailand that would circle and flare, spreading their fins out until they resembled dangerous blue and red flowers in the water, whenever they saw another of their own kind.

Juren, his eyes still locked on Sangris's, said, "Do you mind? You're interrupting."

And then Sangris snapped. A blur went past me and the two Free people shot backward, off the little island in the sky, into thin air. He threw himself at Juren and there was the thud of collision.

Juren moved quickly. But so did Sangris. Wings were everywhere. They circled together until they resembled a sun made of feathers, beating, burning white and gold. I hadn't known Sangris could fight like this. It seemed impossible that he was the same cat who forgot his own name whenever I petted him, the same gargoyle who had begged to kiss my feet. This Sangris was frightening and powerful and screeched like a creature who had scorned the earth millions of years ago. His teeth had elongated, and his hands were more like claws—

"Sangris!" I shouted.

Juren crunched down onto the small island with Sangris on top of him. Sangris, his slanted eyes flashing bright yellow, showed no hesitation or scruple. I heard Juren whimper.

"Sangris," I hissed, "let him go!"

Sangris hesitated. I saw him glance up at me as if he was wondering whether he could get away with pretending to be deaf. I went over and grabbed him by the shoulders, trying to pull him back. I might as well have tugged on a rock.

"Go away," Sangris said, trying to shrug me off without releasing Juren.

"No. When he's a fish, he looks like a helium balloon with fins! You can't kill a *fish*," I said. Sangris didn't seem to be touched by this argument. His eyes were fixed on Juren, and he was inching closer. I changed tactics. "Nothing's more important than a life," I said. "That's why I saved *you*. So let him go!" I took a deep breath. "If you kill him—I won't ever fly with you again."

"You don't mean that."

"Sangris, I'm a vegetarian who refuses to swat flies," I said. "Believe me. I mean it. Remember my father and the bird?"

His eyes were hard, but they flickered when they met mine. Beneath him, Juren panted for breath. A heartbeat passed. "You'll be angry?" he said, finally.

"Yes."

Abruptly, he pulled back, leaving Juren to gasp on the

ground. Sangris stalked away and I heard a *crack* from behind me as he hit the strange little tree.

I knelt beside Juren, afraid for a moment because he hadn't moved. He was staring at the sky, green eyes glazed. On one cheek there was a red stain. Many of his feathers were torn up too. "Are you okay?" I said, my heart still speeding. "Poor Juren." He might be a thoughtless imp, but he hadn't deserved this.

"How did you do that?" he groaned.

"Do what?"

"Get him to release me." He shot a blurry glance at Sangris, who was pacing behind me, hissing to himself from time to time. I didn't blame Juren for looking apprehensive.

"He shouldn't have attacked in the first place," I said, more of my fear turning to disapproval as I thought about it. This was the second time tonight Sangris had put me in an unwanted situation. "He should've had more self-control—"

And then Sangris was there again. "That's enough," he said, pulling me away. He took me around the waist from behind and lifted me to my feet, leaving Juren to sit alone on the ground. "We're going back now."

"No," I said, pushing his hands off. "We need to stay. Look at Juren." I indicated the torn feathers and bloody cheek.

"He's fine."

I turned. "No, he isn't, because you hurt him. Why do you think you're in charge?"

"Because . . ." He couldn't think of a reason—because there wasn't one. There were shadows beneath his eyes as if, all at once, he hadn't slept in a month. It made him look strange. Distressed. The little paper bag of falafel lay crumpled and ridiculous on the ground beneath us.

Then I couldn't argue anymore. It would have been like sticking a pin in him. A pushy Sangris was bad enough, but one with bruised bleak eyes was too much. "We'll go," I said.

I looked over at Juren. At least he seemed to be recovering. He'd managed to sit upright on his own. "Good-bye."

"Earth is too far away for me to visit," he told me in a quick, low voice. "But if you'd ever like to come see me where I live, in a place called Elworth . . . would you?"

"Maybe," I said.

"No," Sangris said.

I flushed. I wouldn't actually have visited Juren, I'd only wanted to leave on my own terms. But Sangris— I got a tight feeling in my chest. He couldn't do this if I had wings of my own.

Greenish eyes slid from Sangris's face back to mine. Sangris watched. His mouth twisted again as he leaned against the tree, folding his arms. In the end Juren dropped his gaze. "Well," he said to me, "good-bye, then."

I nodded and looked at Sangris. He continued to lean against the tree, arms folded. There was an awkward moment.

"Aren't we going?" I said finally. "You insisted."

He pushed himself off the tree. I lifted my arms in preparation, but he didn't pick me up. He shrugged me aside and changed into his feathered dragon form instead.

We left Juren alone on that tiny island in the sky. Sangris's dragon-body moved through the blue air with ease. I sat with my legs crossed on his back, watching the sky part to let us through, and the long soft feathers that framed his face, moving in the wind. He flew in silence.

After a few minutes of this, I said, "He kissed my feet to apologize. Because he'd scared me. He swam up as a fish at first—or maybe he was flying, I don't know—and then he spoke to me and changed forms, and it shocked me so much that I fell over. And that's why I was sitting on the ground." I cast around for more to say. Now that I had explained things to him, I felt better. There, we would patch things up. The sky seemed to loosen around me. I smiled, even though he couldn't see it, and said, "I think I've been traumatized by these experiences. From now on, I won't be able to see an animal without assuming that it's actually a Free person. I might start talking to stray cats by the side of the road. People will think I'm insane. I'll be known as the Crazy Cat—"

"Enough," he said.

"What?"

"Stop babbling. I don't want to hear it," he said, and his voice was shaking. I stared at the back of his head. What? I was willing to overlook things, but *he* wasn't?

"You can't be angry at me. That's completely unfair. I didn't do anything!" I said. "Except prevent you from murdering someone."

"Nenner," he said, "leave it!"

"But—"

He only flew faster. I shut my eyes in the sudden onset

of wind. It was very cold now. I wrapped my arms around myself and waited for it to stop.

We didn't speak for the rest of the journey. When we reached my bedroom window, which was half open, a single square light in the darkness, I slipped inside without looking at him, went to my wardrobe, and threw out his clothes for him to catch.

The room was still strangely uncomfortable without my books. It felt as though it belonged to a different person. Only the bed was mine. I crawled over the sheets and took some comfort in wrapping the blanket around myself. Like a child hiding in a pretend fortress.

Finally Sangris stepped inside, fully dressed. In the peaky, shadowed face, his eyes stung as sharp as electric shocks. "So," he said. Laying the syllable down like a card on the table.

"Can we keep the argument till later?" I asked. Only a dunce wouldn't have been able to sense the storm boiling inside of Sangris. I turned my face away, trying to look at ease, while a chilly river seemed to be streaming right under my heart.

"I'm not going to make an *appointment* to argue with you," he snapped.

"I don't want to wake my father."

"'Poor Juren'?" he said, changing the subject.

"It's called sympathy."

"Oh, is *that* what you call it?"

"Obviously. I just said so."

"'Poor Juren,'" he mimicked again. He spoke as if they were swear words.

"He was poor, and his name was Juren. So what?"

"Don't pretend!"

"Pretend *what?*"

He paced, back and forth, back and forth, over the marble tiles of my bedroom floor. He was wearing his stolen school uniform and despite the windblown hair, he looked almost stiff, more brittle than usual. "So what is it?" he said finally, stopping. "Have you got a thing for green eyes or something?"

"Yes, Sangris," I said in a flat voice, "that's exactly it. How clever of you to figure it out. I insisted on saving him because of his eye color."

"Well, what was it then? The hair?"

I lay back on the bed, staring up at the cracked and discolored ceiling. The tightness in my chest was growing. "I think you're missing the point of nonviolence," I suggested.

Sangris made an interesting, high-pitched keening noise I had never heard him make before.

"You pulled me off him. You protected him at my expense. That's practically like choosing him over me!"

"Because I wouldn't let you kill him? I love your logic."

Sangris continued to list my sins. "And you were *nice* to him."

"Don't be rude. I'm always nice."

"No, you aren't! Not to me!"

I looked over at him and the next second my sarcastic

shell dissolved away. I already just wanted things to be back to normal, if only he weren't acting so unlike himself. "Calm down," I said. Uncertainly, I sat up and reached out.

But Sangris jerked back. "What about when he kissed your foot?" he said, in a fresh wave of bitterness. "When I begged to kiss your foot in Glasgow, you wouldn't let me— not even a foot! Even queens consent to have their feet kissed! But then mister curly hair and green eyes comes along and you *melt*. I've known you for months, but in half a second he—"

Liar. I hadn't been melting, I'd been gaping in shock. I considered telling him this, but it didn't seem as though an accusation would be a good way to calm him down. Instead I said, "Sangris, what could I do? Kick him off?"

"If I'd been the one kneeling there, you would have!"

"Ah, but that's because I know you better than I know him."

He stared. "That's the opposite of the way it should work!"

"No, it isn't. I can't kick a stranger. I only feel comfortable enough to kick you."

"Lucky me," he muttered.

"Anyway, I'm the one who should be upset. I never told him he was allowed to kiss my foot, he just did it. Believe me, I didn't want him to."

"No?"

"Ye gods, no." Sangris's forehead cleared. Encouraged, I said mournfully, "What a night. First—" I stopped. Complaining about his attempt to "talk" to me certainly wouldn't help. "First," I resumed, "stuck in the middle of the sky, then getting slobbered on, then a battle, and finally a flaming argument to top things off. Next time let's just go to Spain."

But he was frowning again. "Then why would you have wanted to visit Elworth?"

"Sangris," I said, "it's not as if I cared about *Elworth*."

"Eh?"

"You were trying to boss me around," I said. "Like—like my father!"

"I didn't mean to," he murmured, not looking at me, but at the window. "Was I?"

"If you don't even know, then what are we arguing about?" There was a long moment. Then he looked at me and we both broke into a smile.

Sangris slipped into a cat and slithered out of the crumpled heap of clothes, coming toward me. It now seemed safe enough to reach out and pick him up. I put him onto the bed beside me and he didn't pull away when I stroked his fur. After a long moment he leaned against me and his eyes slid shut. A light, tentative purring came from the base of his throat. I felt as if I'd just tamed a tiger. "Better?" I said.

"You . . . didn't like him?"

"Nope, definitely not after he did that to my foot. He scared me," I said, and Sangris's tensed-up body softened. Without opening his eyes, he pressed himself closer and began to knead his claws into my shirt. The purring became steadier.

I relaxed. "So, next time, don't try to order me around like that."

"Next time?" he mumbled, in the dazed voice he used whenever I petted him.

"If we ever do meet other Free people. It doesn't have to be Juren, okay. But maybe we'll come across others—ow!"

His sharp cat claws had clutched into me. I don't know if he meant to do it, but it was still a shock. I shoved him so hard that he went flying off the bed, and touched at my side where it was sore. And there was a sensation as if sparks were stuck in my throat, pressing upward, light and heady and dangerous.

"What," I demanded, "was that for?"

"Figure it out," he snapped, not looking sorry at all. My anger frothed up and scratched at my insides.

"That does it, Sangris," I said, standing, getting colder and calmer the more my blood seethed. "I'm sick of your hidden agendas. Conversations that I don't want to have, arguments that I don't want to have . . . You bring your feelings into *everything*."

"And you bring your feelings into nothing!"

"Maybe I don't *have* any feelings. Have you considered that? I hope you realize that even if I did like Juren, you wouldn't have the right to give me a hard time about it. I'm not *yours*, Sangris!"

His eyes paled, the yellow sucked into nothingness.

"I'm not even mine," I said.

It sounded very simple. I raised my shoulders a little, and

spread my hands, to show just how simple everything was. "Okay?" I said.

"But I—" Sangris said. "But I'm—"

I knew exactly what he was going to say next. I could practically see the words in his mouth. He was going to say *But I'm yours*.

Flushing again, with panic this time, I hurried to interrupt him. If he spoke to me like that, I'd never be able to look him in the eyes again.

"You're a Free person. Stay that way," I said.

Sangris's mouth screwed up as if he'd swallowed the words and they tasted awful.

"So what *am* I to you?" he said, and he sounded clumsy.

Everything I'd been thinking for the past months, about how Sangris had given me, not a reason to live—that sounds too dramatic—but an actual life, and how he was my air to breathe and how his face had all the excitement of an unexplored horizon, and how my nights with him, not just flying but talking too, had brought movement back to the sluggish blood that had almost stopped under the weight of a desert sun—there was no way I could tell him. As it came near my mouth I felt the impossibility of saying any of it, and the words died again like a weak lightbulb stuttering, unable to switch on.

Holes opened in him where my silence went through. He didn't move a muscle, apart from the very tip of his tail, which flicked and contorted like the coils of a dying snake. When he began to speak, his voice was steady, but after the

201

first few sentences, his control broke apart, and though he didn't shout, he mumbled, which was worse.

"I'm not a taxi service. I'm not your personal chauffeur. I'm not going to sit aside and twiddle my thumbs while you—and Juren—smiling—kissing your—you—I won't let myself become . . . Get *him* to fly you around if that's all you want. I'm not doing it like this." Crooked bat wings appeared above his back, and then Sangris was gone, leaving me to sit alone in my hollow coffin of a bedroom and blink.

I understood every word he'd said, and I could even understand fragments of the emotion behind them, but when it was all put together, I still couldn't find any answer to make. It was too big to fit inside. The anger was gone as quickly as it had come. There was nothing in me now, just a bit of a chill. Unable to move, I stared at the window as if he might reappear.

The next night, he didn't show up. *It won't last,* I told myself. But he wasn't there the next night either. Or the next.

CHAPTER SIXTEEN

In Which Sangris Admits Defeat

I spent the first couple of days relaxing. I can be very heartless sometimes; it's a useful talent to have. So I didn't pine. I caught up on my homework, I laughed with Anju about how Heritage had been postponed yet again (proof that my school couldn't do anything right), and in art class I got inspired and painted a face that made my teacher shiver.

"Where's the cat?" Anju asked me in the back of the class-room after break.

"Sulking somewhere," I said, trying to write an entire essay using only my left hand. I wobbled all over the page at first, but by the end of the year I would learn to be ambidextrous.

"Oh," she said. She turned back to her own essay without asking why.

On the third and fourth days, and especially nights, I began opening my curtains at odd times, hoping to find Sangris sitting there. When he wasn't, I became a bit disappointed; I told myself that this was because I wanted to fly to other countries and I couldn't without him.

At those times, I wished I could own the sky without

needing to wait for him first. This was what came of relying on Sangris, reduced to borrowing his wings. I didn't *want* to depend on him. *I* wanted to be my freedom, my air, my light. What kind of freedom is it that has to be given to you by someone else?

Every dinner I watched myself closely. Ever since the wadi in Oman, I'd been so afraid I might give something away to my father that I hardly dared breathe. Still, it was a strange, guilty thrill to sit there, knowing I'd never be the daughter he imagined even though he was so determined to believe it. Just existing was a small form of rebellion.

"Your mother needs help. You should wash the dishes tonight," my father said to me on the fifth day.

"Why don't you ever wash them?" I said.

He looked at me impassively for a long time. "Because I'm the father. You're the daughter."

"But if Mom needs help—"

"Go wash them," he said. I went and washed them.

On the sixth day, it rained for the first time all year. I was in class when it happened, but we all got so excited that we poured out of the buildings, leaving our pens and notebooks and bags behind, and milled around as heavy droplets of water plopped in a jagged pattern onto the dust. We tilted our heads back and allowed the miraculous rain to hit our faces. It was light at first, but it kept going, and by dusk the wadis were rushing with fast brown water.

That night, I told my parents I was going on a walk.

"What?" my mother said in alarm. I hadn't gone on a

walk for years. She'd thought the phase had passed.

"If I stand on the edge of the street, I can see the wadi. It's flooding. That hasn't happened in ages."

"You can't go off the street," she said. "Take a mobile phone! Be back in ten minutes. Isn't it too dark?" She looked to my father for help, but he just watched me. Calm and brittle, as though he wanted to observe what I would do next. But this was his rule; he had made it years ago. I decided to plunge.

"The sky's light," I said, and set off into the heat. It wasn't so bad with warm water soaking my shirt. My prison was flushed and animated beneath the blasts of rain—the hammering had softened it, and for once in all these long empty years, movement came to the thin leaves of the trees. It was like seeing a strict spinster aunt begin to dance. The air, usually dry enough to feel starched, was alive in my face now. I breathed as much as I could, taking this one chance to suck it in. No cars were out today because hardly anyone knew how to drive in the rain. I felt my spirits lift. Ten minutes of freedom. My own, for once. I didn't have to rely on Sangris or my parents for this—it was mine, I had won it, and nobody could take it away.

I didn't just go to the edge of the street. I walked a little way off it, a few steps across the damp sand, and then I was at the side of the wadi that curved behind our house. I sat down on the edge and dangled my legs into the floodwater, feeling it pull at my feet, trying to whisk me away. Right now the wadi was swollen, but that wouldn't last long. The sun would have its way in the end. I had to enjoy the flood while it lasted.

The sky was overcast, hot clouds lowering on me, so night came more quickly than usual. I had barely five minutes at the edge of the wadi before I had to return home. I walked back along the bare street, catching raindrops on my fingertips, and, without warning, a long slow ache for Sangris, which would continue straight through the night up until morning, swept from my feet to my head. I didn't need him or his wings in order to enjoy this sudden, rare rain, but I wanted him to be there anyway. That night my dreams were dark and wavering, and I kept awakening to feel the pain of the wave passing through me, before sinking back to sleep.

In the morning, I looked at myself in the mirror matter-of-factly. Almond-shaped black eyes looked back at me from a gold-brown face. From my face alone, a Westerner would have called me Eastern, an Easterner would have called me Western. Wherever I went, I always looked like a foreigner, a stranger from across the seas. Some of the ambiguity of that hung in my sheets of black hair, straight enough to be Japanese; my eyes were slanted enough to be Thai, but wide enough to be Scottish; the long lashes of India, the wide forehead of Italy; the facial structure that kept high cheekbones and long eyes, but also a nose that curled slightly up at the tip. It was all so mixed together that nobody who didn't already know my background would have been able to place me. I'd always thought that it made me look slightly inhuman, as if I didn't belong anywhere at all, as if I could be an elf who simply had taken the wrong turn somewhere.

Now it reminded me of Sangris. I liked that idea. I would be reminded of our common ground, the alien nothingness that we shared, whenever I looked into a mirror.

"Good morning," I said to myself. I had no discernable accent. I had lived in so many countries that the accents had canceled each other out.

I looked back pitifully.

"Cheer up," I said. "It won't last. He'll be back soon."

I leaned closer and saw that my eyes showed traces of my uneasy night. There was nothing to do but splash them with cold water. Nobody would look at me closely enough to notice anyway, I told myself.

I was right.

My father left early, so my mother drove me to school through the dying rain. When the car stopped, she did stare at me sideways, and I thought maybe she'd spotted my eyes—but then she turned her gaze away and frowned at the windshield. "Have a nice day," was all she said.

"We have two periods of biology," Anju told me as I was fetching books out of my locker. Obediently, I reached for the biology textbook.

During class, the rain continued to fade outside, and there was a gust of wind. I heard the frond of a palm tree hitting the window and looked around quickly, but Sangris wasn't there. I didn't want to study after that. "Anju," I said, "I'm sad."

"Because of the cat?" she said. Anju knew me better than anybody in the oasis.

"Yes."

"Well, it's about time."

"What?"

"I was beginning to think you didn't have a heart," she said, in a voice as monotonous as though she were reciting mathematic equations.

She graded my papers for me.

After school, while driving me home, my father said, "You're spending too much time in your bedroom. Tonight you will not stay inside for more than two hours."

He didn't bother to come into my bedroom to check on me, because he knew I would obey. I hid for exactly two hours. Then I spent the rest of the evening staring at the living room wall and imagining that figures were dancing across it as if it were a television screen, moving and acting out stories.

"Help your mother and wash the dishes tonight," he said after dinner. I did so without question.

The ache inside of me was growing heavier and heavier. I didn't miss flying or traveling or exploring anymore. I missed Sangris himself. I carried it around like a stone inside of me.

The very last of the rain died and the oasis was dry once more. Since I couldn't read, I sat at a table and sketched. Not anything much. I tried to draw a perfect circle with one sweep of my hand. Over and over. I was determined to master this, the same way that, a few years ago, I had taught myself to draw straight lines without the use of a ruler; the same way that I was training myself to be ambidextrous.

My circles improved, but they still weren't perfect.

I promised myself things. One day I'm going to be a librarian, I decided. Then I'll be able to spend all day reading and teaching myself useless little skills that nobody else cares about. I'll start the first public library in Phnom Penh. (Or does Phnom Penh already have public libraries?) Maybe somewhere else. Cagliari. Or Negombo. Somewhere you can't find a school that doesn't misspell its own name, and can't find proper bookshops in the entire stupid city. But when I'm older—I'll expand my collection, I'll have not just hundreds, but thousands of books, and they'll become not just the *first* library, but the *biggest*, one of the *best* in the *world*—

I passed the time by promising myself things like that, even though they were impossible. (My father, you see, wants me to be an engineer. Predictable, isn't it.)

I went to sleep early. It took me hours to rest my head on the pillow comfortably. Then another hour to close my eyes. There was a sliver of hot steel pulsing inside my right temple. It wouldn't go away. I felt the heat creeping around the house again, beginning to close over and reclaim its territory now that the rain had died.

At midnight a *tap-tap* broke through my headache and my parched dreams.

I got up slowly, turned on the light, pulled back the curtains, and opened the window. Sangris entered without a word.

He was human, wearing one of his stolen school uniforms.

The wings vanished as soon as he stepped into the light of my room. He looked at me for a moment, and I looked back in silence.

Then he sank down the wall, onto the floor, hung his head, and said, "I give up. You win."

I studied him. He did look exhausted, defeated. His eyes were screwed up as though he had a headache too. "A week," he said hoarsely. "That's all I could manage. A lousy week."

I continued to be silent. After a week of trying to imagine it, having him here again felt like a blow to the stomach. So solid, so familiar.

"You win," he said again. He rested his head against his knees and didn't look at me as he spoke, as if he was ashamed. "I'll be your chauffeur. I won't say a word to you if you don't want me to. If you'd like my wings, then they're yours. I can even take you to see Juren." He took a deep breath. "If you want."

I said, "I win?"

"Yes. Completely. I— Yes."

My fingers twitched. I wanted to brush the hair off his forehead, but at the last minute I stopped myself. He was looking at the floor, and he didn't see. "How did I win?"

He shut his eyes. "I couldn't stay away. I can't. I wanted to prove . . . or at least make you think . . . that I could get along fine without you. And now I'm creeping back like some groveling little *pet* with its tail between its legs. But you—you're obviously fine. I saw you chatting with Anju in class today. I was going to tell you all this then, because

I couldn't wait for nighttime, like the poor sap I am. But that hurt my pride . . . So I went away. But I couldn't wait out another night, and I realized that I don't care about my pride, or anything, as long as you'll let me . . . I don't know. Talk to you. Look at you. Be in the same room." He shook his head. "I'm pathetic, aren't I? For pity's sake, a week—that's nothing. It used to be hard to keep my attention on anything for more than an hour. But now that I *want* to be unreliable, I can't. I'm a cringing *tamed* thing." He said "tamed" with disgust. It must have been an insult for a Free person. "But please, let me stay. Let me be your private chauffeur. Anything. Just not nothing."

To give my hands something to do, I fiddled with my hair. Sangris didn't realize how far removed he was from my reality. We lived in different worlds. But at some point, he had become the real one, and without him, the walls of my desert and my metal-hot sky and the gold spikes of my palm trees, and everything else that composed my reality, was like a cardboard cutout of a life. *I'm in way over my head,* I thought, looking down at him. I wished that he *had* just remained a pair of wings. It would be so much easier than this.

The waves of last night were passing through me again. Warm and billowing and I don't know what else. I waited until they had subsided before I spoke. It was hard to breathe when they were at their peak.

"Sangris," I said, "it's not like that at all." Good grief, this was hard. As if I were pulling my ribs apart. "You're my best friend. Forget the wings. It's you. Um." Why wouldn't he look at me? "I only said those things to you because you'd made me angry." *Sorry,* is what I meant, but I felt that I'd gushed enough. I closed my mouth.

"I know I made you mad. I'm sorry," he muttered. "I was . . . upset."

I knew I ought to mention Juren, and explain that I . . . I don't know exactly. When I tried, I kept coming up against a difficulty with my voice, and I ended up mumbling only, "I gathered that much."

"Sorry," he said again. He still wouldn't look at me.

I went to join him on the floor. It was the most companionable gesture I could think of that didn't involve touching him. We sat side by side, facing forward. "What I want to know," I said, "is what brought on all this stuff about chauffeurs and pets. Is the concept of 'friend' too complicated for you?"

Silence. Then—"I'm not the most important person in the world to you," he mumbled.

That wasn't what I'd expected. "Huh?"

He said nothing.

"You don't hope for much, do you?" I tried joking.

No smile. His face was all pinched and serious.

"There are lots of people in the world," I said. "And living is . . . more complicated than that. There can *never* be one person who just comes along and defines you."

"Yes there can. You named me, didn't you?" said Sangris flatly.

My heart gave a plunging jolt. "Oh."

"And it's not like that for you." He lifted his head to look at me with steady, ill-looking eyes. "Between us, you're the free one."

"Oh . . ." There was a pause, in which I struggled. Finally, I said, "Imagine I met another Free person. Like Juren. Only imagine that I really took to him, and he was wonderful, and sweet and so on."

Sangris twitched.

"Imagine this perfect version of Juren became my best friend, to the point that I wanted to spend all my time with him." I hesitated only for an instant. "Well, the amount I liked him would probably be about a tenth of the amount I like you." And before I could think twice about it, my hand jerked up and pushed aside the hair that fell over his forehead.

His arms slipped off his knees.

"Does that make it any better?" I didn't specify what I was talking about—the touch, or my dismissal of Juren— because I wasn't sure myself.

"A tenth?" he said. Uncertainly, he reached up a hand and felt his head, as if there would be some lingering proof of my finger's passage. I had already turned away and folded my arms back over my knees.

"Almost. Can you live with that?"

"A tenth?"

"Yes."

"A tenth? Honestly? You promise?"

"Yes."

Sangris touched my cheek and leaned forward, looking at me intently. But having him beside me, with my father's itch clawing into my back, my fingers shaky because of what I had just put them through, and things beating to and fro, in one direction then another, inside of me, was already more than I could stand. I shrank away.

He studied every feature of my face, especially my mouth, with a fixed, hungry expression in his eyes, while his thumb gently moved over the skin on my cheek. I leaned as far back against the wall as I could go.

Noticing that I was inching away from him, Sangris let go of my face. His eyes went down from my mouth to the loose nightshirt I wore. I'd only put it on because I hadn't expected him to show up. The sleeves reached my elbows, but the bottom of the shirt didn't quite make it to my knees. My legs were long and bare in the artificial light. He drew back, eyes glimmering amber, and touched my ankle lightly with his fingers. He cupped my heel in the palm of his hands, lifting the foot slightly. He glanced up at me for permission. When I stared back and didn't scream, he brought his mouth to the sensitive area on the narrow arch of my instep, and warmth fizzled through it, up my leg. I clutched at the wall as if I could fall through. The waves were reaching too high.

"Okay," I said hoarsely, "that's enough." Something about the dark flushed look around his eyes, and the way he lingered over my ankle, as if wondering whether he could just keep going, set off alarm bells in my head. Some kind of bells, anyway.

"All right," he murmured into my skin. Delicately, he set my foot back down onto the tiles of the floor. A bit unsteady, hair rumpled, he grinned at me. "A tenth," he said. "I can live with that."

CHAPTER SEVENTEEN

In Which There Are Spiders

"Why are you dressed like that?" my father said when I came out of my room one morning. It was a few weeks after the foot incident.

I halted, awkward as always when he spoke to me unexpectedly. "It's Heritage," I explained. The school had sent out stacks and stacks of newsletters, probably wasting an entire forest, in an effort to keep parents informed, but they'd sent out *so* many, and made so many last-minute cancelations and changes as power shifted from one board member to another, that it was no wonder he wasn't up-to-date.

"Oh," he said. His eyes turned back to the computer screen. "I suppose you have to wear the national dress. But keep your shoulders covered. You never know who's looking."

"Yep."

"Say 'yes,' not 'yep.'"

"Yes."

My Thai dress was basically a purple-and-gold sarong with a light purple, sleeveless tube of a shirt, made of some thin, shiny material, over which I wore a gold-embroidered shawl that draped around my shoulders. I didn't know what the costume was called. That's how much of a fraud I was.

During the drive Mom kept staring at me in my outfit. To my surprise and nervousness she almost looked teary-eyed, and by the time we arrived at school I was yelling at myself to maybe pat her on the arm or something. But as I gingerly reached out a hand, she twitched and muttered, "You're wearing the clothes wrong," so I pretended I'd been grabbing for my lunchbox.

When I got to the empty soon-to-be Thai room, lugging bags of food and decorations along with me, Anju was waiting there. Her sari was white, floating around her dark form like a snowstorm.

"You look interesting," she said, which was the first proper compliment I had ever received from her. "I need to be in the Indian room or they'll yell at me. Farzeen is being all bossy, and she's not even Indian."

"Oh. I'm staying away then. You come and visit later. Any good food?"

"Lots."

Anju left in a swirl of silver sequins.

Strange to see her dressed up like that. She was so quiet and studious that everyone assumed she must be ugly, without bothering to look at her. But in her own clothes, with her kohl and henna on, she was actually quite pretty. Not that I'd ever admit it out loud.

I got the room organized on my own. The hand-painted

parasols with the silk fringe went at the front, in the hope that they'd take up lots of space. They'd been made in China, but they looked kind of Thai. On the door I stuck a poster of an elephant. It was clearly an African elephant, but I doubted anyone else would notice. And I put out a statue of the Buddha, which, unfortunately, I'd got in Cambodia. I was standing on a chair, stretching to drape the Venezuelan flag over the windows (I didn't own a Thai one, but there were no other Thais in the school to know the difference), when a couple of students wandered in. They had probably finished setting up their own rooms and were now searching for food before all the best stuff got taken.

"Not yet," I said, looking back at them over my shoulder.

"Wow," one of them said. I vaguely recognized her. Younger than me, curly haired.

"Reem, right?" I said.

"Yeah. You look cool."

Just then, people wearing nothing but their belly-dancing outfits (daring, but it was traditional, so that made it all right) stopped and told me how exotic I looked. That was always the word: *exotic*. It made me feel as if I ought to be locked up in a cage.

"You should put your hair up," said Reem, once they'd left.

"Oh . . ." I pinned the last of the posters in place. "I don't know. I thought leaving it down would make me look more ethnic. Because people always associate straight hair with Asia, right?"

She fiddled in her pocket and drew out a cheap rubber

hair band, handing it over to me. "Here. This way your hair won't hide your clothes."

Maybe she had a point. My hair did sheet down to my waist. I took the hair band. "Thanks."

But I didn't have a chance to put it on for the first few hours. In the poky assembly room where half the lights didn't work and the doors screamed every time someone walked in, the new head teacher gave a long and pompous speech that nobody listened to. Then the younger kids were forced to parade past in their native clothes. Someone from Fiji danced onstage. Finally, we were allowed back to the secondary school building. Students rushed to get at the food.

They could dash around and eat until it was their turn to man the stalls, but, because I was the only one in the Thai room, I had to stay. I watched as people strolled in, grabbed some food, and strolled back out again. I didn't mind. I even encouraged it, talking loudly about how great the other countries were. If people started looking around, they might realize that my room was about as Thai as I was.

But after a few hours I had reached my breaking point. All the sticky rice my mother had cooked was gone, and visitors had started asking me where the rest was, as if they thought I might be hiding some. I opened my lunchbox and started handing out my own food in desperation.

"Veggie hot dogs?" said someone. "With ketchup?"

"It's very popular in Thailand, all right?"

If the principal walks in, I'm in so much trouble, I thought, looking around once I was alone. All my lunch was gone and word had spread that the Thai room was out of food. Fewer and fewer people were trickling in. And that was good, because I'd just realized that my Venezuelan flag, for some reason, had a conspicuous tag saying *Made in Italy*.

"Made in Italy?" said someone.

I jumped.

"Sheesh, relax."

It was Sangris.

"Took you long enough to show up," I said, recovering.

"I was getting you these," he said, holding out a bunch of orchids innocently. "Thai orchids. From the actual country."

"You didn't steal them, did you?"

"No. They're wild."

"In that case, thanks." I took them from him. "Just as well we have something genuine around here. Next year I'm not doing this. I'll sit in an empty room and when people ask me where I'm from, I'll answer in gibberish."

Some little kid stuck his head in through the door. His eyes widened as he saw the girl with dead-straight, waist-length black hair and the feline, yellow-eyed guy handing her flowers. He took off at a run.

"I think we're scaring people off," I said to Sangris, feeling rather pleased about it.

"You look incredible," was his irrelevant answer. "Like a princess from the rainforest. You have no idea how big your eyes are."

"Sangris, I don't think that this dress affects the size of my eyes," I said.

He ignored me. There was no stopping Sangris once he began waxing lyrical. "Purple and gold and bronze and black. You're the colors of a sunset."

Ew. "What's bronze?" I said.

"Your skin."

"I'm not bronze. Sheesh. Sounds like some macho body builder with a spray-on tan."

"What are you, then?" he said. He went closer to my face and touched my cheek, as if trying to figure out the color. I thought it was just an excuse to touch me. He'd been doing that more frequently lately—ever since the foot incident. And nowadays, I didn't shove him aside.

"Thais are *gold*," I said, lifting my nose in the air.

"Ah," he said, beginning to smile. "Sorry. You're right. I see now that you are gold. Purple and gold and black, then."

"Black would be my eyes?" I said, for something to say. He was standing too close. I looked at the clever, high-cheekboned face that had grown so familiar.

I'm in over my head, I thought, but I hardly heard myself. I had thought it so often over the past few weeks that the words didn't have much meaning anymore. When he'd just been an accessory, a pair of wings, then I hadn't minded shoving him aside, but now, when he stood like this, I didn't know what to do. Things were unraveling. I felt that. But I didn't want him to go away again. Everything was a mess.

"Yes," he said softly, "black would be your eyes." The hand on my cheek brushed against a strand of hair. "And your hair. Have I ever told you that it feels like silk?"

"Yes. Several times."

"It's very long," he said dreamily. *Way over my*— I pulled back, leaving his hand extended in midair.

"You're just stating the obvious," I said. I folded my arms and took another step away. His fingers were making me nervous, and I absolutely refused to seem dizzy in front of him. "Do you think I should put it up? Reem said I should. Though I don't suppose it matters now, because nobody's coming in here anymore."

"Put what up?" he said, hazy-eyed.

"My hair." I resisted the urge to add: "You idiot."

Then, to my relief, Anju came in.

Her eyes went straight to Sangris. Understandably. It was hard not to look at him, he was so out of place wherever he stood. There was always the impression that the universe had just blinked and overlooked him, because there shouldn't have been anyone standing there, and Sangris must be a mistake. He didn't fit.

I saw Anju do a double take. She looked at the thin eager line of his cheek. She looked at the mouth, which was also somehow wrong, because smiles shouldn't be so wicked and so earnest both at once. Finally she looked at the curve he made as he leaned back against one of the display tables. Then she blinked and dropped her gaze. Weird-looking or not, he'd passed inspection; she'd decided it would be immodest to stare at him.

She was only able to take the time to assess him because he wasn't paying any attention to her. He was still watching me.

"Hey, Anju," he said without looking at her.

She blinked at least seven times in quick succession. Then she turned to glare at me. *How does he know my name?*

I adjusted my face until it beamed innocence in her direction. She'd probably faint if she knew that he was the cat she'd once stepped over in the hallway. "Anju," I said, "maybe you can help us. Do you think I should put my hair up?"

"Uh. Yes," she said, "just because you never do."

"Now *that*," I said to Sangris, "was a good, solid, useful answer. Take notes, will you?"

"Anju's the secretary," he said in mild indignation. "She can do it."

"How does he know that? What else have you told—"

I pretended I couldn't hear the hiss of words. "So, Anju," I continued in a loud voice. "What's up?"

Sangris was watching. She had to answer. "There was a riot when our room ran out of food," she said, still slitting her eyes at me.

"Well, this Heritage is going well," I said brightly.

"The new head teacher was fired."

I shook my head. Even by oasis standards, he hadn't lasted very long: about two weeks.

"And the Emiratis' camel got into the primary school building."

I laughed out loud at that.

"So," Anju said, with another nervous glance at Sangris. "I'm going back to the Indian room." She backed out.

"I'll visit soon," I said.

Sangris's attention snapped back to me as soon as Anju had gone. And I felt my smile slip. There was the telltale darkness beneath his eyes again. I had yet to find a cure for that. I wondered if pouring a bucket of cold water over him would help. Or maybe I should run to call Anju back. Preparing to leave, I grabbed the hair band that Reem had given me. But before I could pull my hair up, Sangris stepped behind me and took the band out of my fingers.

"Uh," I said. "I could do that, you know."

But he didn't answer. His hands, a little clumsy through lack of practice, fumbled through my hair, lifting up the length of it and revealing the bare skin beneath. The room began spinning strangely. I felt the A/C blow across my exposed throat and the back of my neck. Sangris twisted my hair together into the band. He took an unnecessarily long time, letting the strands slide through his fingers.

I fidgeted. "Done yet?" I said.

"Almost."

And then his mouth was on the place between my shoulder and the curve of my neck.

I died. My eyes blacked out. Jolting, I jumped away from him. My hands flew up to clutch that spot on the side of my neck. It felt as if he'd—no, there's no other way to put it, because nothing could be worse than a kiss—so intimate, and stolen. "You . . . What was that for?" I yelped. "What's wrong with you?"

"I don't know," he said. "I couldn't help it. Are you okay?"

"No! No, I'm not!" My face stung as if I'd been slapped

there. This, I could not close my eyes and allow. This was the line, this was the boundary of that other country, and I felt my father's finger twanging taut behind my back, straining, and Sangris didn't seem to realize that he was standing in a place where I could not go. "You've never done anything like that before," I said, when I could speak again.

"But I've wanted to."

Sangris looked at me. I couldn't see shame, or contrition, or surprise in his face, though those were what I had expected. There wasn't even that soppy, shadow-eyed expression I'd grown used to. Instead there was a look I couldn't recognize. It frightened me more than anything else I could have seen there. His eyes were burning with something worse than madness; it was a bright, hot sanity, like the death of a thousand stars.

"I shouldn't have done it from behind," he said. "I startled you. I'm sorry about that. It just . . . came over me."

"You shouldn't have done it at all," I said.

"I disagree," he said.

I backed up against the wall.

"I've been a coward. It isn't right to think about these things in secret and not let you know," he said, burning in his private, flame-gold sky. "And I've been thinking about it for months . . . Actually, I've been thinking about it since I met you, but . . . the first time I tried to tell you was before Juren showed up, when we were on that island in the sky. But you got distracted—" He laughed half bitterly, half breathlessly. "And I've been putting it off since then. The last few weeks it's become worse. Since you let me kiss your instep. Nenner, you *have* to listen now, even if you don't want to."

He went closer to me, with his hands held up in front of him, cautiously, like someone approaching a stray dog when they're not sure if it will bite.

"I shouldn't have let you," I moaned.

"But I'm glad you did," he said, more quickly now. His eyes were impossibly bright. "But it is hard, getting a taste and then having it taken away. It made things a million times worse. At least I could control myself before. Now I don't know how to act, and half the time I don't know what I'm saying. I know you noticed. Anyone would have noticed. I've been acting like a . . . a dopey little kid with a crush."

"I was thinking more a dunce with a concussion," I said. I was trying to make the conversation more normal, like the banter we used to have. But he came closer. Close enough to put his arms around me if he wanted to.

I couldn't do this. I willed myself away. I saw purple-gray heather and a distant sky.

"I thought it was like being set on fire," he said. "It burns all the time. And then you look at me, and you smile, or sigh, or look exasperated, or whatever, and suddenly I can't talk."

Hills, like waves that had tried to roll through the earth centuries ago but had fallen asleep in the middle of their journey.

"Can you imagine that kissing your instep could do that to me? Like flames going all the way through me."

Some lakes. There had to be lakes. Sheets of silver.

"It's like that now. Just from touching your neck with my mouth. I can still *taste* it." He flushed. "I couldn't help it. I'd never seen the back of your neck before, and it was like nothing in the world is more important than being that close to you. I want to be the one who's allowed to . . ." He trailed off, going darker.

It would be late afternoon. The sky would be soft, the land sleepy. Not sleepy the way that Sangris had looked when— *No, no, no, no.* I rushed away from that thought. It would be a different kind of sleepy, I assured myself. A *safe* kind.

"I told myself I'd tell you by Heritage. You and Anju were always complaining about it, saying that the date kept being pushed back. 'It's like chasing after a shadow. It's always a little way ahead.' That's what you said. Do you remember? And that reminded me of how I kept trying to tell you this, but kept putting it off, and never managed to make myself do it. By the time Heritage comes, I'll have done it, I decided. See, I was determined enough to set myself a time limit; but I was so pathetic I deliberately chose a date that was always being postponed. I hoped it would be canceled altogether. Stupid, huh? And I've waited until the last minute . . . Because I'm scared of you too, Nenner. I really don't know what you're going to say, and this is—you can't imagine—"

Still I didn't speak. I was off in this other land. There would be a breeze, I thought. Light. Hardly enough to make the seas of grass ripple. To make the surfaces of the lakes pucker.

He said, "I like knowing the houses where you grew up. I like that I've been to all the places you love; that I sat by the sunflowers with you and you let me hold your hands, and that I know things about you that no one else knows, and that you know everything about me. But I want—I want to be able to do things that no one else can do, like kiss that place at the corner of your mouth and stroke your hair and touch the base of your throat and to be able to tell you when I want to do things like that. Instead of dreaming about it like some sick, panting kid. And I want you to reciprocate instead of shrinking away from me all the time . . ."

Clouds at the eastern end of the sky.

"People in this country have different ideals of what's beautiful and what's not." He forced himself to meet my eyes. "You're different from what they're used to. But that's why it's hard to look away from you. So different. You know I love the shape of your eyes? Long and slanted and huge. They remind me of a fox's. But . . . more graceful, you know . . . and they tilt up at the corners." He reached up and touched the side of my left eye, near the temple. His fingers were light and unsteady. "I *love* the way they tilt up at the corners."

Rain. I liked rain. It would be raining in heavy rich droplets that sank into the dirt as soon as they landed. The plants would grow green in gratitude.

"Even when I'm not human, I think that. When I woke up after the Animal Souk, as a cat, and you were holding me, I had no idea what was going on because I'd never been held that way before." One hand remained at my face, and the other, gingerly, reached my waist. "It's part of being a Free person. If you're everything, then really you're nothing. You understand that. When you started petting me"—he tried to laugh—"I thought I had hit my head."

The sun would blaze before the world turned dark, in one massive purple-gold blossom in the west, a light that would catch in the rain and sleet across the vast lakes and touch the sleeping heads of the hills. I saw it in my mind's eye.

Sangris pulled me slowly away from the wall, toward him. "We do this every night," he told me. "You don't need to worry. I hold you all the time. The only difference is that now your feet are on the ground, and we're facing each other . . ."

I felt the hills catch fire under the weight of the falling sun.

His arm went around my waist, a hand on the narrow part where it dipped inward. His other hand supported the back of my head now, touching my neck, unraveling my hair. I felt his chest move. He was barely breathing, I noticed, but I wasn't really paying attention. The door was open. Suppose my father walked through. Suppose someone walked past and saw me. There was a strict school rule against overt displays of affection. But then I didn't care anymore. Sangris was doing an insane thing; we were so far away from normality that school rules couldn't touch us.

Sangris hid his face in my hair. I was close enough against him that I could feel the strain it had taken to say those things to me. I could feel it in his shoulders, the thump of his heart, the shaking of his hands as they moved against me. When my hands had trembled amid the sunflowers of Spain he had held them for me. I wanted to give comfort back now. I pressed myself closer, tighter than he had dared to pull me. For a moment I imagined that I might be able to say yes.

I wasn't Frenenqer now, and I wasn't Nenner either. The two of them—everyone I'd ever been—had escaped far away. I was all that remained: a body, barely the ghost of a mind. I bit back the embarrassment and let Sangris put his arms around me the way that Nenner did when he carried her. He didn't know that I wasn't her. *He'll be disappointed if he finds out*, I thought. *I hope she'll be the one to tell him, not me.*

A minute ago, when he'd kissed my neck, I hadn't known what to do. Impossible to lose him; impossible to let him get so close. But now I thought, maybe this is the solution. I could pretend to be okay with it. I was letting him hold me, wasn't I? He seemed happy enough with my shell. Maybe I could do this for the rest of my life: switch myself off and just never turn back on. Stay with Sangris. His cheek was smooth against mine. But if he tried to kiss me again—I couldn't—and I couldn't think like this. Had to think. *Anju.* Her name came to me automatically. Yes. Anju would know. She would figure it out in her notebook, like a mathematical equation, and come up with an answer the way she always did. I started to head for the door, but when I turned, he tried to keep me there. "Nenner," he said, in a voice that was hoarser than his own, "where're you going?"

"Into the hall," I said. "I'm going to find Anju."

I walked out.

As soon as I saw the peeling green paint of the lockers and the plain white floor, I fell back into my body with a sickening thud. Ye gods, my back itched. My father's finger, pointing at me. I rubbed at it and looked around. Where was everybody? No one was in the hallway. I could hear some racket outside; that was probably where they had all disappeared to. I set off. I'd have to hurry, and—

Sangris had followed me. He caught at my elbow, and when I turned, he pressed me up against the lockers. "Where are you *going?*" he repeated. His voice was ragged now.

"To find Anju," I said feebly.

"Why?"

"I want to ask her something."

He wouldn't turn his eyes away. "Nenner, I just told you that I—that I want—and you're trotting off to find Anju? *Now?"*

"I can't unless you let go of me," I said.

"That's why I won't let go! You need to say something." His face twisted. *"Something.* You can't just walk off and leave me alone after that!"

"Oh," I said. I tried to push his hands off. I couldn't think of anything. "I just . . . let me find Anju. She'll help me to understand things." That was what I did whenever I was lost in class, after all. Turn to Anju.

Sangris leaned closer.

"Nenner," he said, "do you or do you not understand what I was trying to tell you?"

"Um. I think I might."

"You *think*?"

I still didn't know whether or not to lie. The pit of my stomach felt very cold. With an effort, I met his eyes. "You feel some physical attraction," I said. "We'll deal with it. You'll just . . . have to learn how to suppress it."

He stared at me. "You don't get it," he said in disbelief. "You don't get it at all." He continued to stare for a couple more minutes. Since I couldn't wriggle away, I pushed myself back against the locker, as far as I could go. I was uncertain on my feet. I felt like a little seed with the hard outer covering peeled off. A gust of wind would have picked me up and carried me away.

Suddenly I wanted to be back in my boxes, safe. The world out here was too vivid, too raw. I'd been an idiot to hope that I would ever be able to handle it. There was no need to ask Anju about this. I couldn't pretend to be more than I was.

The fragments of our friendship were bright, very bright, in my mind, like shards of an exploded sun, glowing. They were all I could see.

I said, "Sangris, don't you think we can just go on the way we were before?"

He studied me for a long time.

Finally: "You just don't get it," he repeated. His voice was flat. "I'm going to spell it out for you. Nenner, this is for your own good. Try to pay attention this time, because I don't know how I can make it any clearer."

The windows inside the classrooms had been opened for once. The wind coming into the corridor felt warm. Around me little lights reflected off the surface of the walls. Patches of them waved over the white floor, and, on Sangris's face, especially over the line of his left cheek, the broken-up sunlight billowed and swam. Blue sky outside. The slow light was tinted blue as well: a deep near-purple blue. Everything was clean, everything was shining. I had never felt so empty, or so sick of myself.

He tilted his head down and put his mouth to mine. I saw his eyes close. He . . . stayed there for a while. Something seemed to be happening to him. And what had started off as impatience became hunger and tenderness. He moved his body nearer to me too. I was calm. I counted to ten, and when his hands had relaxed their grip I tried to pull away; he mumbled something and went even closer.

I watched from somewhere around the ceiling. The girl against the lockers was holding very still. I could feel the heat from Sangris, but it didn't touch me, and when her lips parted I was mildly disgusted—but only mildly, because I was far removed from the messy softness of whatever was happening down there. But then, too soon, I was her again with my shoulders against the locker doors. I pressed the palms of my hands back against the hard, peeling wood as if it could anchor me.

Then at last, after what seemed like a long time, Sangris sighed and I realized he was done. I drew away immediately. He looked sleepy again, flushed, and his eyes were still hungry, the irises colored like a flame at low heat. He didn't, or couldn't, speak for a moment, and then he said, in a much deeper voice than I had heard before, "You understand now?"

I didn't respond. I was counting down the seconds, listening for the telltale whistle of a bomb. *Three*, I thought. *Two. One.*

Then the shame and the shock hit me.

I burst into tears.

"Nenner?" I heard Sangris say.

I turned away from him, horror shaking me, and put my arms over my head so that he couldn't see my face. I didn't want anyone to see me. I pushed myself against the locker as if I were hoping to disappear into it. The itch in my back was a searing pain.

"Nenner—" Sangris said. He sounded almost as bad as I felt. He touched my arm and I flinched.

Down in the lower level of the school building a flood of noise came as students entered. I didn't know why they'd all been outside. I heard excited babbles about a camel that had peed on the head teacher's car, or something. I didn't care. Sangris picked me up, the way he did when we flew, and carried me through an undecorated door close by. He shut it behind us. Gloom. Only a sharp white light came from the cracks around the door. We were in a closet. The wave of people washed by on the other side of the door, chattering.

He held me uncertainly for a moment. I didn't cling to him and I didn't cringe away either. "Do you want me to put you down?" he said at last. "I can't tell."

"Yes," I said. I found that I was able to speak without too much difficulty. As a matter of fact, my voice revolted me because it sounded so steady.

He put me down. At once I curled up against the wall, putting my arms back over my head to protect myself. I made myself speak again. "Did you," I said, breathing quickly, shallowly, "did you just . . ."

I couldn't even say the word.

"Kiss you?"

Sangris sat beside me and put his fingers on my shoulder timidly. I jumped at the touch. "On the *mouth*?" I said. I couldn't look at him. I said it to my knees.

"That's . . . where people kiss, Nenner."

"Not me! Not me, not me!"

All at once the world was a horrible place. I wanted his hand off my shoulder.

"Why are you so upset? I told you how I felt. And it's not like I haven't tried to do it before," he said, and a little more of the light seeped out of the room.

"Before?" I moaned.

He had the grace to sound embarrassed. "In the tree, before I attacked Juren. And in your room, before I kissed your foot. But I thought about it a lot before then . . . I told you . . ."

There was a chilled, sickly feeling collecting in the pit of my stomach, as if the dregs, dead leaves, and muck from the bottom of a pond were slopping together and congealing in my gut. It was all my fault. I'd hoped that the way I peppered every other sentence with an insult would be enough to discourage . . . this. But obviously not. For months I'd looked the other way, while hanging around a boy who . . . I screwed my eyes tightly shut. I'd been that word my friends hadn't dared to call me. My father put it best. In *Pfft*. I had been walking with Sangris down the streets of *Pfft*.

"I'm sorry I did that. I don't mean to force you," he said in a low voice. His hand, a stranger's now, stroked my shoulder and I flinched away. "It's all right. You should know by now, I . . ." But evidently I didn't know anything. I clenched tighter into my ball. "It's fine. I understand. It's a big step . . ."

"Big. Enormous. Vast," I babbled. "It's practically a canyon. A leap to the moon. So let's just never try to cross it, okay?"

His hand paused on my shoulder. That had jarred him. "What," he said, "*never?*"

"Never ever ever ever ever ever," I said, gripping on to the childishness. "Ever ever!"

To my relief, his hand was drawn back. He was quiet for a moment, and then he said, "Nenner, I don't think you understand how much that hurt."

I had only been restating the obvious. I uncurled a little to stare at him. "Why should it hurt? Didn't you know?"

I could see on his face that it did hurt; that, in fact, he'd been understating it. I knew all of Sangris's facial expressions as well as I knew my own now. At least that was one thing I could rely on. His mouth was curled, the skin beneath his eyes dark gray. But he met my gaze. "I'd hoped—" he said, struggling. "Nenner, why don't you want to?"

Didn't he know that *not* wanting to was the most natural thing in the world? Just the thought of it made me freeze like a hunted animal. This wasn't anything as simple as obedience to my father, or concern over what my friends would say if they knew, or a desire to preserve my honor, or anything that society imposed on me. Didn't his wings mean we could escape from all of that? No, the problem was inside of me—the way I'd been wired and the way I'd wired myself—the invisible finger pointing into my back—the gap where I'd cut my heart away—the itch—I had internalized it, and I carried it around with me like a snake coiled inside my chest, squeezing tight. "I don't need a justification for not wanting to k-kiss you, Sangris," I said.

"Of course not," he said. He flushed painfully. "I was just wondering if there was a specific reason."

"How about that I'm way too young?" I said. "I'm not ready."

"Darling," he said, "you're sixteen."

"Way too young!"

"For what? A kiss?"

"Stop saying that word!"

"It's not dirty," he said, bewildered.

Yes it was.

237

He looked at me helplessly for a little while. I turned back to my knees. "I could wait," he said finally.

"No."

"I'll wait as long as you like."

"Forever, then," I said. I didn't intend to be nasty. I really meant it.

He drew in a breath as if he'd been punched. Another moment passed. "Nenner," he said, trying to keep his voice reasonable, "sooner or later you're going to have to deal with it. Aren't you ever going to marry someone?"

"Not if I can help it. If my father makes me."

A scuffle came from his side of the closet. He'd moved too fast and bashed his head against one of the shelves. "So you'll let your father— Don't you see I have more of a right to kiss you than some idiot stranger picked out by your father?"

That did it. I sat up. "You do not have the *right*," I said. "Nobody has the right to . . . Especially not you. I've told you, I'm not interested. So stop pushing. And, you know what, it's none of your business what my father decides to do with me."

"But Nenner, you need more of a life than—than a set of rules constructed by *him*. Of course it's my business," Sangris said. "And . . ." He swallowed, studying me. I kept my eyes on the floor. There was a spider on it. "And I love you," he said.

A wave of sickness went through my stomach.

"Nenner?" he said, when I did not speak for the next

minute. I watched as the spider scuttled into a crack beneath the wall.

"I hate love," I said at last. "I always have. Love makes people complacent and self-absorbed. They all come to believe that nothing in the world is more important than their chosen one and their love. That's just a form of arrogance, really. But love wraps it up in a sickly sweet bundle so that everyone is obliged to smile at it and act as if it's somehow laudable. And it may draw two people together, but in doing so it alienates them from the rest of the world. 'Look how special we are, look how lucky we are to enjoy a connection that no one else can ever understand!' It's a way for ordinary people who are bored with their lives to fool themselves into thinking that there's something exciting going on. They have to find meaning in other people, because there's none in themselves. Love is cowardice."

A pause. "Maybe sometimes," he said. "I take it you don't love me, then." The shadows around his eyes were almost black.

I didn't have to think about it. "No."

Sangris bit at his bottom lip so hard his teeth cut it and blood showed. He shut his eyes briefly. Then he opened them again and said, "You're unfair."

Indignantly, I said, "Why? Because I don't—"

"No. Because you *knew*."

My lip curled. "What did I know?"

I hate it when people decide that they know what's inside my head.

"You knew I loved you," he shouted. His hair was full of dust from the wall. "All this time. You must have known. I made it so obvious that I wanted to cringe at myself. I told you in a hundred different ways each night. You may be sheltered, but you're not stupid and you're not blind. How the hell can you pretend to not have known?" His face was all crumpled and unfamiliar with bitterness.

"All right, so I knew. But I didn't encourage you," I said. I listened in wonder to how icy my voice sounded.

"You were cold at first," he muttered, "but then you began to loosen up, and I thought . . ."

Another wave of sickness. He was practically accusing me of being—that thing. The s-word that my friends were too delicate to use. "I didn't encourage you," I repeated. Each word was brittle in my mouth. I felt them click on my tongue as if they were made of metal matchsticks. "You wanted to hope, so you did."

A long while passed. He opened and shut his mouth a few times, struggling over his next words. Whatever it was, it had to be something private, something he didn't want to give up. What could be more private than "I love you"?

"But you—" said Sangris. Then he stopped again. He didn't want to say it. He wanted to keep something he'd loved.

And my flat, cold voice said, "I what?"

Sangris wouldn't look at me now.

"You said . . . a tenth," he mumbled to the dirty floor.

Filth surrounded us. Strings of cobwebs dangled from the

ceiling; a stain of water from some cracked pipe spread across the floor. The puddle must be constantly replenished from a leak in the plumbing, I thought. Otherwise it would have dried up. Air-conditioning in the classrooms kept the school cool, but here at the end of the hall, heat had been able to build and the air inside the little closet was stifling. *Our friendship began around the stars,* I thought, *and ends in dust.*

"I'm sorry," I said, also to the floor. "I can't." The words sounded useless.

Sangris unfolded and stood inside the dirty closet. "I want to be alone for a while," he said. He reached for the door. Then he stopped, and stood there for a full minute, his hand frozen on the wood. Finally, he looked down at me. I looked up from my position on the greasy floor. I took in his face properly for perhaps the last time. The slanted pupils of his eyes, the yellow gold glowing in the gloom. The lines of his face, the angles, the planes of shading, I memorized them so that I could sit down and sketch him detail by detail without having to look at the page as I worked. The wavy black hair streaked with dust, the cheekbones, the mouth that he had put to mine. "Should I come back?" he said. Ever, he meant.

My logic spoke for me. "No," I said.

His mouth twitched, but that was all. His face closed up and he nodded. He turned his eyes away, opened the door, and closed it gently behind him. I heard the babble in the hall outside die down momentarily, then start up again louder than ever.

I put my head down onto my arms and allowed my heart to race for the first time since I'd entered the closet. The waves beat through me, faster and faster, roaring now. I tapped my fingers against the floor and noticed with surprise how solid it felt. I'd expected everything to be melting away. But the world held firm around me, like a hard shell. For once I was the one who melted. I cried and cried, not just for Sangris, but also because I didn't know what was wrong with me. My mouth burned where it had been touched.

CHAPTER EIGHTEEN

In Which I Explain a Redless World

Here is what I think *you* think at this point. You think that I was an idiot; that deep down I did love Sangris but that I was just too dense, or too repressed, or too frightened, to realize it; and that in the end the dumb girl will admit she loved him all along and everything will follow from there. But the problem was deeper than that.

When I told Sangris I didn't love him, I meant it.

I wasn't in denial. I just wasn't in love with him. I simply wasn't capable of it. It is true that, if I had been brought up differently, or lived in another country, or in a different family, I *would* have loved him. If I was more like the Nenner who belonged among the sunflowers and less like the Frenenqer Paje my father had sculpted, then I would have been able to say the word *kiss* without shuddering, and I would have adored the Free person with every drop of blood that beat in my body. But as it was, every time a bit of natural feeling began to slide its way through my ribs, it felt like the stab of a knife into my side, and my heart, rather than fluttering sweetly, seized up as if it was allergic.

My father's ever-present fingers at my back reached right through my skin and clamped down around my insides, and then there would be a painful struggle between the frozen fingers and the feeling that wanted to flow, but the fingers had been there longer and love always lost.

Even when I used to read love scenes in my books, I felt uneasy and sick, as though I was witnessing something very wrong. When couples kissed in movies, I averted my eyes and died of embarrassment if my father was there, as he inevitably was, watching the screen with a narrowed, disapproving gaze. "Disgusting," he would say, looking over at me to make sure that I agreed. And my friends . . . If a boy in my class spoke to me, they would sit and watch for any reaction on my part. Just watch. Sometimes with a low, nervous laugh and a whisper. It occurred so consistently that I'd been trained to squirm even if they didn't happen to be there. Even witnessing the affection between a child and a mother, a kiss on the cheek, for example, when a woman came to take her kid home after school, humiliated me.

The shape of the person I was supposed to be fit around me like a full-body brace. My father had trained me too well, constructed me too carefully—to the point that I'd taken over his job myself.

I'd chosen my path as an eleven-year-old kneeling in my bathroom, and I'd chosen the same path that day in the Omani wadi, and I never swerved. I was like a red-blind person walking through a world in which love was colored brilliant scarlet.

After Sangris left me that day, I slunk out of the closet and found Anju. She took one look at me and said uneasily, "What is it?"

Another girl might have hugged me or patted me on the back, or something. But Anju and I weren't like that. We found an empty corner and sat there in silence. She didn't ask any more questions. She brought me food from the Pakistani room next door. Together, we waited for Heritage to be over.

A year has passed since then. I'm older and not much wiser. Nowadays, when I sit on the windowsill in the middle of the night and try to breathe as the heat presses in on me, I do it alone. For the most part I'm calm. I walk, shrouded, down the path my father picked for me. I pretend. My obedience is so exemplary that I'm allowed to read now. I rely on a backbone of books and, most of the time, they're enough to keep me quiet, half drugged with dreams of imaginary worlds. But sometimes it gets too much, and then I have a burst of frenzy. A short while after Sangris left, I had the wild idea that he might be waiting for me at that spot in the sunflowers of Spain. I decided to walk the Camino de Santiago, and when of course my father said no, I determined to earn the money myself. But as always, my father won without having to try. It's illegal for a girl to work in the oasis, and I didn't have a father's or a husband's permission . . . I sank back into my waking coma like rainfall disappearing into the dust.

Somehow, my parents have managed to not notice. One

day my mother attacked my head with a pair of scissors, and even though I had spent years fending her off, now I just blinked as the long locks went floating to the ground. And she didn't notice anything wrong about my reaction. All my parents see is that I read even more than I did before.

A few months ago, my mother came into my room and dug me out of a mountain of books. "You're going to Oman this weekend," she said.

I dropped the book and looked up at her.

"I know what you're thinking—"

"Frogs," I interrupted.

"Oh. All right, so I didn't know what you were thinking," she said impatiently. "But anyway, your father is going to stay with some friends of his. A local family, very respectable."

Ah, yes. My father was proud of his "connections." Local families tended to be rich and powerful. He was always eager to please anybody dressed in a white dishdasha.

"I suggested that you should go with him," said my mother.

I just blinked at her. I hadn't been out of my three boxes for months. I would probably crumble to dust in full daylight.

"The family has a daughter your age. Rhagda. She would be happy to show you around. Your father will be there along with her parents, and she has a personal driver, so it's safe. Come on. You need to get away from these books." She kicked them, unfairly. Their pages splayed out as if they were wounded. "Pack your things."

It wasn't an invitation at all, it was a command. I packed my things. Half the things were books.

I had to skip a day of school for the long trip. My father drove me across the border into the heart of Oman. This time, it was the Oman of my father's world, not the wild and hidden Oman that Sangris and I had shared. All day I sat in the backseat, my face separated from the searing outside air by an inch of glass. Without a word, I watched long plains, covered in nothing but dry stones and white dust, shake past.

When we arrived in the Garden City of Oman, in a place of striped pavements and long sun-bleached roads and white buildings, we met my father's friends under the arched roof of the souk. It was a honeycomb of smooth, dim tunnels filled and filled with stalls beside the startling peacock-blue glory of the sea. I was introduced to a small figure in a black *abiya,* standing beside her father. Rhagda. Her face was uncovered. It was long and thin, with a hooked nose. I looked with envy at the beautiful darkness of her *abiya.* It made her so aloof, so remote. It gave her the chance to hide her body from strange eyes and to float along in her own bubble of black cloth. I would have worn one if I could get away with it.

Rhagda's life must have been just as boring as mine— she was excited to see me. When we got to her house, she showed me around, through massive rooms with expensive, untouched furniture and of course rows and rows of golden chandeliers hanging from the ceilings—a ceiling was naked if it didn't have a chandelier. Sometimes there were more than three in the same room. On the balcony she showed me a tub of water with a turtle inside. She shrugged and said that there used to be two, but then the maid had come in one day and discovered that one turtle had bitten off the other one's head and was eating its neck. I looked at the mad turtle with a shudder.

In her bedroom there were two beds. The room used to belong to her brothers, she said, but now it was hers. She had seven older brothers and no sisters.

"My brothers are nice. You might meet them," she said. She threw herself onto her bed and watched as I got onto mine. Then she added, "But if you meet the one with the beard, don't shake his hand."

I looked at her.

"He can't touch women," she explained. I nodded. Even though this wasn't my native culture, I had absorbed bits of it, and their sunlight had seeped into my skin for so many years that it had become the sea I swam in. It was second nature to hear the muezzin call. The song rippled out over the city, from mosque to mosque, like blood through a heart, and to me that was the sound of the pulse of time. Rhagda pulled out her patterned red prayer rug and I looked away politely until she was done. Afterward, she showed me her "supermodel walk." She put a hand on one thin hip and strutted across the room, black veils streaming behind her. She wasn't bad.

To sleep I wore one of my oversized nightshirts, but I put on shorts underneath too, because anything less would have been inappropriate. The shorts were pink, patterned gaily with pictures of kittens and flowers. I'd had them ever since I was small. They stopped just above my knees. I was a bit worried about my bare shins, but the bright innocence of the baggy shorts reassured me, and anyway there was only the two of us in the room.

At three in the morning I woke up because I thought I'd heard a noise. I looked across at Rhagda's bed, but the dim outline of her sleeping form didn't move. I searched around the unfamiliar room and found the windows. Hidden by thick curtains, of course. I peeked through a window quickly. Nothing but moonlight. I let the curtains fall back into place.

It was wrong to be disappointed, but despite everything, the lack of my best friend was still a hole in the world beside me. I needed to get out of the room. I opened the door gently and slipped through into the darkness of the corridor outside. Persian carpets were beneath my feet, the banisters on the stairway gleamed, and mirrors reflected my dark shape back at me, making me jump. I wondered what Sangris was doing. I hardly believed that he still existed.

Like a ghost, I drifted through the shadowy, aloof opulence of Rhagda's house, the glimmers of the chandeliers floating past above me. I found myself in the living room, opposite the long, wide windows that let the moonlight in. I looked out at the tangled palm trees and the bare garden, and, unthinking, sank down onto the sofa. In the moonlight I could see that the sofa was purple and that the curtains, drawn apart, were probably dark blue. A deep, terrible loneliness beat through me. I always missed Sangris most in the middle of the night.

I couldn't have been there for more than five minutes when I heard a sound. It caught me by surprise and I whirled around. There was a figure emerging from the kitchen. For a fraction of a second I thought of Sangris—but then I saw the glass of water in its hand. One of the inhabitants of the house, maybe one of the mysterious brothers, had come down for a drink of water. I realized that I was sitting cross-legged on their couch and that my lower arms and my lower legs were visible. I uncrossed my legs at once. But there was no way to hide my skin.

The figure came farther out from the gloom of the kitchen, and the moonlight shone on a beard. He put the glass of water down on one of the tables.

I couldn't move. A wave of sick embarrassment went through my stomach and I wanted nothing more than to squirm out of the revealing light of the heatless, heartless moon. I was like the bugs that you find hiding beneath stones, when the stone is lifted away and suddenly they are exposed to the world. A man. He was a *man* and his beard was dark and curly. There was a stunned look behind it. He had probably never seen a girl, or a woman, uncovered in his house before. It must have been the last thing he'd expected, to walk out into his living room and find a strange girl sitting in the moonlight, showing him her knees.

"Sorry," I said, my voice very small. "I didn't think anyone would be awake. I'm Rhagda's friend . . ." I didn't know if he understood English. My voice trailed away. I couldn't breathe. My knees, my knees. I tried to tug the childish, ridiculous shorts farther down. My heart had frozen. I may as well have been dancing around in a bikini. But there was no way to cover myself.

The figure of Rhagda's brother came closer. He looked down at my wide eyes, at the smooth skin on my shins. I watched as his hand came out. He hesitated with his fingers an inch away from my foot, at the place where Sangris had kissed it once. Everything was still for a moment, as though reality hung balanced on a thin line and was not yet sure which way to fall. Then Rhagda's brother turned and ran away. And I was left stranded, blatant, in the strip of moonlight, no better than a harlot.

I scrambled out of the light, holding my stomach and shaky with shame. I stared wildly into all the corners to make sure there had been no witnesses, that my father was not lurking in the shadows, his mouth tight with horror. No one was around. And that, somehow, was even worse. I grew afraid that Rhagda's brother would come back and I fled to her room.

Rhagda's sleeping form gave me no comfort. I wondered what she would say if she knew. I *knew* what my father would say if he knew. I buried myself beneath the blankets and stared at the cloth, concentrating on breathing. I was trembling so much, I shook the bed. It shook until morning. If anybody knew . . . But Rhagda's brother wouldn't

251

tell them. He had behaved honorably. He had run away from me. The blame was all mine. I should never have left the room without covering up first. Maybe my time with Sangris had made me careless. I remembered catching frogs with him, the two of us alone in the mountains. My body was a menace. No, I was a menace.

I didn't speak much for the rest of the weekend. I hid in Rhagda's room, afraid to see him again. I festered in my embarrassment. When the weekend was over and my father drove me back to the oasis, I said nothing for the entire drive, still reeling from my own mistake.

This was my world. This was the background I came from, the sea I swam in. The world my father chose for me. A world where shins, exposed in the faint moonlight, were enough to make a bearded figure halt and tremble, enough to horrify us both, and enough to make me want to cut them off and throw them away. Now do you see why it was incredible that I let Sangris as close as I did? Why it was a miracle that I ever felt comfortable enough to wear a skirt in front of him? And how a kiss could make me feel so violated? Think of the moonlight and the curtains, and the disgrace of my uncovered ankles, and understand.

After the trip to Oman, I covered myself again in books. They numbed me. Soon the memory of Rhagda's brother faded and to me he became no more than a figure in darkness. Sangris, I continued to miss, while the walls in my head stood between us. And then, out of nowhere, Anju's hand raised up and slapped me, hard, across the face.

CHAPTER NINETEEN

In Which Anju Brews Chaos and Destruction

On Monday, Anju and I sat outside on the low stone wall of our school, beneath the shade of a date palm.

"Will you be okay without me?" she said.

She unpeeled a mandarin and handed me some.

"It's halfway through the school year," I said.

She shrugged. "I'm a good student. I'll learn fast."

We both knew it was true. Anju was moving, but she would have no difficulty adapting to a different curriculum.

I took a bit of orange peel and tore it apart without looking. "Where will you live?"

"Qatar," she said.

I nodded. Qatar was a predictable destination. "You'll go to a good school."

"Yeah," she said. "Better than here, anyway."

We were supposed to be in math class. Teachers saw us sitting there, but didn't disturb us. We were good students. We could get away with it.

I blew air across my face. My chopped-up hair lifted, then settled again.

"I won't know which classes I'm supposed to go to," I said. "I won't remember my way to the parking lot. They'll see me walking around, lost, for hours after school ends each day."

"You can find a new secretary," Anju said placidly. She finished the mandarin and crumpled up the bits of peel in her dark hand.

I smiled faintly. "No one would put up with me."

"That's true."

"I'll be very alone," I said.

Neither of us cried. We accepted the way things were. Nobody stayed in the oasis for very long. After my travels, and after all my time in the oasis, I was used to watching friends disappear into the distance. Other than Sangris, none of them ever left a lasting impression. The fact is, you can't be sad every time someone leaves—you'd have no tears left. The only way to adapt is by turning away. After the first few times, it stops hurting.

I thought that I would forget Anju soon enough.

She threw the mandarin peels onto the sand. "Listen," she said, with an energy that was unusual for her. "I've looked after you for two years."

"You put up with my weirdness for a long time," I agreed.

"Yes. Like your stories about Sangris."

I didn't say anything. I just nodded. I had told her everything about Sangris—several times, whenever it needed to come out—because I had wanted to, and because she didn't believe me anyway. Anju was accustomed to shaking her head and ignoring my wild, invented stories. It was one of the things I liked best about her.

"Listen, Frenenqer," Anju said. "You always need me to sort out everything for you, don't you? Your timetable. Your homework. Your life. You're useless at keeping things straight without me."

It was true.

"I'm going to help you again before I leave."

I listened.

"Last night," she said, in her plodding, monotonous voice, as stolidly as she would say: *Plus or minus the square root of b squared . . ."*

"Last night a cat came to see me."

I didn't move.

"Every week," she said, "for months now."

I looked at her. She met my eyes for once. Her face was black and inscrutable against the background blaze of sand; it gave me the impression that light was shining out from all around her, as if she were a sun-goddess. I screwed up my eyes but didn't look away.

"He made me promise not to tell you," she said. "The very first time he showed up, he made me promise. But . . ." she sighed. "But you're my friend."

". . . Sangris?" I said. It was the first time I'd said his name out loud for months. It slid off my tongue just as easily as it used to.

She rolled her eyes. "I recognized him from when he used to hang around you like a stray. I always thought your stories were just . . . I don't know. You being weird. But he spoke to me."

"Tell me faster," I said.

"Don't be impatient. We have half an hour." Ah, Anju. Always solidly sensible. She continued.

"He wanted to hear about you. He made me give him news."

I was immediately alarmed. "What news? You didn't tell him . . . ?"

"That you slope around as if you're half asleep all day and never look up from your books? No."

I relaxed.

"Of course I wouldn't. We're *girls*."

Translated: female solidarity. Sangris was a boy, therefore an outsider, and Anju wouldn't have given him any real information.

"I'd tell him little things. He liked to hear them. He didn't care how little."

"What kinds of things?"

She smiled. "I told him about the day you came into school with your hair all chopped off. I told him about how you'd gone along with it because your mother had wanted you to."

"And because I didn't care one way or another," I reminded her eagerly.

"Yeah, that too. His claws dug into the windowpane so hard, they left marks."

I laughed. It felt sweet to be able to laugh at Sangris again.

"Mainly he just wants to know if you're all right, though. That's what he asks me. Every week."

"What do you say?"

"I say you're fine, of course. Even when you aren't."

"Thanks."

"I told him he should ask you those things himself."

I bit my lip. "What did he say?"

"That you wouldn't want to see him."

"What did you say?"

"Nothing."

Typical Anju.

"Did he say anything else?" I asked.

"Yeah." She gave me another sideways stare. "He said he didn't want to see you either."

I stopped breathing. The heat clutched around me. "Oh," I said. "Oh."

"Because it was too hard," she continued.

"Hard? He knows where I live!"

"Not *that* kind of hard, Frenenqer," she said. When had Anju grown so much wiser than me? "It would be hard for *him*. That's what he meant."

"How do you know?" I said, still not breathing. "What if he hates me because of what I did to him? What if that's what he meant?"

"It wasn't."

"How do you know?"

"Because he's in love with you. Duh," she said. And her voice was so matter-of-fact that I wanted to shake her by the shoulders.

"Still?" I said.

"Yeah."

"That's bad," I said. I thought about it. "If he stopped loving me, then we could be friends again and everything would be fine."

"He's not going to stop."

"How do you know?"

"He's not going to stop because he can't," she said indifferently.

"How do you *know*?"

"Just trust me. It's obvious. He asks 'How is she?' as though the universe might blow up if I answer wrong."

She paused. Studied the sand.

"Why don't you love him?"

"I can't," I said.

"Why not?"

I thought for a moment, trying to find the right way to put it. "If," I said finally, "a dog has water squirted into its eyes every time it goes near a tray of food, since it was a puppy to the time when it grows up, then even if its master is out of the room—even if it is hungry and the tray of food is left lying temptingly on the floor—even if the squirt gun isn't around—the dog won't be able to approach the tray. The fact that it's alone in an empty kitchen doesn't make any difference to the animal."

Anju has many good qualities. Imagination is not one of them.

"You're not a dog," she observed. "And anyway, lots of dogs are disobedient."

"Anju, I know this is difficult for you, but try not to be literal, okay?"

She just looked at me.

"Nothing's changed since last year. I haven't changed. And you know me."

At this, Anju nodded. She did know me.

"Heritage is coming again," I said, "and I haven't grown at all."

She said, "Maybe that's because you've been in hibernation all year."

"Hibernation is the only way to survive life in the oasis."

I poked her henna-laced hand.

"Anju," I said, "help me. Sort things out for me one last time."

And Anju snapped.

I'd finally found her breaking point without even trying to.

It was like witnessing the explosion of a long-dormant volcano. Her eyes narrowed to slits, which shone flat and black, sucking all the light out of the air around us. She actually growled at me, and I blinked when I saw the flash of white from her teeth. She leaned toward me. I leaned back. "No," she said. "No. Do you know how I'm going to help you? I'm going to give you a week. That's the last time Sangris is coming to my house. We're moving after that, so it really is the last week. When he comes, I'm going to send him straight to your room. I'm going to tell him that you want to see him and that it's a matter of life or death. So you'd better be there. And you'd better be in love with him by then."

"Anju," I said reasonably, "don't. You know I can't force myself to love someone."

Anju whacked me on the arm. *Hard.* I couldn't believe she even had the muscles to hit like that. I jumped up. I'd always known that I was the dominant one between us. I was the more energetic, the more creative, the more outspoken. But all the while, Anju had been looking after me, sweeping away my messes, propping me up, unseen, from behind. Did that make her stronger? I had no idea, but my arm was stinging incredibly.

"You won't be forcing yourself," she said.

"But—"

"It's already there," she said. "Well, it's there, but it's not there—"

Poor Sangris, I thought. Just about everything in his life boils down to that. Including me.

"—because you won't let it be! You've dammed yourself up. You *would* be in love with Sangris, if you didn't have so many limits in your mind."

"Yeah," I said, "I know that. But I can't help it. It's who I am."

"No, it isn't. It's who your father wants to make you. You're so mixed up with your father's idea of you that you don't even see . . ." She said, "You know where the real problem is? It begins and ends with your father. Go to your father and . . ."

"You know I can't confront my father."

"You won't be confronting him," she said.

"If you mean I ought to reason with him—"

"You won't be reasoning with him," she said.

I waved my arms around in exasperation. "I won't be forcing myself to love Sangris, I won't be confronting my father, and I won't be reasoning with my father. What *will* I be doing, then?"

"You'll be fixing everything," she said. "You'll be untangling the wires that he crossed when he created you. Your father isn't a very good God, you know. He made you wrong. You're going to have to sort it out."

"How?" I said, hesitating. Anju was sensible. And she was, apparently, wiser than I'd known. Maybe she did have a solution.

"Tell your father that you love him," Anju said.

I looked across the low wall, against the wavy, spiked shadow of the date palm, at the emotionless face of the girl who looked back at me. She was framed against the blinding whiteness of the sand.

"Some fairy godmother you are," I said sarcastically.

"I mean it."

"Anju, you don't realize what you're asking me."

She just raised her eyebrows.

"No," I said. "It's impossible."

"Well," she said coolly, crumbling flakes of paint from the wall between her fingers, "I suppose that depends on how much you want Sangris, doesn't it?"

There was a flat silence. I writhed.

"But—" I tried, "even if I do say that to my father—how's it supposed to help?"

"It will."

"How?"

"Frenenqer," she said, "when I write down your timetable for you, do you ever ask me if I'm sure I've got it right?"

"No."

"And do I always get it right?"

I was still squirming. "But I *don't* love my father. I don't see how lying to him will help me with Sangris."

"Try not to lie," she said. "Really. Try to love your father. Just for a moment. Your father thinks that love is dirty, and he taught you to think so too. Turn it against him. Make sure you tell him, *Daddy, I love you.*" She gave her evil laugh, the almost-cheerful one that suggested tears and destruction were imminent. "You've got until midnight at the beginning of next Monday."

She was like a wicked witch brewing a potion.

"Ye gods, Anju," I muttered. "You're serious, aren't you?"

"Consider it a parting gift," she said. "You said you should have been born with wings. So take them. Your own. If you don't, then you don't deserve any, and it's just as well that you were born without them."

I winced at that. She knew I was sensitive about my imaginary wings.

"Now," she said, "you should start walking to art class." She handed me her notebook with the timetable inside.

She didn't say another word to me for the rest of the day.

I went through my classes thinking that Anju must have gone mad. She had snapped under the stress of moving to Qatar. Or her brain had fried in the heat. I would have to be extra-nice to her for the next week to keep her from breaking down in hysterics.

But that afternoon, my father picked me up after school. And the second I got into the car, I knew that she had pinpointed the source of the problem. Because the minute I saw my father and sat in the same air as him, with my mind still echoing Anju's easy words, *Daddy, I love you,* I started to choke and my heart seized up under the stress. I was ashamed of even thinking those words. They were like maggots in my head. I thought my father would be able to sense them as something unnatural, monstrous, inside of me. I shut my eyes and leaned against the car window. It was worse than being kissed by Sangris. This was the swollen, beating heart of my inhibitions, right here. *He can't hear the words in my head,* I reminded myself. I forced myself to breathe. But I wasn't convinced. I let the words, quickly, run through my mind again. *Daddy, I love you.*

I flinched straightaway. He didn't react. His eyes were on the road. With one hand he adjusted his sunglasses.

I let myself think the words again. *Daddy . . .* And still nothing happened. I found that I could breathe almost naturally.

I didn't say anything to him, though. I couldn't. I watched him uneasily until we got home, and then I escaped straight into my room. Didn't Anju know how . . . *wrong* it would be to say those words to my father? That night I was so disturbed, I couldn't read. My fingers went automatically to a book on my shelf, but the minute I opened it I threw it down again. My thoughts couldn't settle on anything except what Anju had told me about Sangris.

Sangris. That was a word I could latch on to. I would see him at the midnight beginning of next Monday. I sank down onto my bed.

I wanted to love Sangris. I thought of the heather and the sunflowers and the almond-scented tree, and I was taken aback by how much I wanted to love him. I could see, dimly, as if through a foggy glass wall, what it would be like to be with Sangris. I had caught glimmers of it, from time to time—that shade of red I couldn't hold inside of me.

I didn't eat at dinner. I couldn't. My father was sitting opposite me, and the disgusting words still hung in my head.

I left the dining room early. I went into the kitchen. My mother was sitting alone at her table. I hesitated. She'd married him, there must have been *something,* once. I knelt beside her chair. "Mom," I whispered.

She turned her eyes to me in mild disapproval.

"Mom, do you . . ." I lowered my voice still further. "Do you love him?"

As I said it I realized that I desperately wanted her to answer yes.

Her eyes, usually narrow and black, shot open wide in shock. She looked at me as if she thought I was being coarse. I thought I was too.

"Who?" she said suspiciously.

"My dad," I whispered.

Her mouth dropped open. "Go to your room," she said.

I stood uncertainly. "Don't tell him," I pleaded.

I knew she would.

"Go to your room," she said.

She turned back to focus on the surface of the table. I was at the door when she said, "Besides, don't you assume that *I* went after him."

I jolted to a halt. I was afraid that if I looked directly at her she might stop talking, so I only half turned, staring at the door frame. "Sorry?"

"He loved *me*. Chased me," she said quietly, speaking fast. "He'll never forgive me for that."

I couldn't picture my father that way at all. "I don't—"

"You think he would've chosen me if he didn't adore me? For his precious future daughter, wouldn't he want the best possible woman as a mother?"

I'd never considered that. I wasn't able to keep my eyes on the door frame anymore. I swiveled. She was still hunched over her table, a strand of black hair frizzing out of her bun. We looked at each other.

"What happened?"

She didn't speak for a moment. Then—"No one can live up to his expectations," she said, and twisted her mouth into something that was almost a smirk, except that it was sad. "You know that, yes?"

I opened my mouth to reply, probably something clumsy and eager, but a change in Mom's face made me spin around.

He was right there.

My heart contracted. "I—"

"Go to your room," he said to me. His expressionless eyes were on my mom.

I went. Through my closed bedroom door I heard them talking in low tones. I felt as if my clothes had fallen off in public. I sat on the bed, heart racing. Something was going to happen.

After half an hour, when he'd finished with her, my father came in. He stopped in the doorway and looked at me like I was a baboon in a zoo. "Do you have something you want to discuss with me?"

I shook my head. Then I said, apologetically, "I was just asking."

"Why?" he demanded.

"Because . . . we never use the L word in the house. I was curious." I kept my eyes on the floor as I spoke.

"'Love' is a very private matter," he said. Like rude body parts.

"But I'm family," I said. "A daughter wants to know about her parents."

From the look on his face, you would think I'd just asked to hear a graphic blow-by-blow account of how I'd ended up in my mother's body.

"Don't be disgusting," he said. The door slammed shut behind him. With a real *bang*.

He didn't talk to me for the next few days. He kept his distance, looking at me guardedly, as if I was a bomb that might explode at any minute and spew messy fluids all over the room.

On the last day of the week, Wednesday, Anju said to me, "Have you done it yet?"

I didn't need to ask her what she was talking about. I'd been having nightmares about *it*. "He'll be furious," I whispered.

She hit me on the arm. I jumped in my flimsy plastic chair.

On Thursday I kept myself closed in my room. I still couldn't read. My books had transformed into lumpy, dead things. I sat on my bed, closed my eyes, and concentrated on coating my mind in steel. I needed armor for my ordeal ahead. I thought of the sunflowers and of the Nenner who could be bold. It didn't seem to work. I thought of being able to give Sangris my love, like a gift, when Monday began. But it was like visualizing how beautiful a unicorn would be. It didn't actually help.

I planned to say the words to my father on Sunday, the last possible day. I didn't know how I would do it, though. Maybe I'd just blurt them out and run. Lock myself in the bathroom or something. The fact is that no one in my family ever smiled sappily, or held hands, or touched. No one used pet names. And no one in my family *ever* said "I love you."

On Friday, the last day of the weekend, my mother came into my room. It was the first time we'd spoken since the kitchen, and I was shy. I expected her to be awkward too, but even though her words were my father's, if anything, she spoke to me more easily than she had in years. "You will come grocery shopping with us today," she said. "Your father decided that you should get out more often." So that I wouldn't be stewing dangerously in my bedroom, thinking about forbidden things like the L word, she meant.

"All right," I said, because I didn't have a choice.

In silence we got into the car. In silence my father drove us to Al Lou Lou Center. I sat in the backseat, watching my father's reflection in the rearview mirror. I remembered him telling me that, above all things, Frenenqer Paje should be meek. And love, in my father's eyes, was something violent and indecent. This was about more than his idea of propriety, it was about his idea of *me*.

So what was his idea of me? What was I? I couldn't put it into words. The sunflowers, the sky, me cutting out my heart for him. I kept my eyes on my father's reflection.

I trailed behind my parents while they walked through the crowded, air-conditioned aisles of Al Lou Lou Center. I was deep in thought, and I didn't feel my feet as I walked.

"Push the shopping cart," my mother said to me. I pushed it.

My father took his sunglasses off. His eyes were old and crinkled behind them. "Do we need detergent?" he said. He was always vague on household matters. My mom did everything.

"Yes," she said.

"All right. Frenenqer, go get some detergent."

It was just down the aisle. I floated through the crowd of strangers and took hold of a handle. My parents watched closely. "Not that brand!" said my mother. "Get the red one."

The almond-scented tree in the sky, that awful tight feeling I'd had in my stomach whenever Sangris had tried to be soft with me, unable to want him because I'd known I had to slap him away, the harder the better, before I could respect myself. And I was only seventeen now. What would I be like in ten years? In twenty? I glanced over my shoulder at my father and found him watching me.

I was watching me too. Falling into the wadi in Oman with my shirt rushing around my skin, Sangris's eyes amber on Heritage as he struggled to tell me something important, and most of all, the closet with the cobwebs, crying after the kiss, horrified that I might have come close to feeling warmth. And my father calling me disgusting, slamming the door. Like I'd done to Sangris in the closet. Like I'd been doing to myself since I was eleven.

And that's how it happened that, very simply, I came to understand everything I needed to know about my father. He wasn't some enormous mystery. How could a person like him come into being? Like this, just like this.

I carried the detergent back.

"Put it in the cart," Mom said. Where else would I put it?

"Do we need stationery?" my father said. Ye gods, he really was clueless, I thought. This must have been the first time he'd come grocery shopping in months. Usually he just sat at the computer at home. I envisioned him as a thin, dark spider, controlling the strands of his web without moving out of his chair.

"No," my mom said.

"We never need stationery," I said.

He gave me a stern look. He thought I was showing disrespect. "Frenenqer, get us some milk."

I was familiar with the brand this time. I went to get milk, then walked back. I put it in the cart in front of my father.

"All right," he said, "do we need—?"

"Dad," I said.

He didn't respond for a moment. He was taking a huge carton of yogurt from my mother and putting it in the cart. People milled all around us. "What?"

My heart throbbed hard.

"I love you," I said.

He jumped a little bit. His gaze quickly flickered to the strangers standing around. Many were dressed in intimidating white dishdashas. They might have heard me. "Er, that's nice," he said. "Go get some flour."

We didn't need flour. I watched in amazement as the man who had controlled all of my movements for every year of my life squirmed like a stuck bug. His gaze was fixed on the floor.

"Didn't you hear?" I said, raising my voice. "Daddy, I love you!"

A couple of heads turned.

"Frenenqer," he growled, "we will discuss this when we get home. Go fetch some flour."

"You silly daddy," I said. "We don't need flour."

He found my tone of affection disrespectful. "Frenenqer—"

"He is silly," I said to a random passerby. She looked away and quickened her step.

My father dragged me into a corner and slapped me across my face. Quick and flat. He didn't want anyone to see, but he didn't particularly mind if they did. "You're too old for this nonsense," he said.

"Don't worry," I said, touching my stinging cheek. "I love you anyway."

"Is this your idea of fun?" he said. His voice was frozen. It was the voice that always made me feel as though I'd swallowed cold lead.

It didn't do that today. I'd seen his flash of embarrassment. Even now he was slightly awkward. He kept his eyes too steady on my face, afraid of showing weakness. Human. He was human and capable of being embarrassed. A grouchy old man. I burst out of my body, soared up high.

"You're not omnipotent at all," I said to him.

"What?"

I grabbed the sleeve of a passing woman. She turned and looked at me in surprise. I said to her, "I love my dad."

My pulse was so giddy, flying so fast, that I could afford to feel a spurt of real affection. "He's forty-seven and his name is Tiberio," I said. "He's an ordinary person."

She muttered something in Urdu and dashed away.

That stunt earned me another slap.

"Fine," I said, my left cheek burning. "I'll keep it in the family. I won't tell anyone other than you and Mom that I love you." The more I said it, the more I felt as though I was kicking down walls, an incredible kind of power.

"What do you think you're doing?" he said. He grabbed

at the cart and held it between us and the stream of people, like a barrier.

I had never seen my father mortified before. I nearly pitied him. And that was the best thing in the world, because it meant that he was reduced to something *pitiful*.

"I'm done," I said. "Let's finish grocery shopping."

I was obedient Frenenqer for the rest of the night. I still got sent to my room without any food and a strict command not to read, but it didn't matter. I couldn't have eaten or concentrated on reading anything anyway. My blood was humming in my veins.

He wasn't a god. Not even an overpowering father who could make me cramp up all my feelings into a painful knot. He was just a man. Just a repressed man who, in his own way, was a dreamer, who had sat beside sunflowers and thought that he ought to fix nature, and who had made me in his own image. But I wasn't his imaginary daughter, I was *real*. I wasn't going to turn myself into him, not anymore.

The next morning he wouldn't look at me. Mom came out and arranged the breakfast dishes and all the table mats around him in their proper order, and finally he was back in his safe, organized spot, like a person frozen in time. But he looked pale. Or maybe he always looked pale and I was only seeing it now.

For seventeen years, I'd been a plant growing straight toward his sun, or at least that's how he wanted to see me. Did he realize he'd lost his project now? Or was he still holding on to the fantasy? Was that why he wouldn't look at me?

The thought made me sad. I tried to chat with him, following all his rules. I even held my spoon properly. But it didn't work. He ignored me until I let him be. As calmly as he kept himself clamped down, my father, I saw, had the sort of mind that scratches incessantly at itself.

At last I set my spoon down and just looked at him, really *looked*.

His hair had been sheared close to the skull, but it curled anyway, and his face was long. He had wrinkles, just about every kind except laugh-lines.

My eyes moved down. His fingers were carefully positioned around the handle of his fork. It seemed more important to him than eating, I realized.

I wondered if he'd had a similar parent. Maybe it went all the way back through our family tree, a disease inherited from the first ancestor unable to deal with an uncontrolled life, transforming child after child into a bulleted list of rules.

Except I'd broken away.

My father went on avoiding me a little uncomfortably for days afterward. If I loved him, that meant I didn't fear him; and if I didn't fear him, I couldn't respect him the way he wanted. My love had disgraced him.

As for my mother—I think she looked at me with a kind of awe. She saw that I had done something, but she didn't really understand what.

I didn't get to tell Anju about my triumph because she was gone from school. She had already finished her last week.

But I knew she would keep her promise at the moment when Sunday turned to Monday. Anju was always reliable. That was why she'd made such a good secretary. She would do this last thing for me.

Saturday and Sunday went by dizzily. I was adjusting to myself. No itch in my back. No imaginary, pointing fingers. No pretend wings either. I didn't feel them pulsing and bulging at my back anymore. I was light enough not to need them. The heat pressed in and the wadis were dry and scaly and the color green was actually a dull shade of khaki. But it didn't matter. I waited for the birth of Monday. Trembles went through me constantly. I told myself to be patient. Maybe, even if I had healed, I still wouldn't fall in love with Sangris. And it wouldn't come suddenly. I tried not to push myself. I was too afraid. For all I knew, breaking my father's spell might not have helped.

But I felt different. More open. I waited for midnight with a quick, fluttering feeling in my stomach. The excitement came more easily and more naturally than I expected. It crept up on me when I wasn't looking, and at seven o'clock on Sunday evening I found myself in the bathroom, staring worriedly at the mirror. He probably wouldn't like my new hair. My mother had hacked through it with an old pair of scissors so that it hung straight and short, just below my chin. And my glasses—I'd been too absentminded to wear contact lenses lately. I put the glasses away and used my contacts for the first time in months.

Automatically, I felt embarrassed for being so vain. Then

I stopped myself. I didn't want to be embarrassed.

I went into my bedroom and closed the door. I took stock of myself. I'd never been so nervous while waiting for Sangris before. But surely that was a good sign too.

I paced and paced.

CHAPTER TWENTY

In Which There Is a Dark Green Room

By ten o'clock I had changed my mind. My parents were asleep in their room. The house felt empty. The light in my bedroom was artificial and too brittle. I went out into the hallway, put on my shoes, hesitated for an instant with my hand on the knob, and then, softly, let myself out the door.

I didn't want to pace alone in my room for the next two hours, and I didn't want to wait. I planned to go to Sangris for once instead of waiting for him to come to me. Anju's house was only a few streets away. Because I wasn't stupid, I had taken a shawl from my room and used it to cover my head. In the darkness, it could pass for a veil, and it made me less likely to be disturbed by men in their cars.

The night outside was hot and still, as though the world was holding its breath. I set off down the street, clutching the shawl around me. The moon was round and tinged with gold, and the streetlamps were everywhere, burnishing the palm trees with a warmer glow. Bright lights of cars slid by. Of course I had never walked to Anju's house before, but I knew the way. The only problem was that there were no traffic lights or crosswalks on the streets (nobody ever walked outside, so why have crosswalks?) and I had to wait for a lull in the flow of cars and simply run.

Soon I rounded a corner and saw Anju's house down another street. Lamps were everywhere, leading the way. Her house was small and square, painted a peeling, almost-white yellow, half hidden beneath the shadow of a frangipani tree. Right outside her window the flowers opened smooth and white and clean. Their smell was like vanilla but sweeter and freer. I brushed my way through clouds of the fragrance and, heart thudding fast, touched the shabby wood of Anju's window. She'd already opened it for Sangris. I didn't want to startle her, so I looked inside to the faint glow of her room and whispered, "Anju?"

She was sitting at her desk, brooding over an enormous textbook. That made me smile. She looked up as soon as she heard her name. She jumped when she saw my veiled figure, then her jaw dropped as she recognized me. She glanced at her bedroom door to make sure it was closed. "Frenenqer? How did you get here?"

I lifted myself in through the window. "I walked."

"That's dangerous!" she said in admiration.

"Not really," I said. "It wasn't far. And even if cars follow you, they usually don't mean business . . . Believe me, I should know." I took off my shawl and bundled it up.

Her room was smaller than mine. The walls were painted dark green, making it look still smaller. Most of her stuff had been cleared out, leaving only the bed, a few textbooks on a desk, and a night-lamp. I liked the soft, mellow glow a lot better than the blaze in my bedroom.

"I had to come," I said, scrambling onto her bed, where she joined me. "This way you won't have to send Sangris over, see?"

White teeth showed in her grave dark face as she grinned. "You did it, then?"

"Yes."

Fiddling with my hands, I told her all about it. She sat at the foot of the bed, arms around her knees.

"What does your father do now?"

"Ignores me, mainly. But that's the same as before." I glanced at the window again. "When do you think Sangris is coming?"

"Soon," she said. "I asked him to come in human form this time. I told him it made me uncomfortable to speak to a cat."

I shook my head at her. "You had this all planned out, didn't you?"

"I also gave him some of my brother's old clothes," she admitted. Anju had an older brother who had moved out long ago. "I'm sure he thought I was a bit weird."

"He thought correctly," I said, smiling.

I didn't want to talk about Sangris anymore. My insides were tight enough already. We chatted for a bit about Anju's new school in Qatar, but too soon we fell silent. Anju sat at her desk near the window, where the lamp was, and resumed studying. I think it was her way of giving me some space. I was in a darker corner of the room, trying to be calm. The scent of frangipani in her room grew heavier and outside, the crickets serenaded the silence.

When Sangris came, I wasn't prepared for it.

There was a sound as if wind had gone through the branches of the acacia tree outside, and then a tap on the window frame. Then Sangris slipped into the room, lightly, the way he used to enter mine. A shock of familiarity went through me. He looked just as I remembered, and it might have been yesterday that we had stood in a field of Spanish sunflowers and teased each other. The only change was that he didn't look as happy as he had looked then. There was no spark in his eyes when he faced Anju. The black hair fell across his forehead and I saw his cheekbone and the straight line of his nose as he turned to look at her. She continued to work at her desk.

"Anju," he said, and his voice was exactly the same.

At the sound, my heart started to knock at my chest.

"Hello," Anju said in her steady voice. She closed her textbook reluctantly. "I suppose you want to ask about Frenenqer."

"Yes," he said. He became a bit more animated. "How is she?"

"She's fine," Anju said in her blandest, most unresponsive manner.

"What about that art project of hers?"

"She's done. Finished it a few days ago. The new head of administration took it to hang it up in the main office without telling her. She wasn't very happy about that."

"I bet not," he said. "What did she do?"

"She says she's hatching plans for stealing it back."

From what I saw of Sangris's face, it looked like he was beginning to smile. "What else?" he said. There was some of the old tenderness in his voice. "What else is she up to?"

Anju glanced into the corner where I sat. I stared back with sudden panic. *Not yet.* If I had to talk right now I'd choke. She rolled her eyes and returned her attention to Sangris. "I don't really know. I haven't gone to school for the last couple of days. I'm done."

"Oh," he said, and the room went very quiet again. He drew back, and the light of the lamp splintered in the dark mess of his hair and slid along the hollow area under his eyes. It reminded me of the moonlight on his face, the first time he'd come into my room. But now he looked drained. I'd never thought Sangris could look that drained.

"I can't thank you enough, Anju. I know I've been bugging you. But it makes a big difference to me. When I don't know what's going on, I just . . ." He shook his head with impatience at himself. "Now that you're leaving, I don't know what I'll do."

"You could always try talking to her yourself," Anju said. She was probably bored of covering for me. I stopped breathing.

But he didn't even pause to consider it. "You know I can't do that." Absently, still gloomy, he reached out to pick up one of the textbooks. "It's better if she doesn't have to worry about me. It's not fair to hang around like some lovesick kid who just can't let go."

"Isn't that pretty much what you're doing?" Anju said without a visible trace of cruelty. She was probably laughing inside.

Sangris didn't deny it. "I guess," he said. "But at least I never go to see her."

It would have been the perfect time to introduce me, but Anju was having fun now, in her own impassive way.

"Why don't you?" she said.

"Because . . . that would be creepy."

"Don't you think it's slightly creepy to ask her best friend about her every single week?" Anju said. Oh, she was enjoying herself.

"Probably," he admitted. Then, quickly: "You're not going to tell her, are you? You promised."

"I'm not going to tell her," Anju agreed, choosing her words carefully.

"Good." He relaxed. "I know I shouldn't be here. But . . . it's harmless. At least it's from a distance, right?"

She leaned back in the chair. "What would Frenenqer say if she found out?"

Stung, he said, "What I told you. That I'm hanging around like some lovesick little kid."

"Frenenqer," Anju said, looking directly at me with her black almond-shaped eyes, "is that what you would say?"

"No," I whispered.

Sangris dropped the book. He whirled around and saw me.

I stared back from my corner, curled up in Anju's blanket. The darkness beat around us. Anju, ignored, got up from her desk and walked out of the room. She took her textbook with her, picking it up off the floor with a long-suffering air.

Sangris. He was all of my fading memories made solid. It was as if we still stood on the floor of my bedroom while he told me that I smelled of milk and honey, as if we still caught frogs in the hidden wadi of the mountains, as if I had just taken him home from the Animal Souk and cradled him in my arms to warm him. As if I was showing him the guppies swarming between my fingers in Thailand. And this was a new memory too. The faint light and the yellow-hearted frangipani in the night and the little green room that was Anju's. And Sangris—he stared at me as if he was unsure whether he was hallucinating or not. He didn't move for a long time.

"Hi," I said, clutching the edges of Anju's blanket.

"Nenner?" he croaked.

"Yeah."

"I—I'm sorry," he said in confusion. "I didn't know you'd be here. I'll just—" He moved toward the window.

"Don't go," I said. I dropped the blanket around my knees.

"But—"

"Don't," I said earnestly.

He stopped.

His eyes didn't leave me for a moment. His expression wasn't so much one of shock now. It was more the way that a man in the desert would look at a mirage. Wary, waiting for it to disappear, but at the same time, caught. "How . . . long were you there?" he said.

"The whole time."

"You heard . . . ?"

"Yes."

He flushed. "I didn't mean for you to hear."

"I know. Anju told me. She told me all about it. I came here on purpose to see you again."

He sank down slowly onto the other end of the bed. "I thought you didn't want me anywhere near you," he said. His eyes were still fixed on me.

"No," I said. "I missed you."

"I missed you more," he said hoarsely. "Much more."

Maybe it was true. I had a feeling like all the air in the room was sucking me toward him.

Here I was, sailing on a dark green sea, because Sangris had missed me.

My father was just a father. The sunflowers were just sunflowers. And Sangris and I were sitting on the same bed, in the semi-darkness, with Anju's blanket strewn thread-like between us.

The white petals of the frangipani flamed outside the window.

"Why did you want to see me?" he said. "Are you all right? Has anything happened?"

"Something happened," I said dreamily.

Alarm took over his face. He leaned forward. "What? Do you need my help?"

"No," I said. "I've taken care of it."

His keen face. His slanted yellow eyes. The hair that framed his head in blackness. I found it hard to keep myself calm. I wondered if this was what Sangris felt like every time he looked at me. How did he stand it?

"I can't believe she told you about me," he said.

"I wish she'd done it sooner."

"Really?" he said, uncertainly.

"Yeah." I swallowed. "I wanted to hear about you too. Tell me how you've been."

He chewed at his mouth. "But I haven't done much," he said. "My life's been a bit incoherent, like before the Animal Souk. I jump around from place to place without any particular reason."

"Humor me," I said.

He did as I asked.

"This is the first time I've turned human since Heritage."

"Why?"

He looked at me. I understood.

"And you?" he said.

"My mother cut my hair," I said, choosing something he already knew.

He hesitated, then said to the embroidered pattern on the blanket: "I think it looks cute."

"My mom practically cut it with a pair of pliers," I said. "You're biased."

We both smiled, but not at each other. He didn't see me. He was studying the blanket, twisting it in his fingers. And I was watching his long nervous hands. "No, really," he said. "It looks like you're wearing a cap. And it shows your neck." He stopped suddenly, probably remembering Heritage. I wasn't sure what I felt, but warmth was a major part of it. He changed the subject hurriedly. "I've been going to new countries. I was angry at first, for—you know. In the closet. But then I thought, it's not your fault if you don't—you know." He winced at how awkward it sounded, and rushed on. "So I thought of revisiting the places where we went together, but that was too much. I went to that sunflower field near Santiago, and . . . Um. It was bad. So I've stayed away since then." He stopped himself again. "Sorry," he said, still not meeting my eyes. "Too much information?"

"No." I had to tell him. Now.

I drew a frightened breath. Everything was very vivid now. I took in the clumsily built, deep green walls around us. They leaned in, as if they were green hands clasping us together. I took in the night-lamp on the desk and the textbooks in the corner and the closed wooden door. I saw the white flowers gleaming outside like moons caught in the tangled foliage. And Sangris, on the edge of the bed, his head bent as he fingered the blanket. The lamplight directly behind him made him appear dark in contrast, but his eyes were clear, clear yellow, aflame in his face, brighter than anything else in the room. And I was aware of the light sliding along my own arms and down my exposed neck as the hair tumbled short and helpless around my ears. A pain like a high, thin note of music slanted through me, straight through the chest and down, deep inside.

"Tell me what happened," he said. "The thing that Anju helped you with."

"I defeated my father," I said.

The blanket fell through his fingers and his eyes shot up to mine. The pain and the sweetness grew, and things were flowing into me.

"Your father?" he repeated dumbly.

"He's not a god anymore," I said. "He's just a man. I told him that I loved him and I broke down everything he'd done. I'm not a figment of his imagination now, and he doesn't have any hold over me, and every part of me is *mine*." Nerves vibrating, I leaned over across the bed, leaning into the lamplight. Gingerly I took the blanket out from beneath his hands. I tried my best not to tremble. "It also means there aren't any walls in my head."

In pure astonishment, Sangris stopped breathing. "Nenner?"

Frangipani and darkness and heartbeats. On my knees on Anju's bed, bringing myself closer toward him. The little room was absolutely silent.

"I'm sorry I made you wait," I said, with the last of my breath. With a lightheaded feeling as if I was throwing myself off a cliff, I moved through the dark green air, leaned farther across the bed, and kissed him timidly. On the cheek at the corner of his mouth, first. Then, when he still didn't move, I brought myself to his mouth and kissed him there too, my head tilted. There was a brief moment of sweetness and heat. Then I began to draw back.

But before I could, Sangris's hands were on my back and he was leaning forward too. He kissed me and when he found that my mouth moved in response, his whole body came to press against mine and we fell backward onto the hard little bed as the frangipani burned, seeping its scent into the room.

A long while passed. Sangris wouldn't let me talk. Or rather, I couldn't talk because he kept distracting me. His fingers were in my hair, or stroking my throat, or at the base of my back, feeling through the loose cloth of my clothes. And his mouth—whenever I tried to catch my breath he pulled me back greedily. A slow crimson flame was beating between us. We drowned in the little dark green room. Occasionally I would resurface and see the brilliant white of the frangipani flowers before he drew me back, and the warmth of their whiteness stayed in my mind as I touched his cheek and found an area at his throat that made him gasp for air when I kissed it. He spoke occasionally, but most of it was incoherent, or mumbled into my skin. He said my name a lot; sometimes I heard him moan something about warmth and milk and honey. But most of the time we were wordless, cupped in the green hands of the room.

Because I was still me, I stopped him when his fingers unconsciously tugged at my shirt. "I'm seventeen," I reminded him. He groaned and held me tighter. His eyes were shining canary yellow; they stood out above everything else. "And besides," I added, "you have to give me a moment to breathe so that I can tell you I love you."

Sangris looked down at me, his hair in disarray. "Say that again," he said breathlessly. "What did you just say?"

I laughed and refused to speak.

"Say it," he begged. I reached up and put my arms around him, curling, my insides fizzling.

"I thought we were too busy to talk."

"Tell me!"

"Tell you what?" I said against his neck. "That I love you?"

"Yes. Tell me properly," he said. "It's not fair. You already know how I feel." For a little while he lost track of his argument, because he'd dipped his head down. He didn't seem to be able to keep his mouth away from mine for more than ten seconds at a time. But then he was insisting again, "You need to say it."

He refused to be distracted even when I targeted that spot in the hollow of his throat. "Come on," he said, though he couldn't help tilting his head back. "Say it. *Please.*"

"Not here in Anju's room. That's weird." I smiled at him through the drowsy light. "Maybe you should take me somewhere else."

"Anywhere."

"The sunflower field. It'll be dark in Spain now, though . . ."

Sangris didn't care. He picked me up straightaway, kissed me again, and brought me toward the window. I noticed his hurry and it made me feel as hot inside as if I'd swallowed the sun. At the last minute I remembered to ask, "Shouldn't we say good-bye to Anju first?"

"I'll bring you to see her in Qatar," he promised. "We can thank her then, and you can chat and be polite all you want. But right now we're headed for Santiago." He already had me out of the window and in the scrubby herb garden near the flowers that gleamed white in the darkness under the acacia tree. "You're not going to get out of this one."

"Why would I want to?" I put my head on his shoulder, almost causing him to forget to grow wings before we took off. When we left the ground, there was a sensation as if someone had upended a packet of sparkles into my stomach. But maybe that wasn't just because of the flight. It might have had something to do with the way that Sangris moved as his wings beat. I had never allowed myself to press close enough to notice it before. Looking up at his flushed face, I said, "And after we spend a while in Spain, let's go to Thailand and see if the orchid gardens are open. Or maybe we could find a beach somewhere that's quiet, with waves that glow green at night and sand that's still hot from the day. I know a place near the Arabian Gulf." I could tell, from the way he kissed me in midair, that he liked that idea.

But first he took me past Santiago, over the gold dust of city lights, to a place where the land was dark and the sky was cluttered with tiny stars like points of light shining through a velvet cloth, and everything else was hidden beneath blackness. We heard the roar of the oil-painted trees. I dipped my hand into the cold water of the well. I couldn't resist splashing Sangris while he was impatiently waiting for me to say the words. He wrestled me down under the sunflowers. And there, in the place where my father had tried to plan me, with the roaring of the trees drowning out all other sound and the heavy petals of the sunflowers forming a second sky over our heads, I told him that I loved him.